Angel in a Devil's Arms

"Mrs. Breedlove," he said quietly.

She dropped the curtain and whirled about.

She couldn't quite manage to get her guard up in time and he saw what was beneath her reserve: a sort of wild joy and heat.

He couldn't help it: he moved toward it as he would toward a chink of light in a cell.

He was grateful he'd gotten that one glove off, because the next moments were filled with shocking little pleasures: her satiny cheek against his bare hand, the warmth of her head tipping into his palm, the silk of her hair as he threaded his fingers through it and tugged gently back. She was rigid with surprise for about a heartbeat.

In the next he saw her eyes go hazy and dark just before they closed, just before his mouth touched hers.

By Julie Anne Long

JULIE ANNE LONG

Angel in a Devil's Arms

THE PALACE OF ROGUES

DISCARD

AVONBOOKS

An Imprint of HarperCollinsPublishers

ANGEL IN A DEVIL'S ARMS. Copyright © 2019 by Julie Anne Long. All rights reserved. Printed in the United States of America. No part of this book may be used or reproduced in any manner whatsoever without written permission except in the case of brief quotations embodied in critical articles and reviews. For information, address HarperCollins Publishers, 195 Broadway, New York, NY 10007.

First Avon Books mass market printing: November 2019

Print Edition ISBN: 978-0-06-286749-0
Digital Edition ISBN: 978-0-06-286750-6

Cover design by Guido Caroti
Cover art by Juliana Kolesova; © Can Stock Photo/Ollyy

To Patty, for being an original FT,
for the shelter, for the laughter,
for the incomparable forever friendship.

Acknowledgments

‚∞‚∞‚∞

*M*Y GRATITUDE to . . .

. . . my splendid, insightful, understanding editor, May Chen, and super publicist Kayleigh Webb, and to all of Avon's brilliant staff for their patience, kindness, and flexibility.

. . . to the countless lovely fellow authors, readers, friends, and colleagues who reached out and flew into action in the wake of the Camp Fire—Dabney Grinnan, Pam Jaffee, Julia Quinn, Grace Burrowes, Patty Hansen-Judd and Gerry Judd, Josh Morgon, Pam Rosenthal, Meg Tilly, Melisa Phillips, and so, so many others for their generous offers, loving friendship, time, energy, and shelter, and for making it possible for me not only to finish writing a book I loved, but to imagine, and begin to rebuild, a life after the fire. It means more than I can adequately express.

I truly could list everyone whose words of kindness and offers of help lifted my heart over the past several months. I will never forget it, and I'll view life from now through a lens of gratitude. I hope to one day be able to pay it forward. May your kindness return to you a thousand-fold.

. . . To my agent, Steve Axelrod, and his wonderful staff, Lori Antonson and Elsie Turoci.

And a special shout-out to my genius nephew Sam for the heroic, eleventh hour recovery of a hopelessly corrupted Word file!

Angel in a Devil's Arms

Chapter One

❧❧❧

Mrs. Angelique Breedlove stared at the little token—a sort of half unicorn, half lion—nestled in the man's palm. The firelight nicked a glint off the signet ring gleaming around one of his long fingers.

The kind of fingers poets and musicians are said to possess.

And excellent lovers.

Also, probably stranglers and pickpockets.

For God's sake. Fingers were just fingers. It was just that staring at the token was easier than looking into the man's face. She still had vertigo from the last time she'd done it—thirty seconds ago.

"I don't know *what* he is, Mrs. Breedlove, but I don't think I shall ever forget seeing him" was how their maid Dot had described the man when she'd admitted him to The Grand Palace on the Thames all of minutes ago.

Normally Angelique and Delilah would meet with potential new guests in the reception room, but in the parlor across the foyer the party celebrating three marriages was still underway, and everyone was just drunk enough to think that a round of pianoforte and singing was a good idea. She turned her head and was treated to a view of the vast dark O of Mr. Delacorte's wide-open mouth, through which a surprisingly decent, albeit loud, baritone poured. Everything Mr. Delacorte did lacked nuance.

She'd warrant the man in front of her was all nuance.

Suddenly the black-and-white marble foyer floor between her and the party and the parlor seemed like an ocean.

She cleared her throat. "I'll allow this token bears a close resemblance to half of the token Mrs. Hardy and I have in our possession here at The Grand Palace on the Thames, sir. Of course, I suppose it's always possible you've murdered our mystery guest and stolen his half of the token, and then came straightaway to The Grand Palace on the Thames to take up our best room."

Well. That emerged a little more waspishly than she'd intended. Apparently her senses were overwhelmed and were mounting a defense.

"Do I look as though I'm capable of such a thing?"

He sounded as though he genuinely wanted to know.

Angelique raised her eyes and found his expression oddly grave. His eyes were a crystalline green, like moss agate, or mist over a moor. It was as peculiarly difficult to hold his gaze as it was to hold a lit coal. It was far too . . . *alive* . . . and complicated. He aimed this gaze out over cheekbones that called to mind a pair of battle shields arrayed side by side. His mouth was a long, sensual curve. Not a classically beautiful face. It was something better, or perhaps worse: it was fascinating.

She flicked her thoughts away from that notion the way she would flick her skirts away from an open flame.

"Rather," she said shortly. "But then, I suspect we all are, given the right circumstances," she added. "Humans are capable of so many things."

"You begin to interest me, Mrs. . . ."

She tipped her head pityingly. "Begin?"

Was she flirting? Surely not. She would no sooner do that than blithely step out in front of a runaway barouche. In her life, the consequences would have been identical, at least metaphorically.

But all at once she could feel the difference in the quality of his attention. As if someone had lit a candle in a pitch-black room.

When he began to smile she redirected her gaze to a safer place, which turned out to be the flowers in the vase on the mantel, which were drooping as if they'd all been dosed with laudanum. She enjoyed a bracing dose of exasperation for Dot, whose job it was to make sure they were fresh.

Where the devil *was* Dot?

Ah, she could hear her now, as a rattle of teapot and cups on a tray approaching. It was a perilous journey for Dot every single time. Dot and gravity had an uneasy alliance.

At last she appeared in the doorway.

Thus began the slow, delicate journey to settling it on the table between the settees.

The man watched this with apparent fascination.

"I don't believe you mentioned your name, Mr. . . ."

"It's Lord, I'm afraid."

"Oh, of course it is. Who but a lord would find it amusing to communicate through tokens."

"Necessary," he corrected evenly, sounding as insufferable as that supercilious little man who'd appeared one night weeks ago with half of a token and paid them three guineas to hold a room for a mysterious stranger. "Necessary to communicate through tokens. My name is Lucien Durand. Viscount Bolt."

The tea tray crashed noisily into place.

The perfidious Dot's shoes were already clicking across the foyer at a run.

Leaving Angelique alone with a madman.

"I agree that humans are capable of nearly anything, given the right set of circumstances," he said conversationally, as though he hadn't just claimed to be someone the entire *ton* knew had been dead for a decade, and who, before that, had taxed the broadsheets' ability to come up with hysterical adjectives. "Although murder certainly seems a good deal of effort to go through for an opportunity to stay here at the . . ."

A faint puzzled frown settled between his eyes as he took in the pretty but well-worn settees facing each other before the fire, arrayed atop the thick but faded rug (frays artfully hidden beneath furniture legs); all of those in shades of rose, the hearth facade fashionable decades ago, the table with its nick out of one leg, also skillfully disguised.

Since they'd combined talents a few months prior, Angelique and Delilah had seen any number of people glance around just that way: bemused, but not necessarily censorious. As if wondering at the source of the room's charm. One could not place a finger on its source any more than one could bottle sunshine or air. Its charm was that it was well-loved and it knew it.

Madman or not, it seemed her pride was at least as powerful as her sense of self-preservation. She would not sit idly while someone criticized their beloved room.

She cleared her throat. "Lord . . ."

On the off chance she'd heard him wrong the first time.

"Bolt," he confirmed, pleasantly.

Hell's teeth. She drew a sustaining breath.

At best he was a charlatan.

A gorgeous, gorgeous charlatan.

"The comfort and security of our guests is paramount at The Grand Palace on the Thames, so Mrs. Hardy and I—we are the proprietresses—typically like to have a conversation with a potential guest to ascertain whether someone is mad or otherwise unsuitable before we invite them to stay."

He studied her.

"Invite them, do you?" His tone was skeptical. But his voice was suddenly startlingly soft.

Instantly, alarmingly, it was easy to imagine that voice in her ear, from the next pillow, whispering the things he'd like to do to her.

"Yes." The word emerged absurdly huskily. It sounded rather like she was giving permission to something. "Yes," she repeated firmly. "Ultimately we give careful consideration to who we invite to stay, as we'd like all of our guests to feel comfortable and safe. And our business is thriving, much to our gratitude. We're even contemplating a little expansion. And in case you've any doubts, the king himself sat just there not long ago."

His eyes followed her gesturing hand to the pink settee.

He examined it a moment.

He turned back to her.

"Now who's mad?" he said gently.

"Excuse me, Lady Der—Mrs. Hardy."

Delilah—the former Lady Derring and new Mrs. Hardy—gave a start when Dot stage-whispered hotly next to her ear. She was panting as though she'd come at a run.

"What is it, Dot?"

"A man has arrived to inquire about a room and Mrs. Breedlove is speaking with him, but . . ."

She sank her teeth worriedly into her bottom lip and said nothing more.

Delilah's eyebrows arched aggressively, prompting Dot to continue.

"Well, I think perhaps you ought to join her."

Delilah exchanged a swift glance with her husband. He was planning to leave for Dover with Sergeant Massey for a short spot of business in an hour or so, and she wanted to soak up his presence.

But Dot was not in the habit of making recommendations. Cheerfully following orders, and occasionally getting them right, was her forte.

She had proven to be rather a savant at describing guests, however.

"Is he behaving in an . . . ungentlemanly manner, Dot?"

"Well, no. He is one of the most gentlemanly gentlemen I've seen, but not in the way you'd expect. His kit is very fine and his boots, well, they're Hoby, and the way he stands is very . . . and you know how they are, Lady Derring—I mean Mrs. Hardy. Gentlemen, that is."

"I do indeed know how they are."

"He has only said a few words. His voice is very fine and low. He is merely standing there, mostly."

"So the trouble is . . ." Delilah coaxed. She could feel the fine strands of her patience groaning like the buttons on Mr. Delacorte's vest.

"Well, there are two troubles. Mrs. Breedlove's cheeks have gone pink."

Well.

This was fascinating.

"*Where* are they pink?" Delilah asked swiftly.

"Here and here." Dot pointed to places high on her cheekbones.

Angelique typically sailed through her days like a swan on a sea of jaded wit and cool aplomb, all born of worldly experience. Very little occurred to change the color of her face, unless it was the heat of the kitchen on baking day.

"I see. What was the second thing, Dot?"

"Oh, you'll think me silly . . ."

"I would never dream of thinking such a thing," Delilah lied.

"I believe I saw the letter 'B' on his ring!" she said excitedly. "Oh, Lady Der—that is, Mrs. Hardy—do you suppose he could be . . ." she lowered her voice to another stage whisper, pressed her knuckles to her lip ". . . *the* Lord Bolt? It's just he looks so . . . so . . ."

She clasped her hands together and gazed at her mutely, blinking her huge pale blue eyes.

Apparently not even the broadsheets—which Dot read with religious fervor—could provide her with a sufficiently hysterical word.

Delilah silently counted to three to fortify her

patience. Ten would have been better but time seemed of the essence.

"That poor misguided young man drowned in the Thames a *decade* ago. A life wasted. Unless you're a newspaper that peddles gossip, in which case they profit from him still."

"But the broadsheets said someone who looked *just like him* walked into Mantons last week and shot the heart out of every target and walked out again without saying a word. Scared everyone silly, they said!"

"But, Dot—"

"And that someone who looked *just like him* walked into his favorite glove maker in the Galleria and paid for a pair that Lord Bolt had ordered specially just before he died, black with brown wrists, and walked out again! Right dear they were, too."

"Dot—"

"And that Lady Wanaker claimed her loins had started up a burning out of nowhere like they always did when Bolt was—"

"Dot, please!"

". . . and that a mysterious wager appeared in the betting books at White's, signed and dated with the word 'Bolt,' and it said 'I wager every penny I possess I will have revenge.' I ask you! It fair made me shiver, it did! And *no one saw who did it*." She pressed her knuckles against her teeth.

"DOT."

Dot raised her eyebrows as if she'd made her point.

Delilah sighed. "Oh, Dot. Didn't we discuss the wisdom of believing all the gossip you read? I admire your *enthusiasm* for reading, but might I suggest something more calming? Mr. Miles Redmond's book about the South Seas usually puts me right to sleep. It might be just the thing."

Dot looked crestfallen. "Yes, Mrs. Hardy. Of course you're right. It's just he told Mrs. Breedlove that his name was Lord Bolt, you see. So I just assumed."

Delilah went still.

She darted another glance at her husband. Who arched a brow.

"We won't be longer than a few minutes," she told him.

And if they were, he would be there in moments, because Captain Hardy's unique gift was knowing when she needed him.

LUCIEN WAS ACCUSTOMED to the stares of beautiful women. Countless times he'd watched conclusions made and discarded scud across their faces like clouds on a breezy spring day. They noted the flawlessly sleek black coat, clearly sewn by the lads at Weston. The gold watch fob. The signet ring. The English accent so elegant and precise every consonant seemed to have been turned on a lathe. The exquisite manners, the charm precisely calibrated to weaken feminine knees.

But then there were the contradictions: the childhood French that haunted the contours of his words and syntax. The long, lean body clearly not raised on great platters of English roast beef. And no proper Englishman went around with eyes like his: *Vert, comme un chat*, one woman, tangled in his sheets, had purred on a memorable occasion. "Like a devil," another had hissed on a very different memorable occasion. There was indeed something just shy of feral about him, something that implied that one could never predict what he'd get up to, and the fact that this unpredictable man was dressed up in aristocratic finery made them deliciously uneasy.

He had once cared that he did not fit anywhere.

Until he'd learned that he could use this to his advantage.

He was not in the business of making anyone feel more comfortable about anything.

So he let the beautiful ladies of The Grand Palace on the Thames stare, and he said nothing.

On the little table between them, the two pieces of the token lay locked together like lovers, reunited at last. Mrs. Hardy had fetched the other half from upstairs.

Mrs. Hardy's dark eyes were soft and curious and she wore a gentle smile. Mrs. Breedlove seemed to actually be pressing herself back against the settee. Her chin was up a little, and her hands were folded perhaps more tightly than they ought to be, though her expression was decidedly cool. As though nothing ever surprised her. Their dresses, one red, one golden, overlapped in a shining spill of silk on the seat between them.

Mrs. Hardy's eyes went to his new gloves, which he'd removed and laid aside on the settee next to him. Black leather, with brown wrists.

They fixed there for a time.

He spoke first.

"I should have thought you'd surround the settee with velvet rope and erect a plaque if the king sat here."

"Ah. Well, we've only the two pink settees at the moment, you see," Mrs. Hardy said.

She poured the tea from a pot painted all over with periwinkles.

"Ah," he said, taking great pains to sound fascinated.

She eyed him sardonically as she handed his tea to him. They both knew this exchange was inane.

He took it with a gracious nod. He drank it without sugar, without cream. It was a habit of childhood he could not abandon and it niggled him a bit. It spoke to a time when such things, the niceties and enhancements of life, simply could not be had.

"I once, in fact, sat on the king's knee. At the sort of party ladies such as you would certainly not be invited to attend. I was three years old."

It was a deliberate, testing bit of wickedness.

Neither of them even blinked.

Which he liked.

"Lord . . ."

"Bolt." He'd happily say his name just like that, all day long, knowing full well the impact it had and not giving a damn anymore.

"Very well. We thought we'd perhaps have a conversation before we admit you to The Grand Palace on the Thames, since we know only what we've read about you, you see," she said.

"You have me at a disadvantage, then, as I have read nothing about you."

They didn't laugh.

Mrs. Breedlove gave him a tolerant little smile. "And it is *such* a struggle to remain out of the broadsheets."

When he grinned at this, she turned her head away ever-so-slightly from him, toward the mantel. The line of her fine jaw and the slope of her throat, and the way her skin took the light like a pearl, suddenly struck him as almost insufferably lovely. It made him feel fleetingly restless, as if someone had dragged a hand over his fur backward.

"Perhaps the most pertinent thing we're read about you is that you're dead," Mrs. Hardy pressed on.

"Boo, I'm a ghost," he said mildly and fanned his fingers in mock fright.

Two strained smiles greeted this.

"Lord . . ." This was from Mrs. Hardy.

"Bolt."

"May we presume that you're claiming to be the very same Lord Bolt who raced a high flyer down Bond Street?"

"Not at all."

There was a pause.

"You're *not* claiming to be the same Lord Bolt who fought a duel with the Earl of Cargill and shot him in the shoulder?" Mrs. Breedlove also had an interesting recollection of his exploits.

"No."

"And you're not the Lord Bolt who wagered a thousand pounds by writing in the White's betting book that a hummingbird would—"

"No."

"Or that you wagered five hundred pounds that you could get a donkey to kick Lord—"

"No."

"But . . . then . . ." This was Mrs. Hardy.

"It's the word 'claim' I feel I must take issue with," he clarified. "It rather implies a defense must be mounted, wouldn't you say, in support of an assertion? Shall we choose a different verb? I was born Lucien Durand. My father is the Duke of Brexford. He was not married to my mother. My mother, Helene Durand, was beautiful, kind, and a bit of a fool. Hence my existence in the world." He gave them what was meant to be a bit of a self-deprecating smile. "For which I am certain you are grateful."

They regarded him with tiny polite smiles of their own.

He had the sense they wouldn't have minded sliding the hairpins from their coiffures and jabbing him.

He liked their composure and their obvious intelligence. It wasn't boring. He loathed boredom and he found it more and more difficult to tolerate dull people with anything like grace.

"To further expound, my father, the Duke of Brexford, persuaded the king to confer upon me the title and the modest lands when I was ten years old. I was in favor then, you see." He said this very, very ironically. "It's safe to say I am no longer. But I am still a viscount."

"I feel I must point out that this portion of Lord Bolt's . . . history is rather widely known in London and in other parts of England," Mrs. Breedlove said gently. "Among those who read the broadsheets, most particularly."

Bolt gave this the tiny taut smile it deserved. "Some weeks ago you decided to choose to accept one half of the token on the table and three guineas from a small, maddeningly efficient, nondescript, supercilious man, the sort who manages the sorcery of both blending into the wallpaper and nettling like a burr beneath a saddle, to hold your finest room for his employer, who would be me. His native dialect is irony, which you would probably come to understand if you spent a few years working for me as well."

Their silence told him they remembered him well.

"I don't believe *that* was mentioned in the broad-sheets," he concluded.

"Does this supercilious man have a name?" Mrs. Hardy said suddenly.

"Exeter. Mister Exeter."

"Mister E," Mrs. Hardy repeated, wonderingly, on a hush. The women shared a secret, a swift little mirth-filled glance he could not quite interpret. "And he's your . . ."

"Solicitor. After a fashion."

"Are we given to understand that you did not, indeed, drown in the Thames? There was a funeral, you know."

"More after the fashion of a celebration, in some quarters," he said calmly. He was certain he knew precisely who celebrated. Just as he knew precisely how he'd wound up in the Thames.

"It was reported that some women rent their garments," Mrs. Hardy told him, dryly.

He smiled placidly. "They generally do when I'm about."

Mrs. Breedlove had turned to study the flowers on the mantel with a little frown.

He knew this because he'd looked immediately for her reaction.

Mrs. Breedlove leaned forward a little. "Help us to understand something, Lord Bolt . . . If you didn't drown, then . . ."

"As I was leaving a gaming hell I was accosted by two men and hurled into the Thames. I survived. Don't know who the poor bloated soul was who was fished from the river and presented as proof of my demise, but it wasn't me. I was on my way to China by then on a serendipitous clipper ship. Scooped from the water. I'm fortunate I did not wind up in a pie, like an eel."

"This is London. One should never take for granted what winds up in a pie," Mrs. Breedlove said evenly.

Frankly delighted by this, he transferred the whole of his attention to her. The later afternoon light through the window burnished her hair the color of an old doubloon, a shade or two darker than her gown.

"Words to live by," he said gravely.

She turned ever so slightly away again, as though *he* were the sun, and not the great orb aiming beams through the window.

A silence ensued.

The room was comfortable, he'd grant it that. The proportions were gracious and pleasing. Through the sturdy closed doors came the strains of a muffled reel. A bit like the way it would sound if ghosts were having a party. Lucien had reached adulthood feeling both on the outside of things and at the center of things (usually gossip), and for an instant he felt that way again.

"As for that duel . . . It takes particular skill to avoid a target as big and black as the Earl of Cargill's heart. He can still use his shoulder, but I'll warrant he thought twice about using his mouth that carelessly again."

They went perfectly still.

Mrs. Breedlove leaned forward just a little, and it took every scrap of breeding his father had insisted he acquire to keep his eyes on her face and not where they yearned to go, the expanse of creamy décolletage. "Lord . . ."

"Bolt. Or Viscount Bolt, if you prefer."

"If you could help us understand why you've chosen to . . ." she paused ostentatiously ". . . favor . . . our establishment with your resurrection? And what are your plans for the future?"

Oh, *well* done, Mrs. Breedlove, he thought. He had a weakness for a good, irresistibly subtle piss-taking.

He met her direct gaze evenly. Her eyes were hazel, full of soft greens and golds, a surprisingly gentle color in such a coolly possessed woman. A bit like a spring dawn. The gears of time suddenly slipped. He was nine years old and back at his father's house in the country, and the joy of it pierced the breath from him. For one moment he'd felt like a window had been thrown open in a stifling room.

For a mad moment he wanted to be alone with that feeling, if only to remember who he once was.

He was not that person now.

"You were selected after a bit of research conducted by Mister Exeter, primarily because you hadn't any guests at all at the time and it seemed as though you never would, but also because your location is conveniently proximate to a bit of business I intend to transact. And I wished to keep my reentry into London society entirely secret at first. Hence the token, a cheap bit of sub-rosa nonsense I bought in a bazaar in Morocco. I do not intend to keep my presence a secret any more. And if after this conversation you still doubt me, read the broadsheets tomorrow."

He took a sip of his tea as they rigidly, with wide eyes, took this in.

"Oh, and my plans are to open a gaming hell," he added brightly. "And I shall need you to get in Lapsang Souchong tea while I'm here. I cannot possibly continue to drink whatever this is."

"DEAR GOD. HE can't stay here! How do we get him to leave?"

Too late, Angelique realized she sounded like someone who burst onto the stage in a pantomime waving their arms about.

It was Delilah and Angelique's habit to confer about potential guests before making a decision. And since the party celebrating three marriages— the Farradays, the Masseys, and the Hardys—was underway but showing signs of winding down, they were speaking in loud whispers on the stairs instead of in the opposite parlor.

"He's not a . . . a . . . tusked boar, or some such, Angelique, who's inadvertently wandered in. We can't just shoo him out. He says he's Viscount Bolt. I'm inclined to believe him, based on what I know of viscounts."

"He's *insufferable*."

"Yes. That's what I mean."

"And he wants to open a *gaming hell*. What manner of pastime is that for a grown man?"

"A lucrative one, I should imagine," Delilah said practically.

Angelique went mute in astonishment.

"Do you see?" she said darkly after a moment. "Usually I'm the one who says things like that. And then you exclaim 'Angelique!' in shock, and *I* laugh, and *you* learn. He's already upsetting the natural order of things."

Delilah laughed, rather proving Angelique's point. "I *am* learning from you. Thank you. Pragmatism is a fine quality."

Angelique snorted.

"I wonder if that's why he's doing it."

They were quiet for a moment of furious thinking. They would need to go in and bid farewell to Mr. and Mrs. Farraday and the Masseys, as they would be leaving soon, and Delilah would want a moment alone with her husband.

"And he has those . . . those . . . eyes."

Angelique fervently wished she could unsay the words the moment they left her mouth.

Delilah stared at her. "Bolt does? Do you mean the ones in his . . . head?"

Delilah was beginning to sound a little concerned. About Angelique. Not Bolt.

They stood on their toes and peered into the parlor. They could see Bolt sipping his tea. Regretfully, probably. Given that he drank only Lapsang Souchong. For God's sake.

His hair touched his collar and it gleamed in the light, like his signet ring and his boots and his eyes and his buttons. But even from here Angelique could see there were faint shadows under his eyes. He did not look debauched. When he didn't know he was being watched, he in fact looked a little weary.

She didn't want to feel anything like sympathy.

Where had he been during that ten years' absence? Did she and Delilah have the right to know? It was and it wasn't difficult to reconcile the legend of the newspaper gossip with the arrogant, seemingly immovable man who sat on their pink settee.

"I'm sorry. I can see you're upset, Angelique." Delilah had lowered her voice even more. "Do you know him from . . . That is, has he . . ."

Angelique went still. Delilah's delicacy was both touching and mordantly amusing. The tacit agreement was that Angelique would prefer to forget her past. Entire days went by when she didn't think much of it at all, so content, so busy, was she here at The Grand Palace on the Thames. She had begun to think it had ceased mattering to her.

Which was why she was surprised to discover that Delilah's delicacy brushed against a raw place in her soul she hadn't realized she still possessed.

"No," she said finally. Her voice lowered. She sighed. "I've never met him until today. And to be honest, he hasn't *done* anything in particular to upset me. You—and only you—know the whole of my history with men, Delilah." Angelique had provided Delilah with a painful summary, sans emotion and details, on the day they'd first met. It could be summed up in one word: "disastrous." Or, if one were to use more than one word: "a faithless squire," "a feckless lord," and "Delilah's perfidious dead first husband, the Earl of Derring," all of whom had partaken of her and left her flailing, terrified, and in the end, jaded.

She was not entirely faultless. What mattered was she was standing, and that was very much in *spite* of the men who had populated her life.

And yet it wasn't entirely out of the realm of the possible that she would have seen Lord Bolt at one of the Earl of Derring's little parties, comprised of men and their mistresses and much appalling drunken tomfoolery. The Duke of Brexford *had* made a brief appearance at one, after all. It really wasn't the very proper duke's sort of thing.

Of course, it hadn't been Angelique's sort of thing, either, but at the time she hadn't had much of a choice in the matter.

"I suppose Lord Bolt simply rubbed me the wrong way, Delilah," she said finally. "It's been some time since we've had to contend with anyone we didn't take to at once."

"Oh, he'll probably be insufferable for a time

and then he'll be off, because can you imagine a man like that agreeing to abide by our rules of conduct? We will not make an exception for him, of course. Including our epithet jar. And if you and I have expertise in anything at all, it's managing insufferable men."

Angelique bit her lip. And then she sighed. "And this one did give us three guineas, and hope, after a fashion, when we had none. Though it was hardly gracious of him to remind us. Alas, my sense of fairness thinks we owe him."

"If he proves intractable beyond even our expertise, I'll ask my husband to intervene."

Delilah still blushed and faltered a little over the words "my husband." Angelique thought it was adorable even as it whipped her own cynicism into a bit of a white-capped froth. If she were a wagering woman—and she certainly wasn't, at least not beyond Whist, as the trajectory of her life was a testament to the fact that she was bad at it indeed—she'd put money on the fact that Delilah would say those words in a complicated variety of inflections as the years went by, not all of them flattering.

Delilah seemed to be waiting for Angelique to say something.

Angelique finally made a bored, noncommittal sound, something like "peh," a syllable she was certain she'd never before uttered in her life, and lifted her hand vaguely.

"I expect we'll find he's quite manageably human, as are all men, ultimately," Delilah mused. "We just have to find his weakness."

That was the trouble. Standing next to him had been a bit like standing next to a mountain, or an obelisk. She'd detected no weakness at all.

Chapter Two

LUCIEN COULD find no fault with his room, really.

It wasn't for want of trying.

The fire was lively, and it warmed every corner. Not a hint of lint or a shadow of a wrinkle disturbed the surface of the blue-and-white quilted counterpane, which was crowned by two tempting, plump white pillows. Sunlight ricocheted from the spotless, gleaming wood of a handsome little writing desk opposite the bed; a handful of blossoms sprang from a blue-and-white porcelain vase perched on its right edge, and on its left edge rested a little rosewood writing box, presumably so the tenants here could write letters to their friends and relatives extolling the virtues of this inn by the docks.

And as he looked at the desk the memories crashed over him like slops dumped from an upper-story window. Of other blossoms in another room. Of a music box that had lit his mother's face up like the sun.

And of a letter that had killed the light in her forever.

Lucien had born witness to both moments. But

the duke had been present for only the first. The coward.

Lucien was anything but a coward. He'd proven that to himself time and again. He was hardened and jaded and his confidence was a formidable thing, built up like muscle—or scar—over the past brutal, satisfying, edifying decade. He'd created his own wealth, then lost it through speculation and wiser for it, rebuilt it. At the age of thirty-three he'd learned that anything—pirates, illnesses, storms, wealth, mistresses, being hurled into the Thames in the dead of night—could happen at any time.

But damned if he could yet reconcile the jovial, smiling man who'd given his mother that music box with the man who had written that letter. Because one man had carried him on his shoulders when he was three years old, paid for an Eton education when he was thirteen, bought him a watch when he was fifteen years old because "a man ought to have one," got him elected to White's at seventeen, and had brought them to live in a country house when he was very small, where his mother gaily stuffed every available vase with blossoms.

The other man had cut them adrift with a few words scrawled on foolscap. Abandoned them, like the slops out the window.

And now this man had a *proper* wife and a *proper* son and heir. Which was essentially the primary responsibility of a duke, after all.

In his more honest moments Lucien sometimes suspected his failure to understand this was more an unwillingness to understand. Because a cold, quiet fury stirred when his thoughts touched on it. And fury tended to blind.

When he was at last satisfied he was the man his father could never be—when he was satisfied that he was the man *he* wanted to be—Lucien had invested in cargo sailing for England. He'd sailed home ahead of it. Because England *was* indeed home. It had been a decade. And it was time.

He would get answers to all of his questions. He would get justice, and if it was the last damned thing he did, he would get his mother's music box back.

He ventured forward and idly, almost tentatively, lifted the lid of the little writing box, as though he half-expected it to play Mozart, like his mother's box. Inside he found foolscap, ink, sand, everything he needed to write his memoirs, if he so chose. He smiled tautly. He could call them . . . oh, *Always a Bastard*.

Perhaps in the ludicrous eventuality that his plans for opening a gaming hell did not come to fruition—it had been a full ten years since he'd failed to accomplish what he set out to do—he would write them. Because one way or another he was going to make certain his father and his duchess would never be able to do what *they* had set out to do all those years ago: erase Lucien and Helene Durand from their lives.

He closed the lid crisply and sat down on the edge of the bed to test it for bounce.

Which it possessed.

Next he decided to test the pillow for softness. He fell backward and let his head sink down onto it.

The next thing he knew, he was jerking awake from a dreamless sleep.

He turned his head and was startled to discover the room's window revealed a slice of the night, a rooftop, and a bit of a crescent moon.

He fished in his pocket for his gold watch and confirmed that it was after the dinner hour.

"I'll be damned," he murmured. It was a magic bed, apparently. When his bed was a bit lumpy or the pillow less than cloud-like, his dreams were sometimes dark as brackish ocean water, and he turned and turned helplessly in that dark, struggling to find his way to consciousness again.

Points to Mrs. Breedlove and Mrs. Hardy.

He lay still for a moment, getting a feel for what it was going to be like to wake up in The Grand Palace on the Thames, listening, thinking of the times he'd awakened in hammocks, on dirt floors, in mattresses stuffed with vermin-infested straw. He would be damned if he ever again slept in anything other than the best.

He shifted and something crackled in his pocket. He fished it out.

Ah, yes. The list of rules for living here at The Grand Palace on the Thames. The saucer-eyed maid, her hand trembling, had pressed the little printed card upon him when she'd led him up to the room. Her features arranged in equal parts glee and terror, which wasn't an unfamiliar expression to him.

He was just about to crunch it in his fist and test his cricked arm by hurling it into the fire. Then he decided he could use a laugh. He read it.

> *All guests will eat dinner together at least four times per week.*

"The *devil* I will," he muttered, blackly amused. "Why in God's name would utter strangers want to watch each other eat four times a week at a boarding house near the docks?"

It only got more entertaining from there.

> *All guests must gather in the drawing room after dinner for at least an hour at least four times per week. We feel it fosters a sense of friendship and the warm, familial, congenial atmosphere we strive to create here at The Grand Palace on the Thames.*

"Familial, congenial atmosphere." He could think of nothing more oppressive. A faint sense of alarm stirred.

> *All guests should be quietly respectful and courteous of other guests at all*

*times, though spirited discourse is
welcome.*

"Well, if spirited discourse is what you want,"
he murmured wickedly. Lucien was nothing if
not spirited.

*Guests may entertain other guests in the
drawing room.*

"I suppose that rules out the orgy I'd planned,"
he mused. He imagined saying that out loud to
Mrs. Breedlove and Mrs. Hardy, just to see how
they managed to keep their faces still.

*Curfew is at 11:00. The door will be
securely locked then. You will need to
wait until morning to be admitted if you
miss curfew.*

What the dev—*curfew?* Suddenly this wasn't
amusing anymore.

*If the proprietresses collectively
decide that a transgression or series of
transgressions warrants your eviction
from The Grand Palace on the Thames,
you will find your belongings neatly
packed and placed near the front door.
You will not be refunded the balance of
your rent.*

Good God. It was Newgate with blue-and-white quilted counterpanes.

Obviously he could not be expected to tolerate this.

Awake and charged with purpose now, he bolted from his room and had gotten down one flight when he encountered Mrs. Breedlove on the landing, heading upstairs.

"Curfew?" he expostulated without preamble, smacking the rules with the back of his hand. "Courtesy? *Camaraderie?* You can't possibly expect me to adhere to this nonsense."

"Well, that is *devastating* news, Lord Bolt," she said brightly. "We'll miss you."

She took another step up the stairs, then suddenly feinted to the right, clearly hoping to move past him.

"Mrs. Breedlove."

She stopped.

Their eyes met. Little flecks of gold floated in the green of her irises, like coins in a wishing well, and her eyelashes were dark gold with burnished tips. He had the absurd impulse to ruffle his finger across one. Just to see how quickly he could get himself thrown out the door of The Grand Palace on the Thames.

He tried a reasonable tone. "I'm a grown man, Mrs. Breedlove. Not a boy still at Eton. Some of my pleasures and pursuits may, shall we say, preclude returning before midnight."

"While I appreciate that you may have an arduous schedule of frequenting gaming hells—and while I appreciate that you spared me the details of your other pleasures and pursuits—we'll happily allow you back into the boarding house the following morning. Where you stay in that interval is entirely up to your discretion. And as you're a grown man, and not a boy at Eton, I'm certain you'll be resourceful enough to find shelter."

For a silent moment he inspected Mrs. Breedlove, experiencing twin impulses to laugh and growl.

"Given that we may well soon be neighbors, Mrs. Breedlove, perhaps some exception might be made for me."

It was a little gauntlet, thrown down.

There was a silence.

"Neighbors?"

"Oh, yes. I think the building next door is a fine location for a gaming hell. It's for sale, as it so happens, and I intend to purchase it. Which is the primary reason I am your guest."

Interesting, her little hesitation here. She was good, Mrs. Breedlove was. Very cool. Not one eyelash flickered. Her lovely mouth did not so much as twitch.

But she'd gone quite still.

For a moment they did nothing but lock eyes.

"I suppose you would know better than I would about fine locations for gaming hells, Lord Bolt," she said smoothly.

He narrowed his eyes.

He gave the rules a little smack again. "And this bit about the drawing room. What manner of mad—"

"Lord Bolt." Her tone was practically a caress, and yet he had a feeling she could command the attention of a crowd with that tone. Certainly he'd be dying to hear anything she had to say if she used that voice. "If you'll allow me to save you a little breath and time. Our rules are not negotiable. I believe they could not be more plainly stated, so prolonged discussion will not likely yield more clarity. None of our guests find them unduly onerous. Perhaps you won't, either. Our party guests have dispersed, and if you like, I can introduce you right now to the guests you will come to know during your stay. If you choose to stay here."

He listened to this little discourse as well as *felt* it. And what he felt was a woman who knew herself well. She had confidence, no doubt earned. And more interestingly, this woman perhaps gave not one damn whether he stayed or didn't, but perhaps had a slight preference for the latter.

Which of course made him determined to stay.

"Given how eventful your life has been, surely this shouldn't pose an undue challenge?" This arrived sympathetically. They both knew this was a goad.

He wasn't so stubborn that he would resist as a matter of principle. He knew winning strategies often involved an acquiescence or two.

At first.

"Lead the way, Mrs. Breedlove," he said silkily.

To SAY LUCIEN'S presence was instantly felt in the little parlor was a bit like saying earthquakes were felt by the foundations of buildings.

Silence, of the confused and wary sort, descended. The room was full of guests—tonight it was Mr. Delacorte, Mrs. Pariseau, and Mr. Cassidy, along with Dot and Helga, their cook—who tipped their heads up to Angelique uncertainly. It was as though she'd left the room to bring in lemon seed cakes and nonchalantly returned with a leopard on a lead instead.

Mr. Delacorte was the first to offer her a tentative, forgiving smile: Did you *mean* to lead a leopard into the parlor? We'll all politely look the other way whilst you lead it out again.

Angelique cleared her throat, said brightly, "Good evening, friends. We've a new guest. We're delighted to present Lucien Durand, Lord Bolt. I hope you'll help us make him feel welcome."

Another brief but notable silence ensued as the word "Lord" had its usual impact on mixed company. Suddenly no one was quite certain what to do. No one eyed her or Delilah with a sense of rank betrayal, but she had the sensation that they were tempted.

And then Lucien bowed. And it was so very polite, such a thing of beauty and grace, that lean body of his folding like an animal languorously stretching, that Mrs. Pariseau's eyebrows flew upward like skeet and her mouth pursed in a silent whistle.

She was on her feet to offer him a rather rusty curtsy by the time he was upright again, and when she was finished, she gave her skirts a little fluff.

He favored her with a smile.

Everyone was on their feet by that time, so Angelique made the introductions.

Mr. Cassidy, any woman's definition of handsome, was also courtly and well-spoken and had so far behaved faultlessly, but every now and then he deployed a sort of slow, crooked smile that lit up his blue-gray eyes and made the maids alternately act like idiots or bicker among themselves over who brought things up or started his morning fires. If he was not precisely an open book, well, that described most men. He hadn't a pedigree and he wasn't wealthy, which was a bit of a relief.

"Mr. Hugh Cassidy. A pleasure to meet you, Lord Bolt."

"Likewise, Mr. Cassidy. An American, I see."

"Indeed, sir. All the way from New York."

"Americans are always telling one where they're all the way from. So helpful."

Mr. Cassidy went still.

Angelique held her breath.

A beat or so of too-interesting silence ensued.

"I suppose it's just that we enjoy reminding

Englishmen of all the fine places you lost in both wars," Cassidy said finally, easily. "Especially since I helped defend New York against the British just a few years ago."

Lord Bolt's faint, pleasant smile remained in place as he regarded Mr. Cassidy in unblinking silence.

Intriguingly, this wasn't something Mr. Cassidy had yet shared with any of them. He'd have been not much more than a child, surely, when the British burned the American capitol. One caught glimpses of something steely beneath the amiability now and again, like scenery flashing past a carriage window.

There really was reason the little hairs on the back of Angelique's neck should stand up. Then again, men were such perverse creatures that exchanges of insults could lead either to fast friendships or duels.

"The farther one travels across the world, the more one realizes the futility of any empire attempting to prevail. The exception will be England, of course."

But Lord Bolt said this ironically, and Mr. Cassidy smiled, and Angelique exhaled. No blood would be shed. Yet.

Men.

"So you're the chap clever enough to claim the best room here before anyone else could!" Delacorte was still a little too full of bonhomie from the earlier gathering. "Or ought I to bow, as you're a lord?"

"I shall accept a bow or a handshake in the same spirit. I leave the choice to you, Mr. Delacorte."

"If you bow, I expect you can see yourself in his boots, Mr. Delacorte," Mrs. Pariseau offered, rather wickedly. "I had a look meself and quite liked what I saw."

Angelique exchanged a startled glance with Delilah. They'd all known Mrs. Pariseau was spirited, but a frisky Mrs. Pariseau was unanticipated.

"And *I* can see an entire column of myself in your waistcoat buttons!" Mr. Delacorte sprang forward, bent, and peered roguishly at Lucien's sternum. "Just what the world needs! Three more Stanton Delacortes!"

Either the silence—abrupt and total—or the sudden twenty-degree drop in temperature in the room made Mr. Delacorte flick his gaze up.

To find Lucien's expression rather reminiscent of an executioner measuring the neck of a criminal to determine which axe to use.

Mr. Delacorte cleared his throat and took a step back.

Total silence reigned for another startled moment.

Lord Bolt ignored the eye daggers aimed at him by Angelique.

"What brings you to The Grand Palace on the Thames, Lord Bolt?" Mr. Cassidy was not easily daunted.

"Revenge." He said this with a little smile as if this was entirely self-evident. "You know, the same reason one goes to Brighton or Bath."

Angelique clamped her back teeth.

"I'm sure we'll all grow accustomed to Lord Bolt's sense of humor. And if you find the adjustment a bit of struggle, rest easy, because he won't be here forever. Lord Bolt, you might like to have a seat near the gas lamp in the corner." She gestured to a little table in the far corner. "Perhaps reading quietly would suit you better than polite conversation."

He fixed her with a stare that teetered on the mutinous.

She returned it with an "off you go" eyebrow hike that brooked no argument.

He turned and went.

Everyone watched him go, then sank back into their chairs.

"Mrs. Breedlove, may I ask you a question?" Delilah said sweetly from her own chair in the corner. But the words emerged through gritted teeth. They barely just escaped being a hiss.

Angelique stifled a sigh.

She returned to sit beside Delilah.

Nearby, Dot was embroidering words on a hoop, while Mrs. Pariseau had taken up reading aloud a horrid novel they'd been enjoying. The heroine was about to unadvisedly go up the stairs to an attic.

Delilah gazed at her in silent incredulity while Angelique pretended not to notice.

Angelique took up her knitting—it was meant to be a coverlet for one of the bedrooms—but she merely held it. Then lowered it to her lap again.

"I know," Angelique muttered crossly. "And I'm sorry. I ought to be able to manage more graciousness."

"Are you *certain* you haven't a history with Lord Bolt?"

"I suspect my history with the type of men who believe they are better than everyone by virtue of a title and money, even if this one is a"— she dropped her voice to a whisper in deference to their epithet jar, which was currently empty, much to their pride—"bastard, in every sense of the word, may be influencing me just a little."

Delilah's eyes widened.

Angelique felt faintly wretched, which she resented. Because she knew this wasn't the entire truth, and she had been nothing but truthful with Delilah since they'd met. The entire truth was difficult to put into words.

Then again, Delilah knew her rather well.

"*And* he mentioned that the building next to ours might be a fine location for his gaming hell. That's why he found it so convenient to stay here."

Delilah's jaw fell open. She clapped it shut at once. "No! The one *we* wished to buy?" Emphasis, alas, on the word "wish."

Angelique nodded grimly.

They sat with this little unwelcome bit of news for a moment.

"Perhaps you can talk him out of it," Delilah said, not sounding confident.

Angelique only snorted. "I wonder why he hasn't yet bought it if that's his intent. Because we surely would have heard, given our expressed interest in it."

"Good question."

They were silent another moment, and then Delilah sighed. "Perhaps you ought to go and establish a détente with Lord Bolt, for your own sake and for the sake of our other guests. And if there's even the slightest possibility he'll be our neighbor . . . well, we might as well attempt to establish cordial relations. If anyone can do it, you can."

It was the very last thing Angelique wanted to do. But Delilah was right. It was probably necessary.

"Very well. And you're right. It *should* be child's play." This was bravado.

Angelique did indeed feel more like herself, bolder and more confident, now that she was across the room and safely beyond the riptide of his charisma.

He'd produced a little book from somewhere

in his coat and seemed occupied with it. Perhaps a list of his enemies, or the whores he wished to call upon, or a list of items to check off as he went about getting revenge, or of items he would "want them to get in." He reminded her of her father on Sunday mornings in church, barely enduring their well-meaning but uninspired vicar.

The pleasant little ambient sounds that made up their evenings at The Grand Palace on the Thames—the click of knitting needles, the murmur of Mrs. Pariseau reading aloud, the sounds of chess pieces gliding across the board and gently tapping against one another, and Mr. Delacorte making his "thinking" sound, a sort of clicking against the roof of his mouth with his tongue—had resumed, much the way birds start up singing again when the cats are out of view.

Angelique listened to it all, marveling at what she and Delilah had created. Her heart felt full, and that gave her confidence, too.

She glanced up at Lord Bolt, who had turned a page and had not once looked up.

"Off I go, then," she said to Delilah.

"Good luck," Delilah said fervently. She did not quite wave a white hanky in farewell but the spirit was just the same.

Chapter Three

❧

ANGELIQUE SIDLED over to the little table in the corner where a decanter of brandy was kept for any gentlemen who wished to imbibe, and filled a little snifter.

Bearing this gift, she navigated the sea of carpet. Absurdly, her heart accelerated with every step.

He began to rise as she approached. "Mrs. Breedlove. To what do I owe the pleasure of your visit to Elba?"

She gestured him back into his chair. "In this room we are very casual, Lord Bolt. No more than one bow per night is usually necessary. Captain Hardy used to sit at this very table when he first arrived, and he liked a brandy when he read his book. We thought perhaps we'd bring one to you, too, by way of welcome."

He eyed the glass she held critically. "What sort of brandy?"

The cheek of him.

"The wet, brownish kind."

"Oh, well, in that case. "

She placed it in front of him. He eyed it a moment, pensively.

"Won't you sit down with me for a moment, Mrs. Breedlove? Unless you're absorbed in the story Mrs. Pariseau is reading. Will you have a sherry or is such debauchery as that not allowed in this . . ." he intercepted her warning stare and abandoned a perhaps more colorful word in favor of ". . . sanctum?"

"It is allowed, but tonight I thought I should like to have my wits about me. I will sit for a moment, thank you."

He'd nudged the other chair out with his foot.

"I'd help you into it, but I fear the startling formality will shatter the tranquility of the room."

She sat.

Then he lifted the glass in a mocking little toast and took a sip. His eyes flared surprised approval. "Calvados."

He held it before his eyes and peered into its depths as though it were a crystal ball.

She waited.

And waited.

Say thank you, you supercilious—

"Thank you, Mrs. Breedlove," he said gravely. He looked up at her at last. But the light in his eyes suggested he'd gleaned something of the flavor of her thoughts and he 1) was amused; 2) didn't care.

"You are welcome, Lord Bolt. Are you going to tell us what brandy you expect us to get in?"

"This will do."

"I am *so* relieved."

He smiled at her.

"How do you find your room?" She actually genuinely wanted to know. Not that they would change a thing.

"The appointments are as expected."

"As wonderful as that?" she asked brightly.

"I find they are in keeping with the singular appointments elsewhere in The Grand Palace on the Thames."

Here was her opportunity to make her point.

"And the singular people?"

He took another sip of the brandy. He sighed.

He seemed to consider this.

His brow furrowed slightly as he looked out across their beloved parlor.

"Americans always seem as though they've been hewn from a log with an axe, don't they?"

Angelique stared at him in astonishment.

"A big log. A dull axe," he clarified, turning to her, as though her silence was instead a request for specifics.

"Perhaps they thrive away from the dismal English climate and the shade of the towering importance of notorious aristocrats."

His grin grew slowly, wickedly, as if he thought this was a darling, *darling* thing to say. As if he'd known she'd had it in her.

That grin stole her breath. It spread in her chest and heated her veins like a bolted liqueur. No doubt petticoats slid to ankles of their own accord when he deployed that smile, much the way snakes are said to undulate from baskets when a charmer blows a flute.

For a distinct instant, she was dazzled blind.

She was hardly a green girl. It was only a smile. And like liqueur, the effects would eventually fade. It meant nothing at all in the long run.

How lucky she was to be mature enough now to realize these things. And just two days ago she'd found a tiny fine line next to her left eye. She liked that line. It suited her, frankly. And it meant she was still alive and thriving and nearly thirty years old and she needn't feel a *thing* about this man if she didn't want to. She'd begun looking forward to discovering the ways in which she would become dashing, like Mrs. Pariseau, who sported two broad silver stripes in her raven hair.

His mouth returned to its usual state until his expression became something more difficult to interpret. "Speculative" she might have called it. Perhaps even a bit "troubled."

"And Mr. Delacorte . . ." He studied the man, who was chortling over a move he'd just made in chess.

He turned to her in all seriousness. "What *is* Delacorte?"

It was a fair question.

"Enthusiastic and kind-hearted," she said firmly.

He tipped his head in a "oh, come now" gesture.

She said nothing more. She pressed her lips together.

He took another sip of brandy.

"Mrs. Pariseau seems a delight," he offered.

"All of our guests are delights," Angelique said evenly.

For some reason this made him smile. He gave his fingers a drum on the little table. "I find I should like a cheroot. To take the edge off of the nerves, you see. The tension of the chess game and the knitting and the *embroidery*. How many times does she stab herself nightly?" He gestured at Dot.

"You've noticed."

"My dear Mrs. Breedlove, I notice everything."

The sudden clash of their gazes turned the word "everything" into an intimacy. She decided she would not look away. Perhaps one became more accustomed to Lord Bolt if he was administered in a series of consistent small doses, like opium or whiskey or one of Helga's foul tisanes.

"'Mrs. Breedlove' will suffice," she corrected evenly.

His little smile was confident. "For now," he said easily.

She struggled with the impulse to cast her eyes ceilingward.

His smile deepened, as if he knew.

"As for your nerves, Lord Bolt, if the brandy is insufficient to steady them you will have an opportunity to smoke with Mr. Delacorte and Mr. Cassidy in a room set aside for the gentlemen."

A hunted expression flickered across his face.

He gazed at his brandy as if wondering if he could swim away in it.

"Gentlemen?" he echoed, finally, with a certain black amusement.

"Surely you, of all people, should understand the gradations of the word."

He studied her with amazement.

"'Me, of all people,'" he quoted slowly, sounding impressed and perversely pleased.

Hell's teeth. It was safe to say she'd veered badly from her original diplomatic mission. And yet like a cart hurtling downhill, she couldn't seem to control it.

The little smile lingered on his lips. There was a dimple at the corner of his mouth and it took all of her fortitude, suddenly, not to stare at it.

"I generally like Americans, mind you, Mrs. Breedlove," Lord Bolt said conversationally, as if this had been the topic all along. "They're forthright, on the whole. Less prone to machinations, as it were. They're useful when the mast of your ship has toppled and you need some brute to shove it upright again."

"Ah. Is your own strength not up to the task, Lord Bolt?"

He leaned back in his chair, relaxing as a theatergoer might when it became clear the show he'd paid to see was going to be entertaining. When he crossed his legs, Angelique saw that Mrs. Pariseau was right: his boot toes reflected the little chandelier overhead. They were proud of that chandelier: it meant they weren't only surviving, they'd actually made enough money to buy a new chandelier for this particular room. Everything else in the house had been cobbled together from ingenuity and scraps. It was beautiful. She had only lately dared to want more.

And that's what that little building nearby represented. He had *better* not turn it into a gaming hell. They had only just succeeded in persuading a certain stubborn and permanently drunk gentleman to lie against another building, and they had made inroads into the number of men who relieved themselves within view of the guests' windows.

"Whilst I am capable of assisting in shoving a fallen mast upward again, getting men to do the mast shoving for you is the difference between strength and power. Guess which one I find more appealing."

"The one that makes you feel superior would be my guess."

He did not reply. Unless eyebrows diving a little could be considered a reply.

Instead he regarded her thoughtfully.

She wondered if these silences were strategic. It gave them naught to do but stare at each other, and the longer she looked at him the less she preferred not looking at him.

He frowned faintly. "Have I given you some reason to dislike me, Mrs. Breedlove?"

Hell's teeth.

She'd asked for that.

Moreover, she deserved it.

But she also rather liked it. Angelique was not fond of machinations, either. Nearly her entire life until she'd met Delilah had been a series of compromises and contortions primarily designed to suit some man's whims.

Most of the reasons she disliked him were, more accurately, reasons he ruffled her composure. She sensed he'd very much like knowing he ruffled her composure, so there wasn't a chance in Hades she'd tell him. The entire point of Lord Bolt seemed to be composure ruffling.

"Lord Bolt . . ." She leaned forward a very little, and began with some effort at her usual dulcet tones, "My friend Mrs. Hardy and I founded The Grand Palace on the Thames from what was essentially a ruin. It is thriving beyond our wildest dreams, for which we are grateful. It is our home. We cherish—I see your eyebrow has twitched at the word, but nonetheless—our guests and we find that their comfort is owed in large part to the company they find here. We take great pride in their enjoyment of each other. And furthermore, I like these people. I fear I cannot tolerate hearing them insulted or witnessing them made to feel uncomfortable when you know better. It pains me greatly."

He was absolutely motionless. He appeared to listen to this with every evidence of absorption.

It was a tick or two before he spoke. Behind

her, she heard the tiny "click" of a chess piece be-ing removed from the board.

"You like *all* of them?" He said this skeptically.

"Most of the time, yes."

He smiled at this, as if that had been a test and she'd passed.

"Ouch!" Dot muttered behind them.

"Mrs. Breedlove . . . what do you suppose I did between the time I was fished from the Thames a decade ago until the moment I walked through your door?"

"I can only surmise you spent at least a few minutes with an excellent tailor."

He gave a short nod again, as if she'd scored a point.

"The reason I know about falling masts, Mrs. Breedlove, is because I learned everything there is to know about a ship—from how to repair nets to how to sail one to how to make fortunes in cargo—after I awoke from a fever, only just alive, in the hold of one sailing to China. They had fished me from the water in the dead of night a few moments after I'd been cast in. Cold filthy water sobers one rather swiftly, in case you find yourself in a position requiring rapid sobering." He offered a swift, taut smile here. "I'd managed to swim to an opposite dock after I was cast in, but I'd gone under three times, and I'd decided the fourth would be the last. I was told later they'd wagered on whether my thrashing in the water was a rat drowning or something else. A coin flip saved them shooting me to put me out of my misery. They hauled me out of the water."

Angelique was motionless. Her ears were very nearly ringing with an onslaught of emotion, as though someone had clashed a cymbal nearby.

"The captain was a Dutchman named Janssen, working for the East India Company. The price of my life was labor. That, and my boots. They took my boots straight off." He smiled faintly. "Gave me a pair stolen off a dead pirate in exchange. My fencing and shooting lessons endeared me to Janssen. And coincidentally I know everything there is to know about how to convert a pirate from living to dead, thanks to that journey and the ones thereafter."

Somewhere during this recitation she'd begun to hold her breath. The terrifying plunge. The sink into the black dark. The despair, frustration, and exhaustion. Swords clanging, straining against each other in a great glinting metallic "X" in the air, hovering between life and death. He'd left the adjectives and the emotions out of his story, just as she had when she told Delilah her own story—the one and only time she'd told it in her entire life—but she felt them all the same.

Along with a ferocious, almost helpless, admiration. Devil's blood, indeed.

He waited.

She said nothing. Her stomach, however, had contracted as though she'd just been thrown into the brackish harbor waters.

"At no point did I think it was an unfair trade for my life, either the work I performed or the boots," he continued. "It's how I became who I am now, which is, frankly, wealthy. But I will never again wear boots that are anything other than the best that can be had. Or anything else for that matter. Life is short, brutal, and confusing. And because I'm able to do so, I see no reason I should not arrange it to suit my tastes or preference. Which happen to be excellent and particular."

He concluded this with an almost bored finality. As though his right to arrogance was inalienable.

She cleared her throat.

"What unusual luck you've had, Lord Bolt, of every variety. I am sorry if you've experienced suffering. I imagine you learned to be resilient. Adaptable to circumstances. So admirable. I doubt many men would survive such arduous, frightening conditions. You are to be commended."

Other men would begin basking in the compliment at this point. He was no fool. His sardonically uplifted brow told her he knew she was setting up a point.

"And somehow, the reward of this resilience is that you have become a man who needs to bend to no one. You have acquired wealth and, I suppose after a fashion, power. You don't normally do a thing you don't wish to do. You don't accommodate anyone you don't wish to tolerate for more than a second. And now and again you can't even be bothered with manners, and yours, I've noticed, when deployed, are exquisite. So as an ironic result of your resilience, you're more rigid now than ever you were. And much like the proverbial ship's mast in a storm, rigid men are a trifle prone to, well . . ."

She held out her two fists together and flicked them down sharply. *Snap.*

Then she tipped her head in mock sympathy.

He'd gone motionless. He stared wonderingly at her fists.

She put them back in her lap and laced her fingers neatly.

Then he lifted his eyes back to hers.

He gave a short, stunned laugh.

That is, if a sound resembling a laugh but lacking all amusement could be called a laugh.

"One might, in fact, describe it as a weakness. It's funny how wealth does that to a person, no matter how it is acquired," she added lightly. "Well, wealth, and being born a man."

It seemed she had decided détente was not her goal, after all.

Their gazes met and locked. She could *feel* the concentrated life force of him, like a blast of wind coming off the sea. She sensed there were limits to Lord Bolt's patience, but the frisson of danger wasn't unpleasant. It meant she'd found a vulnerability in him. She realized suddenly she'd been in search of that since he'd walked in. Something, anything, that made her feel more sure-footed around this man, whose very presence demanded everything of her senses from the moment she'd laid eyes on him.

When he spoke, his voice was low, deliberate, ironic. "And doubtless you have learned over the years that a stunningly beautiful woman can get away with saying nearly anything."

Her breath stopped in her lungs.

His words detonated in her like a little firework in her chest.

Perfidious vanity. But there it was.

And he knew, of course. Bastard. Because his eyes gave her no quarter.

They were hot and too intimate and yet deadly serious. In other words, very like how they would look glowing above her in a room lit only by a low fire, his arms planted on either side of her nude body as she arched her hips to—

She dug her nails hard into her palm.

The little pain was instantly as sobering as a cold plunge into the Thames.

Yet the next breath she took was both shallow and hot.

And to think she'd thought she was safe here at The Grand Palace on the Thames. And safety now meant freedom from desire—from her own, and from the kind of men who would pursue and then partake of her as thoughtlessly as they would a cigar or Belgian chocolates. In other words: most of them.

"I credited you with more insight than you

possess, Lord Bolt, if you think a woman of any kind is at liberty to say whatever she thinks without suffering consequences."

She managed to say it with some semblance of her usual aplomb.

One did not allow men like Lord Bolt to think they'd found a vulnerability.

She gave a little start and whipped around at the sound of a "Ha! Ha ha!" behind her.

Every chess win was as exciting as the first time for Mr. Delacorte.

Mr. Cassidy was muttering good-naturedly. He knew better than to swear. The epithet jar remained a reproachful presence.

Delilah caught her eye. Angelique gave her a quick smile and turned back to see Lord Bolt take another sip of brandy.

And for a moment they sat in a silence that seemed to be comprised of resettling impressions of each other. It was not a comfortable silence. But troublingly it was infinitely more interesting than any silence she'd ever before known.

His expression as he studied her was somewhat abstracted, as if she were a map to an unfamiliar place.

"Have you considered, Mrs. Breedlove," he began, "that I may, in fact, be in need of some comfort?"

She blinked, astonished.

His expression remained unreadable. He asked this question as if it were a question of academic interest. A debatable philosophical conundrum. It lacked even a shred of insinuation.

Which was a shame, because it would have been much easier to dismiss that sentence as euphemism: What could be more "comforting" than a quick tumble, from a man's perspective? That sort of thing. But she was pretty certain Lord Bolt was not a coy man.

Something about the careful way he'd said the words sneaked them past the spike-topped, thick-walled ramparts around her heart, and escaping from Newgate was easier to do than getting past those. She understood that this man's life had not been shaped by kindness. Perhaps he craved a little respite from whatever relentlessly drove him.

The one remaining undefended corner of her heart ached to reach over and stroke away the shadows beneath his eyes. Because nurturing was a woman's gift, and she had a gift for it, too. Maybe even a need for it.

And to think she'd just lectured him on the hazards of rigidity. The true danger was softness. Because men who were not shaped by kindness were ultimately hard. They sought their comforts from the softness of women. And some woman eventually paid the price.

She did not want to care. She did not *have* to care.

She was done paying that price. Period.

"Our staff here at The Grand Palace on the Thames will make sure your room is scrupulously clean, that you're well-fed and warm, and it's our policy not to allow anyone to kill our guests, unless they truly deserve it."

He laughed, surprised. A genuine, good laugh.

And something in her eased.

He sighed. "Tell me, Mrs. Breedlove. How did a woman like you come to be a boarding house proprietress? Something tells me you may have once, metaphorically speaking, been fished from the Thames. Because I know of a certainty one does not come by a predilection for lecturing here at the docks."

Oh, if only he'd been a little more stupid. He'd be so much easier to dislike.

Of all the things she'd been in her life— "daughter," "mistress," "ruined," to name a few— she told him the one thing that required the least explanation. Because she was not about to exchange intimacies with Lord Bolt.

"I was once a governess."

His smile was disarming and utterly charming. "Shocking."

She found herself smiling back at him. "You'll be happy to now have an opportunity to exercise your resilience when you join Mr. Delacorte and Mr. Cassidy for cigars and brandy. Go on, they're going now. I warrant they'll be kind to you."

"Very well," he said with an entirely feigned air of martyrdom. "I'll do it for you. But only because I yearn to be as treasured as your other guests."

She stood up from her chair. Slowly and gracefully.

He didn't bother to disguise that he watched every bit of that motion, the way one might watch a sunrise or any other beautiful thing one wanted to remember.

She didn't attempt to disguise that she knew he was watching.

"I want for nothing, Lord Bolt, so do not bother on my account. Do it for yourself . . . that is, if you wish to remain here at The Grand Palace on the Thames."

She delivered that with the kind of smile that ensured the last thing she saw before she walked away was Lord Bolt's expression.

And it was dazzled and transfixed.

SHE RETURNED TO sit beside Delilah.

And she lowered herself gingerly onto the settee. Her entire body seemed to be humming just a little, like a plucked string. She found she wanted to sit with the sensation. She didn't want to make another sound yet.

"Well, I heard him laugh," Delilah murmured. "So . . . well done?"

Poor Delilah had clearly been knitting twice as fast as usual out of nervousness. She'd regret those tiny stitches when she had to pick them out later.

Angelique wondered if she wished she could unpick some of the things she'd said to Lord Bolt tonight. It was too late now. Something was underway.

How was it that she had forgotten the difference between life with desire and life without it? It was like the difference between life with music and life without it.

"He did indeed laugh," she said finally.

"Does that mean it went well?"

She considered what to say.

"I think we shall be able to abide peaceably beneath this roof for the duration of his stay."

Chapter Four

❧❧❧

MUCH LIKE Lucifer himself, Lucien was no stranger to sudden evictions and abrupt changes in atmosphere. From impoverished waif to favored child. From favored child to pariah. From dry land into the Thames. That sort of thing.

And now—in truth, out of curiosity as much as anything else—he found himself back in what felt like the equivalent of the Thames. Or in other words, a little parlor set aside for men to do things women apparently wanted no part of, and where he most certainly did not want to be.

He did not want to be here, but he was curious.

The curiosity was about Mrs. Breedlove.

A decade ago, on the day when he was finally able to climb up a ladder to the deck of the ship that had rescued him, his beard was so long he could clutch it in his fist and he could all but strum his ribs like the bars of a cell. The sunlight slashed like razors across his skin and his eyes. He'd tipped his head back to watch a silver gull cut across the blue sky; when he closed his eyes, he could still see its outlines in blurred gold emblazoned against his eyelids. Perhaps for the first time he understood that simply being alive was a glorious thing. Perhaps it was enough for anyone.

Watching Angelique Breedlove walk away reminded him of that moment. She felt burned against his eyelids. A glorious irritant.

A woman like that made a man glad purely to be alive.

He had not anticipated the sort of distraction a campaign of seduction would present. But he could always make room in his busy itinerary of revenge.

Mr. Cassidy, Mr. Delacorte, and Lord Bolt had claimed three separate corners of the Gentleman's Room and not one seemed able to think of a word to say, which was probably Lucien's fault.

He couldn't bring himself to care very much.

He kept a wary eye on Delacorte, who reminded him of a friend's spaniel who, given the slightest opportunity, would hump his calf. Lucien had always needed to keep an outstretched booted foot gently pressed against the dog's sternum while its claws scrabbled the floor in the vain hope of gaining some kind of purchase. He could still see those doggie eyes gleaming in manically joyful, determined desperation.

He inspected the room. The carpets were a brown-and-beige scrolled pattern, the curtains hung in great panels of tobacco-colored velvet, and roomy leather chairs arrayed about the type of worn wood tables upon which men could heave boots. For God's sake.

"They really do think we're simple creatures, don't they?"

He hadn't realized he'd said it aloud until he heard it echo in the room.

"Women, you mean?" Mr. Cassidy said, proving that he, at least, wasn't a simple creature.

"That is . . . do they think colors will upset us?" Lucien was darkly amused. "Prove too stimulating? Prompt us to break out into duels and fisticuffs and fits of curse words?"

Mr. Cassidy gave a short laugh. "I like brown, frankly. Dirt, manure, gunstocks, my favorite mare. All brown. All wonderful things."

"I had a Moroccan mistress whose eyes were the most beautiful chocolate brown," Lucien mused.

Mr. Delacorte and Mr. Cassidy went still. They stared at him as if this Moroccan mistress had strolled nudely into the room and stretched out on a couch.

"Ah. Not a mistress crowd, I see," Lucien said regretfully. He inhaled a lungful of cheroot smoke. "My apologies."

"No need, Lord Bolt," Delacorte said kindly, as if Lucien had instead quietly broken wind. As if it could happen to anybody.

But he'd unfortunately created the kind of nonplussed silence that threatened to last the duration of the cheroot.

Lucien occupied himself by inspecting his companions through the veil of smoke.

The young and craggily handsome Mr. Cassidy had rather piercing blue eyes. His mouth smiled easily but there was something determined about the set of his jaw, and a sort of . . . suppressed impatience about him. As though he harbored a burning secret ambition or purpose. All determined men looked rather like that. Lucien had seen that kind of man look back at him in the mirror. Mr. Cassidy played his cards close, of that Lucien was certain. He wasn't certain he cared enough about the reason for it.

"Perhaps it's not because they think we're simple," Mr. Delacorte volunteered suddenly, causing the other two men to pivot toward him abruptly. "Perhaps it's more the way they would look after a pet. It's out of concern. Women don't trust us to look after ourselves and so they make it easy, you see. I had a blind aunt. We did the same in her house. Made sure she couldn't trip on or break things. Kept her path clear and simple like. They think we're like my blind aunt."

When both Lucien and Mr. Cassidy laughed, Mr. Delacorte's face was fulsome with happiness.

Lucien fixed Delacorte with a warning glare, foot at the ready should he become too enthusiastic and leap forward to peer at his buttons again or clap him with great cheer on his back or bellow "what ho!" or the sort of things Lucien was certain Delacorte did.

"No disrespect meant to your aunt, Delacorte," Mr. Cassidy added, hurriedly.

"Of course not." Delacorte waved his cigar dismissively, glowing with bonhomie. "She had a wonderful sense of humor. But Brownie and Goldy are all that is kind and solicitous and I don't think I shall ever wish to leave."

"Brownie . . ." Lucien said slowly, with wicked, gleeful disbelief ". . . and Goldy."

"Oh, I would never call them those names to their faces, mind you. I shouldn't be able to bear their disappointment if they heard me call them that. You won't tell them?" Delacorte pleaded up at him. His eyes were a rather lovely sort of misty blue. One would think they were the eyes of a dreamer if they weren't embedded in Mr. Delacorte's solid, pleasant face, which was perched atop a body reminiscent of a Welsh pony. His hair tufted out about the tops of his ears, however, which called to mind a red squirrel.

"I wouldn't dream of it," Lucien said, which was a lie. If a strategic opportunity arose, he absolutely would inform the proper Mrs. Breedlove that her nickname was "Goldy" just to watch the fascinating way in which her expression would change.

"I know the former Lady Derring is now married to a certain Captain Hardy. What do you know about Mrs. Breedlove?"

He didn't see any reason to be subtle about it. As he'd told her, life was short. He wanted information.

"As kind as the day is long," Mr. Delacorte

maintained stoutly. "Like waking up and every day is sunny, with the two of them in charge here."

"She has a clever wit and she is everything that is fine and proper," Mr. Cassidy contributed.

Lucien fixed Cassidy with a brief narrow look. This was a careful response. Mr. Cassidy doubtless had other thoughts about her that he wasn't about to share. What red-blooded man wouldn't?

Lucien would warrant Mrs. Breedlove knew *very* well how to be improper. She moved as though she knew the pleasures life had to offer, in bed and out of it.

Imagine the pleasure in teaching her not to be proper, if the opposite proved to be true.

Mr. Cassidy shifted restlessly from one leg to the other, as though he'd like to be outside gamboling through the woods or whatever it was Americans did since they'd freed themselves from England's smothering clutches.

"Where is *Mr.* Breedlove?"

"She's a widow," Delacorte said somberly.

Lucien nodded silently. Better and better.

"Perhaps you've both noticed that they're both beautiful," he said idly.

After a moment, Mr. Cassidy smiled slowly, ruefully at that. A tacit acknowledgment that all men of the species, no matter how formidable, were at the mercy of beauty.

And said nothing more.

He might get to like Cassidy.

"Have you got a wife, Bolt?" Delacorte ventured.

Lucien made an impatient sound. "Dear God, what would I want with one of those?"

They all laughed.

And when they were done laughing, Delacorte cleared his throat. "Actually I'm hoping to get me one of those."

"Of course you are," Lucien said. He blew a lazy ring of smoke into the room. "Perfect thing for you."

"She'd knock the rough edges from me."

"*Just* what I was thinking," Lucien said.

He suddenly remembered Mrs. Breedlove's expression, and her fists in the air snapping down. He felt his back teeth clamp. The *temerity* of the woman to lecture him that way.

But the restlessness he felt were her words scraping against his conscience. His own scrupulous sense of honesty forced the question: Was she right?

Perhaps he'd become the sort of man who could no longer recognize the good in others. Who could no longer respond to kindness with kindness. A little too dismissive. A little too like his father.

The notion made him uncomfortable.

"You'd be amazed what women want, Delacorte," he added. More conciliatorily.

"You, I would expect," Delacorte said sadly.

"Usually," Bolt agreed vaguely. Sympathetically. "But a woman will come along who has eyes only for you."

Did he believe this? He'd never really given it

any thought. He'd known love in his life, but it came hand in hand with devastation. He had not even bothered envisioning an ordinary life; he still felt a bit like he was at the mercy of the heaving wave of fate that had taken him across the world. He was back with a mission. He would be glad when it was done. But beyond that he hadn't yet imagined.

He'd made Delacorte smile, however.

"What about your mistress?" Delacorte seemed to relish the opportunity to casually use such a controversial word in a sentence.

"She left me to marry a wealthier man than I was at the time. I cannot say that I blame her."

Somehow, once again, he'd created an utter nonplussed silence.

"Do you . . . miss her?" Delacorte ventured.

Lucien fixed him with a long, pained stare. A man could only endure so much. "For heaven's sake . . . Delacorte. What on earth about me makes you think I might be a sentimental man?"

Delacorte was uncowed. "It's just that it always struck me as rather sad when people leave."

He has a kind heart, Mrs. Breedlove said.

It had been years since Lucien had felt a twinge of shame.

"It is," Lucien said shortly. "It is a sad thing."

He realized he very much didn't like to think about people leaving.

"But no," he added. "She doesn't haunt my memories. Thank you for your concern."

Delacorte nodded. "I like how you talk, Bolt. 'Haunt.'" He quoted dramatically, as though Byron might have written it.

"What brings *you* to London, Cassidy?" Bolt asked.

Cassidy took a deep breath and sighed it out. He seemed to be choosing his words carefully, which intrigued Lucien just a little.

"I am searching for a woman. You both may lower your eyebrows. It's rather after the fashion of . . . an assignment. For the sake of the lady in question, I am not at liberty to divulge more than that."

"Naturally," Lucien said gravely. "I believe I understand."

"Flew the coop, did she?" Delacorte chortled.

Lucien laughed.

Cassidy scowled quellingly.

Silence descended again.

Standing here with these two was indeed a bit more interesting than Lucien had anticipated.

Lucien wondered what the women of the house were doing now. Had they gone up to their rooms, to read, to laugh, to talk about all the men? He thought about Mrs. Breedlove unpinning her hair. He imagined the golden waves of it fanned over a white pillow.

In the midst of this reverie Delacorte's voice crashed. Lucien suspected he was frequently a reverie crasher.

"Lord Bolt . . . there is something we are wondering . . . that is, Mr. Cassidy and I . . . if we may be so presumptuous . . ."

Lucien sighed. "Yes, Mr. Delacorte. Nearly everything you've read about me is true."

Cassidy whistled, long and low. Teasing him.

And Delacorte seemed to have nothing to say. Which he supposed made it worth it.

"That was a decade ago. As you can see, I'm a grown man now. Do I look as though I intend to race a horse down Bond Street? Challenge a man to a duel? Make absurd wagers?"

Neither of them looked prepared to commit to the answer "no."

"Apart from revenge, I can't be bothered now with the rest of it."

This wasn't an answer designed to make anyone feel comfortable. Lucien had never been in the business of making anyone feel comfortable.

"There was never any question about your character in my mind, you see. Your character must be sound if Mrs. Hardy and Mrs. Breedlove think so. Such delightful people walk through that door."

He smiled tautly. "That is such a relief to hear, Delacorte."

"Where did you end up after you wound up in the drink, Bolt?" Delacorte wanted to know.

"China."

"Floated there on the currents, eh? Ha ha!"

Lucien eyed him with great, strained patience. "Was picked up by a ship. Learned everything about ships and imports and exports. And fighting. Made a pile." His cheroot was almost finished.

"You don't say! I import cures from China. Sell them to apothecaries."

Bolt went still and regarded him curiously. Now this was interesting, too. "What kind of cures are you talking about, Delacorte?"

"Oh, some of it is bollocks, mind you. Wouldn't cure a pimple. And some of it is, in *fact*, bollocks. Also, eyes and hooves and horns and snouts and tails and whatnot. Ground up, mixed with this and that. Most of it is made of herbs and you can take them in teas. Some of it works a treat. I try to sample my wares and know what I'm selling and I've good customers all over. Hard to get a wife when I travel so much," he said wistfully. "I expect that's true of you. Man goes thither and yon, and a woman wants to stay and have a family."

Bolt waved a hand noncommittally. "Is this a good business, this niche of yours, Delacorte?"

"Oh, I make a fair bit. A fair bit."

"I import silks and satins, spices, things of that nature. From the same region."

"Isn't that interesting? Captain Hardy just bought a ship and he's up to the same."

"Indeed. I look forward to meeting him. Some of the Chinese remedies are very effective, Delacorte. I say that with the utmost seriousness."

"You don't say." Mr. Cassidy was intrigued now, too. "Say, if I've a sore elbow—"

"Sore elbow, eh, Cassidy?" Delacorte chortled. "Doing a bit too much of this, eh?" He performed an astonishingly rude, explicit gesture with a pump of his fist.

Lucien and Cassidy dropped their jaws.

The silence nearly reverberated. It was so appalling it achieved a sort of transcendence.

It was also one of the funniest things Lucien had witnessed in his life.

In large part because Mr. Cassidy was eyeing Delacorte with the rankest astonishment he'd ever seen on another human's face.

"No," Mr. Cassidy finally managed. In a voice positively frayed with incredulity and great, strained patience.

"How much have you dropped in the epithet jar so far, Delacorte?" Lucien asked mildly.

"Three pounds twenty," Delacorte admitted. "But I feel I am becoming more and more of a fine gentleman every day, thanks to it."

"Well, that much is clear," Lucien said easily.

Mr. Cassidy grinned at Bolt.

Delacorte was still brisk. "Well, I've a salve I could sell you, Cassidy, for the elbow. Stinks like the inside of a hog pen. Good for aches and the like. But you could take the acupuncture cure, too. They stick needles into you so's you resemble a hedgehog, and snip snap your trouble is gone."

"Delacorte, have you gone mad?" Poor Cassidy sounded stern. His credulousness was taking a buffeting.

"I swear on me mum's grave."

"I won't swear on that, but they can do wonders with those needles," Lucien concurred easily. "Ancient remedy, tested by time. He's completely right."

"I know where we can all go get jabbed for our ailments. Take in a boxing match, get jabbed with needles," Delacorte said. "A pub meal."

This was what men were bound to get up to when they were segregated from women. Talk inevitably veered to stabbing, hitting, shooting, and masturbation, all followed by a greasy meal.

"Count me in, Delacorte," Mr. Cassidy said firmly.

Seemed the American was adventurous, but then he'd have to be, living in the colonies.

"Gentlemen, it's been a pleasure, but I must be off" was what Lucien said before he could be roped into acupuncture and boxing. "I've an appointment."

"Happy Revenging," Delacorte called after him cheerfully.

THE VIEW FROM the top of St. James Hill hadn't changed in a decade.

There it stood, for centuries the ultimate arbiter of whether one was a gentleman or not. Whether or not one *belonged*. White's. That he'd never been blackballed was purely a miracle, but they did seem to like their quotient of eccentrics and bastards, literally and figuratively. It made the members feel that much more superior. And his father was a duke, after all. By virtue of that alone his blood was bluer than most of the men who passed through the doors of White's.

Whether ghosts were ever admitted was another thing altogether. Ghosts did what they pleased, he suspected.

The famous bowed window was aglow with lamplight and blurred with the smoke of London's elite.

When he entered, he found the place teeming; conversation was lively and the hum of it meant attention was fixed elsewhere when he walked in, which was precisely what he wanted.

Head down, Lucien slipped through swiftly, found an unoccupied table in a dim corner next to a wall, and settled into one of the incomparably comfortable chairs.

After a moment or two of leafing through a newspaper someone had left behind, he accepted a drink from a passing waiter. A face he recognized. Older now, of course. As was he.

"Brandy," he said. He let his hand rest in the soft beam thrown by a sconce.

The waiter lowered a glass, and as he did, his eyes naturally were drawn to the gleam of gold circling his finger.

They lingered on that signet ring with its emblazoned "B."

Then slowly rose to Lucien's face.

Lucien regarded him with utter neutrality.

The man's expression didn't change at all as he backed away and moved to another table. But he was positively vibrating with suspicion.

Lucien smiled to himself.

He heard Lord Cuttweiler laugh—a great loud shout of it—at something one of his companions said. Cutty had always been quick with a laugh.

And Mr. Exeter had said Cutty would be here at this time, because he always was.

Lucien rose from his table and sauntered in that direction, his head down until he passed Cuttweiler's table.

At which point he looked Cuttweiler full in the face for the count of one . . . two. That was all it took.

Cuttweiler reared back as though acid had been dashed in his face.

And Lucien had the pleasure of seeing him blanch the color of the flawless napkins as he passed and disappeared swiftly out the door.

Chapter Five

࿇

BOLT IS BACK!

Dᴏᴛ ʟᴏᴡᴇʀᴇᴅ the broadsheet. It was a veritable shout, that particular sentence. Her reflex was to give it a little distance.

She'd read it aloud in the kitchen and Helga and the other maids gathered around, as had become their habit.

What were the men smoking at White's yesterday? One could not be blamed for thinking they had traded in their cigars in favor of passing about a hookah. Because at least five usually sober citizens swore Lucien Durand, Lord Bolt, everyone's favorite bastard, was sitting at the table behind them, reading a newspaper and sipping a brandy.

Ghosts don't drink brandy, gentlemen.

Are things in London about to get livelier?

"Well, then. He did say to read the broadsheets," Angelique murmured.

She had slipped into the room to stand over Dot's shoulder. Dot and all the maids gave a guilty start.

What was Lord Bolt playing at? He seemed to be, out of mischief or some larger plan, establishing a general air of nervous dread or drumming up fanfare. Which was either sinister or rather funny, depending upon how one wished to view it. Her instincts told her it was meant to be some combination of the two.

Wherever he'd been last night, he'd come back by curfew without a fuss, as the chambermaid who had lost the coin toss and was forced to wait upon him this morning reported to her on a whisper. Angelique did not want to examine too closely the quality of the relief she felt. It felt a little too much like gladness, and surely gladness was an unnecessarily specific way to feel.

"Wouldn't it be exciting to see your name in the newspaper, Mrs. Breedlove?"

"Good heavens, Dot. No." Angelique was exasperated. "You should not aspire to appear in the newspaper or gossip columns. It is not as glamorous as it seems. I should hope none of us *ever* are. It's not the kind of publicity that typically benefits an establishment, and do keep in mind your behavior here and elsewhere reflects on The Grand Palace on the Thames. So if you all could kindly refrain from frequenting gaming hells, we would appreciate it."

All the maids giggled.

But the muscles across Angelique's stomach suddenly tightened. For years they'd all known Lord Bolt as entertainment to be consumed, a pithy paragraph to read over the morning porridge. What must it have been like for him to know that all of London knew he was the rejected bastard of a duke? He seemed to have handled it with panache. But when she imagined her own bad luck, heartbreaks, and shame presented for public consumption and preserved for posterity, she couldn't breathe. The girl she once was would have been shocked to learn how much she cherished this extraordinary, ordinary life.

"Ladies."

When Mrs. Breedlove used that tone it made them nervous because it meant business. She was stricter than Mrs. Hardy. But they liked it, too. She expected more of them and she felt they were capable of excellence. It made them feel as though they were part of something important, and Mrs. Breedlove saw them as people. And Mrs. Breedlove was responsible for improving Dot's reading and spelling.

"Lord Bolt is our guest. As such, we have ascertained that he is proper and fit company for our beloved boarding house, and so, as we do for other guests, we will cherish his privacy and not mention him to another soul outside of our home. Is that clear?"

"Yes, Mrs. Breedlove." They nodded eagerly.

"Thank you. We appreciate your discretion."

She smiled at them. "And if I learn that any of you have betrayed his confidence, there will be consequences." She paused and fixed them with a meaningful raised-eyebrow stare to emphasize her point. "Now back to work."

"Discretion," Dot mouthed as they scattered to obey, saving that word up for use in a sentence one day. "*Consequences.*"

Fortified by a surprisingly accomplished breakfast of perfectly prepared eggs, sausage, and Lapsang Souchong miraculously and touchingly brought in for him, during which Delacorte and Cassidy didn't speak because their arms were blurs that ended with flashing forks and their faces were lit with absorbed, satisfied wonderment, Lucien set out on a very particular errand.

The Grand Palace on the Thames occupied a spot at 11 Lovell Street, which wasn't so much a street as a bit of fringe, like a loose thread on a sleeve, poking out onto the main street. The façade glowed white, which seemed rather a miracle given the twin insults of London weather and London coal, and it was tidy all around. Only two other buildings, plus a little pub that seemed to be called The Wolf And, according to its battered sign, shared the street.

And that's when he saw her.

She seemed more vivid than anything else surrounding them. She was standing very still, a vision in a green walking dress and heavy shawl, the faintest of furrows between her eyes. She was staring at something with such concentration she called to mind the quivering needle on a compass.

"Mrs. Breedlove. Good morning."

She pivoted.

There passed a moment, a little hiccup or snag in the flow of time, during which neither of them could seem to speak, as looking at each other was frankly all they wanted to do.

She'd tied her green bonnet ribbons in a neat bow beneath one ear, and it suddenly seemed like an arrow pointing to where he ought to put his lips. Right in that silky secret place where her pulse beat.

"Good morning, Lord Bolt. I expect you have a busy day of unnerving people ahead of you."

Little did she know how closely this hewed to his actual agenda.

"Naturally. Fine weather for it. Saw not one but *two* gentlemen pissing against the side of the building across the street this morning and that struck me an augury. The way seeing two ravens is and whatnot."

She quirked the corner of her mouth and sighed. "Yes, that is a bit of a risky view, though that window does offer a good bit of light and a lovely view of the moon. And by the way, that's an example of an observation you might not want to share in the drawing room in the evening, at least in precisely those words."

"Once a governess, always etcetera. Never let a lesson go by unuttered."

"Precisely."

"Perhaps I shall utter one epithet after another in rapid succession and flip shillings into the jar the way one casts aside the shells of roasted chestnuts."

He watched incredulity, irritation, hilarity, and a sort of wonder mingle in her expression like the awkward assortment of humans in the parlor. That little furrow formed between her brow again. She regarded him as if he were a marvel, a confusing natural phenomenon, something she would never believe existed unless she'd seen it with her own eyes.

There were worse ways to be stared at, of a certainty.

"We would welcome the revenue. And the opportunity to perhaps refine our rules," she said.

He grinned.

She turned slightly away from him then, rather swiftly, to stare at whatever she seemed to have been staring at previously. A moment later she aimed a sidelong look through dark gold lashes and smiled. He felt that smile like a sharp, sweet kick in his solar plexus.

Her top lip was a little shorter than her bottom.

Her mouth was, in fact, rather like a lush, pale pink heart.

Before too long he would need to do something about getting Mrs. Breedlove into his bed.

Because if he felt this restless now, he would be well nigh on savage within days.

The notion made his mood soar.

He stretched luxuriously and inhaled deeply. "Ah, the docks."

He was only being partially sardonic. He'd been to dozens of worldly cities, but he frankly loved London, replete with all of its smells. Ocean, food, feces, humans, animals, coal, lashing winds off the ocean, *life*. And a beautiful woman who seemed out of context here at the docks, and yet something about her was like the first flower poking from barren ground in the spring.

"Oh, yes, the *docks*." She mimicked his cheerfully ironic tone.

He sensed the docks would not have been her first choice of home.

"Don't you have urgent business to attend to, Lord Bolt?"

"Oh, no business occurs if I'm not present for it. If I may be so bold, you seem to be out here on this fine day staring avidly at nothing, Mrs. Breedlove. You call to mind Nelson on the deck of a ship with a spyglass."

"I am, in fact, staring at this patch of dirt here between the buildings. And waiting for Helga to emerge with her basket so we can go to the market. A scullery maid needed a talking to. They generally do."

"Helga is . . ."

"Our cook."

"Indeed. She is gifted."

"She knows."

He smiled at that.

"*And* our excellent food is one of the *many* reasons people enjoy staying with us at The Grand Palace on the Thames." She turned to him, delivering this little advertisement pointedly.

He nodded, with exaggerated gravity. "Does this patch of dirt hold significance, Mrs. Breedlove?"

The patch of dirt in question was surrounded by cobblestones. What might have once been a tree occupied the center. It was stripped bare now and sported two sad spindly branches. It could just have easily been a twig blown violently in off the ocean and hurled like a trident by the wind in muddy ground during a storm.

She hesitated. "I imagined a garden here. With benches and flowers. Surrounded by perhaps a little wrought iron fence with a gate. Leading to the building we'd like to buy."

He went still. "The one I might buy."

"Why, yes," she said brightly.

They stared each other down.

"That is fascinating, indeed, Mrs. Breedlove," he said idly. "One would think you would have mentioned it yesterday."

"I suppose one would think that," she agreed pleasantly. "Why haven't you bought it yet, Lord Bolt?"

"Why haven't *you* bought it yet?"

Neither one of them took that up. Lucien was waiting for a ship.

"Buyers aren't precisely clamoring for it," he said. "Given its location. So one of us is bound to eventually be the proud owner. But why the devil do you need this building, Mrs. Breedlove? One building near the docks strikes me as enough of a liability."

She sighed. "We imagined it as an annex to The Grand Palace on the Thames. Delilah and I envisioned it brimming with happy families in London for, oh, a bit of a vacation. Or Londoners needing a place to stay if repairs or renovations are being performed on their homes. Children running about, perhaps. It would be . . . lively. Heavenly, even."

She sounded wistful.

"What a coincidence. I pictured it fair teeming with drunk young bloods eager to lose their fortunes. Which is very nearly the same thing as a place teeming with children."

"The upper three suites are *perfect* for lodging families," she added, as though he hadn't said a thing.

"I thought those suites would be perfect for accommodating gentlemen to stay after a long, hard evening of gambling. I'd call the suites . . . Drunk, Drunker, and Drunkest."

She fought and lost a battle to a smile. "You are indeed a man of vision."

He smiled at her. It seemed improbable that she

could say so many things in a row that made him look forward to the next thing she might say. But there it was.

"The *ton* would be shocked if they truly understood the degree of my ambition."

"If only you were to apply it to something more worthy, Lord Bolt."

"What could be more worthy than my gaming hell? Staff would tenderly care for all of those young men while they recovered from their evening. It would all be very safe and genteel and no one would be robbed or murdered."

"Well. That is everything a young man could possibly hope for."

He laughed.

"Lord Bolt, I have a question for you. Given that you're currently a merchant, shall we say, what on earth do you know, if anything, about running a gaming hell, apart from how it's a wonderful place to lose money?"

"A good deal, as it so happens. Gambling was how I supported myself and my mother between the ages of eighteen and twenty-three, the latter being the age I was thrown into the Thames," he said shortly. "No one wanted to hire me as a dancing master or Latin tutor."

"Did you *really* try to be a dancing master or a tutor?" She was startled.

He merely grinned at that and dodged the question. "Gaming hell owners liked my notoriety, you see. It was good advertising for them, so they were indulgent when I exercised my idle curiosity and asked questions about how to run a gaming hell. I am nothing if not thorough, Mrs. Breedlove."

Her expression—some hybrid of sympathy and censure and admiration, all of them warring a little—was a window into her thoughts. But she didn't reply.

"All right then, I have a question for you. Why buy a building *now*, Mrs. Breedlove? When you have only lately set up in business? I ask that as a businessman accustomed to assessing risk."

Oddly she hesitated. As if she were trying to find precisely the right words, or uncertain she wanted to tell him. "Well, Mrs. Hardy came into the property here at Number 11 Lovell Street, The Grand Palace on the Thames. And we are now doing more than just surviving. Ambition seemed a luxury at one time, and I didn't dare harbor any. Ambition means we are *thriving*, and can hope for more."

"And you want to hope for more." He was, for an instant, unaccountably a little moved.

"I suppose so." But she sounded abstracted. Then she gave herself a little shake, as if she'd revealed more than she'd intended. "And the nearby livery is so useful—"

"Oh, yes. I thought so, too."

"—because if a family should wish to hire a carriage, or shelter their own horses, it's merely a short walk away."

"I thought I'd keep a carriage there to convey gentlemen home again if they're too foxed to give their direction to a hack driver or to get there under their own perambulation. Provided of course they haven't *gambled* away the family home."

He thoroughly enjoyed the appalled amusement in her expression.

"*But* . . . the chief attraction is the ballroom," he prompted with a flourish. As if they shared a script.

"I agree. That is Delilah—Mrs. Hardy's—dream to have cozy musicales where everyone who can form words will be invited to sing them instead." She sounded resigned.

His own face must have registered horror then. "And do *you* have other ideas?"

"But I thought . . . given the proximity to the livery . . . and to comfortable accommodations . . . we might charge now and again for quality musical evenings. A fine soprano, perhaps. Excellent musicians."

"Hmm. Enterprising of you. Sound idea."

"I thought so."

"I've known a few fine sopranos in my day."

"I am certain you have."

He smiled.

There was a little silence.

Without either of them realizing it, with every sentence, they'd moved just a little closer to each other, as though pulled by some invisible tide.

The distance between them seemed to pulse, the awareness so dense he could almost grab handfuls of it.

Oh, how he loved the delicious period between nascent lust and the animal satisfaction of it; he loved the serrated anticipation, the not knowing, and yet knowing. He was going to enjoy every bit of it while he was here. Widows were the *ideal* temporary lovers.

"And I intend to call it the Duchess of Brexford's Den of Iniquity," he said softly.

Her eyes flew wide in astonishment.

Her jaw dropped.

And then she released a full-throated shout of mirth that showed all of her teeth, and good God that laugh was the best thing he'd ever heard.

"Oh." She wiped her eyes. "Oh, my."

He was basking. Quite stunned, really.

"I take it you're familiar with my stepmother, then."

"A gaming hell is a perfect tribute to her. She is an *awful* person," she said fervently.

"You don't know the half of it, Mrs. Breedlove."

He wasn't about to enlighten her. He wagered she'd look at him another way entirely if she knew what he suspected.

"She is always trying to steal our cook. Our cook learned her lesson the hard way and will not work for her at any price. And she also once fired Dot."

"Dot? Is she the maid with eyes like a baby

owl's? Ye Gods. She dropped the coal scuttle in my room this morning and it wobbled for a good ten minutes if it wobbled one and it took another year of my life. I suppose my stepmother always did have impeccable taste in servants."

"Poor Dot must have drawn the short straw if she was the one building your fires this morning. I think they're all quite in awe of you. Which is another way of saying they are terrified of you."

Mrs. Breedlove was teasing him and he considered this a triumph. A milestone. An augury of things to come, like the ravens and the pissing men.

He rewarded her with a smile.

And she abruptly turned her head just a little away again. Something about it—the turning away—called to mind a woman tugging her shawl more snugly about her to cover the bare places. A protective gesture.

"Delilah has a kind heart. And Dot came along with Delilah. Dot is ours forever, I think," she said resignedly.

"That *is* a shame. Doubtless your resilience and fortitude will pull you through," he said gravely.

She smiled at him again. And it was the kind of smile that made him feel as though he'd bolted champagne.

"You'll need wrought iron flowers as well as a wrought iron fence if you'd like them to survive here by the docks, Mrs. Breedlove."

"I think the fact that The Grand Palace on the

Thames is thriving is proof enough that miracles happen, Lord Bolt."

"I think," he mused, "your bottom lip is a miracle."

She went still.

Her breath left her in a little shocked sound.

It hovered near her parted lips, a tiny white ghost between them for a few seconds on the chill February air.

Caught in the beam of each other's gaze, they were both motionless. Fascinated. Wary.

A breeze seized and tossed her bonnet ribbons.

And then he noticed her shoulders rising and falling, rising and falling with swifter breaths.

He exulted.

The next breath he took was hot and unsteady.

Then both turned at the sound of footsteps racing up behind them.

"Begging your pardon, Mrs. Breedlove, the girl is lazy as the day is long but she's me sister's—oh, my goodness it's . . . Lord Bolt."

She put a hand to her heart.

Helga was a handsome and formidably tall woman, with glowing cheeks, a pile of gray and gold hair, and biceps many a man would envy, earned from pummeling bread and hoisting roast haunches, stirring delicious things, no doubt. She was tugging her shawl about her.

"You must be Helga. I was just telling Mrs. Breedlove how much I enjoyed breakfast. You have a gift."

He left two speechless and radiant women behind him when he strode off.

BOND STREET WAS its usual lively deafening
throng of men and carriages and horses, and,
frankly, he'd missed it. Lucien waded into it as
though it were a balmy sea, letting the shouts
and laughter and furious arguments of pedestrians, the pye men and costermongers bellow-
ing their wares, crest and break over him. But he
kept his head down. A decade ago this had been
one of his haunts, and little had changed about
the storefronts. He was also, and had never been,
an inconspicuous man, and his plans today, part
of a multipronged plan, rather hinged upon ano-
nymity.

He passed the watchmaker who'd repaired the
watch his father had given him.

He passed a maker of fine stringed instruments.

He passed the jeweler where his father had
bought for him the singular signet ring he wore.

And when he'd nearly reached Oxford Street,
he ducked into an alley between a tobacconist
and a haberdasher and waited. Mr. Exeter had
done his research well.

At half past nine Lord Cuttweiler strolled
briskly by, the picture of cheerful self-satisfaction.
There was a good twenty pounds more of him
than the last night Lucien had seen him, but the
nose pointing skyward was unmistakable. The

gold tip of his walking stick winked and tapped merrily on the ground.

Lucien slipped from the alley and fell into easy stride alongside him without saying a word. And such was the throng that one would scarcely notice a brushed elbow.

So when Cuttweiler glanced left, it was really more a reflex than anything else. He didn't seem to notice a thing.

But something primal must have jerked his head back around in that direction again.

And when he did, he met Lucien's gaze full on.

Cuttweiler stopped abruptly.

Another man tripped over him and uttered an oath.

Lucien didn't blink as he stared at him.

Cuttweiler's throat moved in a swallow. And before Lucien's eyes he blanched to the shade of buttermilk.

"Oh God . . . Dear God . . . No . . . please no . . . it can't be . . . no . . . No. No. NOOOOOO."

Somehow Lucien doubted an innocent man would scramble backward with every "no" and turn the last one into a wail.

Cuttweiler ricocheted like a billiard ball off the pedestrians in the crowd, staggering, spinning, tripping, never quite getting control of his balance until he finally hurtled backward into a costermonger's cart.

The stacked pyramids of apples exploded and

rained down on the crowd amid shrieks and epithets.

That would do for now, Lucien thought with grim satisfaction.

He scooped up a rolling apple and rubbed it on his shirt.

And Lucien quietly melted away.

Chapter Six

❦

"MRS. BREEDLOVE, if you move closer to the fire, it will be easier to get a good portrait of you."

Angelique looked up from her knitting at the chair that Mrs. Pariseau was gesturing to.

Unfortunately "closer to the fire" was almost comically on the nose. It was much closer to where Lord Bolt was sitting, that little book in his hand, long legs outstretched, radiating impatience.

"By all means, Mrs. Pariseau."

Lucien looked up and saluted her with a raise of his eyebrows. He lingered on her face.

I notice everything, he'd said.

Thanks to him, she'd caught herself several times today softly dragging a fingertip across her bottom lip.

She'd forgotten, somehow, the shivery, subtle pleasures that hid in that tender place. If the right person knew how to coax them out.

She wondered if this was his strategy. *Your bottom lip is a miracle. A stunningly beautiful woman.* Perhaps when he set out to seduce, he placed these sorts of words about like little lit coals in a straw house. Strategically, here and there. Enough of them and the house was eventually, slowly, bound to burst into flames all on its own.

Thinking of it as strategy was what kept her finger off her lips for the rest of the day.

Mrs. Pariseau had decided to draw everyone at The Grand Palace on the Thames in turn.

"I should like to draw you, too, Lord Bolt," Mrs. Pariseau said, as she rotated the chair Angelique sat upon. As though he were a three-year-old being promised a sweet.

"Everybody does, eventually," he said absently.

He didn't look up at all.

And it was as though he felt Angelique's admonishing glare.

"Thank you, Mrs. Pariseau," he added. Amused. Pointedly.

Mr. Delacorte, Mr. Cassidy, Delilah, and Dot were engaged in a rather harrowing game of spillikins, interrupted now and again by shouts of cheerful dismay when the wrong pillikin was moved.

And it was Delacorte, impatiently waiting his turn, who asked the question that Angelique longed to know the answer to but did not want Bolt to know she longed to know the answer to.

"What are you reading, Bolt?"

Lucien looked up and said the one word guaranteed to create a nonplussed and perhaps permanent silence.

"Poetry."

The silence did indeed ensue.

It certainly was perhaps the last thing Angelique expected to hear but she wasn't about to say that out loud.

In a room that contained Delacorte, silence was destined not to last.

"Never say poetry, Bolt!" Delacorte was stunned. "Is that why you go about using words like 'haunt' when it's naught to do with ghosts? Instead it's to do with Moroccan mist—"

A fascinatingly black warning look Bolt aimed at Delacorte shriveled his words on his tongue.

Angelique was immediately curious.

"But . . . why?" Mr. Cassidy seemed sincerely troubled. "I never understood the 'why' of poetry. To go out of your way to sit and ponder and write about things when you could go out and simply *be* in the world. Smell it. Taste it. Touch it. Climb it. Sail it."

Bolt was studying Cassidy expressionlessly, but his eyes were very intent and bemused. Angelique could almost hear his single thought: *Americans.*

"Indeed, Mr. Cassidy. But I like it because the world is a chaotic place filled with millions of things that require us to think and feel, and poetry distills it in neat couplets and stanzas that are very like music. There is something soothing about it, and I think there's something masterful in the attempt. And I feel it focuses the mind, the rhymes and images. Not every poet goes on about daffodils."

Angelique watched him, suddenly breathless

with reluctant fascination and a near traitorous, restless ache she patently did not want to feel. *Have you ever considered that I might be in need of a bit of comfort?* He'd endured horrors and hardships with an inimitable aplomb. What, if anything, softened the contours of his life? Apart, of course, from Lapsang Souchong, gaming hells, and the truly wonderful pillows here at The Grand Palace on the Thames.

He turned her way as if he sensed an opportunity to drink in her gaze.

It took a moment, but she managed to avert her gaze again and resolved to keep it averted.

I am not so easy, or foolish, as that, Lord Bolt.

"Read a bit of poetry, if you would, Bolt," Delacorte called out.

Dot had collapsed the entire pile of pillikins when she'd attempted to take her turn at pulling one and they needed to start the game all over again.

Lord Bolt sighed. "Very well, Delacorte."

And in a sonorously beautiful voice he read:

"But oh! that deep romantic chasm which slanted
Down the green hill athwart a cedarn cover!
A savage place! as holy and enchanted
As e'er beneath a waning moon was haunted
By woman wailing for her demon lover!"

Holy—!

Everyone was *quite* surprised.

Not one person moved a hair.

"'A savage place, holy and enchanted,'" Bolt repeated, mildly. "Reminds me of this drawing room."

Angelique stifled with her knuckles what threatened to be a shout of laughter.

"You could go on stage, Lord Bolt, with a voice like that," Mrs. Pariseau declared.

"Yes, if your gaming hell should not work out, you must absolutely consider the stage," Angelique agreed.

He was smiling at her. She could feel it as surely as she could feel the sun through a window. She dare not look. To look was to court that sweet sharp jolt she felt in the region of her heart, and, if she were being honest, the region of her loins.

"Mrs. Breedlove, kindly do not laugh while you are posing. I am trying to draw your mouth."

"Would it be possible to do my ears first?"

"I have done your ears." Mrs. Pariseau was strict. "Mouthless faces are simply eerie, dear."

Angelique sighed. "Oh, very well."

"I recognize that as Samuel Taylor Coleridge, by the way, Lord Bolt," she murmured between narrowed lips. With a rebellious glance at Mrs. Pariseau.

Mrs. Pariseau paused to glare her into silence.

"Yes." He sounded surprised that she knew it. "I was curious, because I'd heard he wrote it in the midst of fever, and so I sought it out. One sees the most remarkable things in the midst of fever dreams."

There was a silence.

"Go ahead, dear," Mrs. Pariseau sighed. "I can feel that you're fair quivering to make some sort of point."

"Here is the part *I* find most compelling, Lord Bolt," Angelique said.

> *"And all who heard should see them there,*
> *And all should cry, Beware! Beware!*
> *His flashing eyes, his floating hair!*
> *Weave a circle round him thrice,*
> *And close your eyes with holy dread*
> *For he on honey-dew hath fed,*
> *And drunk the milk of Paradise."*

She punctuated her delivery with an eyebrow launch.

He'd heard the "beware, beware" bit precisely as she'd intended him to. Their gazes met and his eyes were virtually dancing. He was entirely undaunted. His lips curved just a very little.

To her horror, she imagined drawing her tongue along the long swoop of the bottom one.

"Mrs. Breedlove, please don't look *down* suddenly like that or your chin will turn out very odd indeed. You are as wriggly as a toddler."

Thusly Angelique was forced to look straight at Lord Bolt again, much to his amusement. He took unchivalrous advantage by staring unabashedly straight at her.

Surely Mrs. Pariseau couldn't object if she aimed her eyes sideways.

"Demons, dread," Delacorte mused. "Sounds as thrilling as a horrid novel, that poem. I should like to read the whole of it. I only know one poem by heart, and it's shorter."

"Perhaps you'll favor us with it, Mr. Delacorte," Delilah encouraged, trying to distract him because she needed a little more time to choose her pillikin.

"Well." He cleared his throat, flattered and a little bashful. "You should not expect a performance quite as impressive as Lord Bolt's, but I shall do my best."

He rose and put a hand to his chest, and in stentorian tones he declaimed:

"Six times did his iron by vigorous heating,
Grow soft in her forge in a minute or so,
And as often was hardened, still beating and
*   beating,*
But each time it softened, it hardened more slow.
With a jingle bang, jingle bang, jingle bang, jingle,
With a jingle bang, jingle bang, jingle, hi ho!"

Every single jaw in the room dropped as though their hinges had collectively snapped.

Mr. Delacorte took the gaping as a tribute,

and beamed. His smile gradually faded when he took in the expressions above those gaping jaws. Shock, horror, and rueful resignation (Cassidy), and gleeful hilarity (Bolt).

It was Bolt who spoke first. "Not a poem, I'm afraid, Mr. Delacorte," he said lightly. "It's about a woman whose husband is no longer virile and she meets a young blacksmith who—"

"I think we *all* know what it's about, Lord Bolt, thank you," Angelique interjected sternly.

Delacorte's shoulders slumped and he sighed. "Well. My brother had one over on me, then, when he taught me that. How much should I put in the jar?"

"Fifty *pounds*," demanded Mr. Cassidy. He was pretending to be incensed. "Because now I shall be going about singing 'jingle bang, jingle bang' in my head for weeks, damn you."

"It's unprecedented," Delilah said soothingly. "Though it's undoubtedly a wholly inappropriate poem for mixed company. Mrs. Breedlove and I shall need to discuss it later to decide. But how about a pence for now, as usual?"

Delacorte heaved another sigh, stood, and plinked a pence into the epithet jar.

Followed by Mr. Cassidy, who, being a man of honor, dropped in his own pence for the "damn" without being asked.

"If you've done with spillikins, Delacorte, Mr. Cassidy, we shall have a cheroot and I'll tell you about a poem you can recite in mixed company. It makes the ladies swoon." Bolt issued this surprisingly magnanimous invitation.

One could only hold in all epithets for so long, she supposed.

Mr. Delacorte and Mr. Cassidy were up for some time with men only. They shot to their feet.

Bolt languidly rose from his chair and lead a caravan of sorts to the Gentleman's Room. "The poem goes a bit like this:

"She walks in beauty, like the night
Of cloudless climes and starry skies;
And all that's best of dark and bright
Meet in her aspect and her eyes."

"Oh, my . . . right beautiful, Bolt," Delacorte breathed.

"I so agree," Bolt murmured idly as he swept Angelique with a look as sultry as a caress on his way out of the room. "Don't look up, Mrs. Breedlove. Mrs. Pariseau is working on your eyebrow."

Chapter Seven

༄༅༄

*L*UCIEN SELDOM frequented the north end of London Bridge, but Mr. Exeter had told him that this was where he ought to be at two o'clock in the afternoon. And of all the things Lucien had learned to place his faith in—his sword arm, his W.A. Jones pistols with the saw-handled butts, his charm—he perhaps ranked Mr. Exeter's suggestions at the top. Of the precious few qualities that he and Exeter shared, thoroughness was one of them.

Lord Cuttweiler, his step not quite so jaunty and assured now—his aspect might even be described as a trifle *twitchy*, Lucien noted with grim satisfaction—came into view.

Lucien waited until Cuttweiler was flush with the place he stood. And when the gold tip of his walking stick flashed flush with his hiding place, Lucien stepped forward and shouted, "NOW!"

Cuttweiler shot straight up into the air and spun about like a drunken mill wheel, his limbs flailing all at once in every direction, swinging his walking stick through the air as though at invisible attackers. "Ah! No! Ah! AHHHH!"

A few passersby eyed him warily and picked up their pace.

Lucien enjoyed this spectacle for the space of about four seconds and then raised his own voice. "For God's sake, don't piss yourself, Cuttweiler. It'll make this conversation even more unpleasant than I intend for it to be. I'm alive. Not a ghost. Do shut up."

The reasonable tone finally got through to Cuttweiler. He got hold of himself and stopped the flailing and the little terrified shouts.

Cuttweiler inspected Lucien with a dumb-struck fascination.

Lucien allowed him to do this for a quarter of a minute and took great pains to look bored.

"Bolt. Well. So the rumors are true. You're look-ing well," Cuttweiler tried finally. With a certain cautious friendliness. He dared to allow a wobbly smile to begin to form.

Lucien fixed him with such a look of cold amaze-ment that all hope drained from Cuttweiler's face and left it gray.

Lucien allowed Cutty to chill in that gaze in silence.

"Are you going to kill me, Bolt?" Cuttweiler was trying for defiance. He missed it by about an octave. His voice emerged like the strained blat of a broken flute.

"Why, do you think you *deserve* killing, Cutty?" he said conversationally. "Got something on your conscience? Or do you think killing would be easier than merely haunting you for the rest of your life? Leaping out of nowhere and so forth? You'll never, *never* know where I might turn up. I'm perfectly willing to do either one."

Cutty was mulling his choices.

"Well, I really don't want to die." Cutty's voice was trembling now.

"Nobody does, Cutty," Lucien said with great faux sympathy. "Nobody does. That is, I certainly didn't. And yet one moment there I was, happily drunk, heading home from a club with one of my dearest friends—that would be you—and the next I heard your voice say 'NOW . . .'"

Cuttweiler's Adam's apple undulated in his throat with a hard swallow.

"—and just like that, these two mongrels, two brutes, appeared from nowhere, got hold of my arms and legs before I could get hold of my weapon, and threw me into the drink. The most *remarkable* thing." He furrowed his brow in faux amazement. "You'd have thought that everyone involved *wanted. Me. To. Die.*"

He issued those words with an icy ferocity and banged out each one with his walking stick.

Cuttweiler flinched every time.

He was now greenish around the mouth. His words clicked out aridly, in stuttering bursts. The battalions of sweat beads ranked at his hairline began to make their way down his face. "Awf-awful thing, Lucien. I was gutted. I tried to save you. I, er, shouted for help, I did."

Lucien snorted. "Come now, Cutty, even that lie lacks conviction."

For a moment they stood in a silent stalemate. Cutty seemed trapped in Lucien's remorseless stare.

"If you're going to kill me, I wish you'd do it sooner rather than later, Bolt," he said. With great noble suffering. His voice was hoarse now.

"Why oh why would I kill you? Have you a guilty conscience, Cutty? Two men are standing here, and only one of them is a murderer. Here's a hint: it's not me."

Two white dents lay alongside the man's nostrils and Lucien could actually see the little hairs fluttering in them as he siphoned in shallow breaths.

"Even when I shot a man in a duel I made a point of *not* killing him."

"Lucien . . ."

"Even when I stabbed a pirate to death boarding the cutter I was on, it wasn't murder, given that he was trying to kill me. I certainly know how to do it in a number of ways, but it isn't pleasant nor is it precisely easy to kill a man, Cutty, not if one isn't evil. And I'm many things, but I'm not that. Although . . ." Lucien drummed his chin. "I suppose it's easier to kill someone if your only job is to say '*Now.*'"

Cutty blinked through all these words as if they were hailstones landing on him.

And then he was silent.

The fight had gone out of him. Then again, the

quotient of fight in him was probably minute to begin with. He was waiting this encounter out the way a man waits for his turn at the gallows.

"Why, Cutty? That's what I want to know. Then we'll discuss how you'll make restitution."

Had a word ever sounded so sinister as "restitution"? It certainly made Cutty wince.

"Lucien, I have scarcely slept a night since. The remorse has been a blight upon my life. I have missed your company. It wasn't worth it. It wasn't worth it." He did sound sincere. Cutty hadn't the sort of subtlety that went into making convincing liars.

"Well, I imagine you feel that way now since your murder didn't quite *take*."

Cutty turned his head toward the water. He was probably wondering whether jumping in was more advisable than standing here.

Lucien was growing weary of the conversation. He'd once counted this man as a friend and he didn't know why, except that "friend" meant very little back then—someone with whom to drink and gamble and exchange prurient anecdotes about women, he supposed. Cutty had been good for a laugh and he hadn't cared that Lucien was a reckless bastard, and that had mattered, too.

It was a singularly lovely day. A feathery white cloud hovered above them in the blue sky; the surface of the river was a blinding, rippling silver beneath the sun.

"Isn't it ironic that we're right here next to the water, Cutty, where last we saw each other? I'm not adverse to doing a little damage to your person in order to get the answers. Perhaps tipping you over the side. I like the poetry of it. You'd sink like a stone now. Clearly you've been so distressed by my death that you haven't had a bite to eat since."

Lord Cuttweiler sighed bleakly. "Fine," he said evenly. "Do what you will, Lucien. I understand. I deserve it. I know the kind of man I am and so do you—a weak one. But I was desperate. You knew the kind of debt I was in. I would have ruined my family, my prospects, my future, the *shame* of it. And Bolt, she paid my debts."

Lucien went still. "She . . ."

But he knew. He supposed he'd always known.

Hearing it said aloud was another thing altogether.

"Your stepmother. The duchess. Sent an emissary to me and told me she'd pay my debts and all I had to do was walk with you by the river and shout 'NOW!' at precisely that time of the night. And though nothing was stated explicitly, I suppose I did know what was about to happen. I haven't been able to get it out of my head since, Bolt, and that's the truth. I'm not evil. Weak bastard, perhaps. Not evil."

Lucien was still.

Hearing his suspicions confirmed was not quite the liberation he'd expected.

It heralded no cleansing surge of triumph. The sadness, however, was a surprise.

But it mattered that it had been said aloud.

The duchess—the former Lady Medger—had swept into the duke's life years ago and ruthlessly swept everything out of it, and that meant Lucien and his mother. Apparently she'd intended to be even more thorough about it than Lucien realized.

"She did write to you, Lucien, remember. She begged you to behave—what was the word that made us laugh? You and me and Hallworth roared about it that time we were thrown out of the Rogue's Palace?"

"'Decorously,'" Lucien said absently. "'Decorously' was the word. She wanted me to behave decorously."

She had indeed written. She'd said his father wanted nothing to do with him and would frown upon her writing to him, and would not see him even if he was contacted. But if Lucien had a shred of decency—this was how she put it—he would strive to remain out of the broadsheets to spare the Duke and Duchess of Brexford and her little son embarrassment.

"I'm not positive she wanted to do you in, Loos," Cutty said quietly. "Maybe just frighten you a bit. Maybe get you to go away for a time."

"Do you know who those men were who got hold of me?" He said this abstractedly. He was reeling.

"No," Cutty said.

Lucien believed him.

He and Cutty stared at the water below in an odd sort of peaceful communion. Doubtless the knowledge had indeed plagued Cutty, and the confession was a release. Lucien had no pity for him. He was the last person inclined to offer absolution to anyone.

But oddly he found he didn't even care what Cutty did now.

Lucien wasn't a fundamentally somber person. To shift the sudden weighty bleakness, his thoughts felt about for comfort and landed, to his surprise, on Mrs. Breedlove. He pictured her standing and staring at that stick in the ground outside The Grand Palace on the Thames, a little furrow between her eyes, daring to dream her modest dream of a future, while he stood here and addressed the ugly, ragged ends of his past.

"You can't prove a damn thing, you know," Cuttweiler said, after a moment. Though he sounded weary and even sympathetic.

"I know."

Another little silence.

"Funny thing is, Loos . . . they liked to say you had devil's blood and whatnot and we used to laugh about it . . . I think she really does."

HE LEFT CUTTWEILER by the river with the grimly cheery warning: "I'll be in touch to let you know how you can make it up to me, Cutty. I'm back in London for good now. Don't even think about contacting the duchess, because I'll know."

Because Cutty deserved to have his day thoroughly ruined, at the very least.

Cutty vowed his behavior would be faultless. He seemed resigned to some sort of restitution.

And yet Lucien wasn't positive he *would* be in touch. He wasn't certain he was prepared to let Cutty go for good with a "cheers, got that settled, then!" Extorting the man until the end of his days was only what Cutty deserved. But that meant he would be a part of Lucien's life until the end of *his* days. Which struck Lucien a bit like refusing to cut off a gangrened limb.

Lucien had just pulled one glove off with a sort of violence, as if it were the very source of the dark mood clinging like a film to him, when he came upon Mrs. Breedlove standing at the window nearest the landing, clutching the parted curtain in one hand.

He was yanked up short, as though his senses were a team of restive horses.

The afternoon sun poured amber over her. Her expression was so wistful, so very nearly dreamy, that she almost looked like a watercolor of Angelique Breedlove rather than a flesh and blood woman. She was, in fact, so far away in her thoughts she hadn't yet sensed his presence.

Of whom or what was she thinking?

A rogue, irrational emotion surged through him: he wanted it to be him.

In fact, if he'd been given his choice of additional powers in that moment—flight, or invisibility, or the ability to turn back time so that he'd never been thrown into the Thames—for just that moment, he'd choose the power to put that expression on her face.

He remained motionless, one glove off, one on, one foot on the landing, one on the stairs. His breath was held. The part of him still convinced everything of beauty or grace would be whisked from him froze him in place.

"Mrs. Breedlove," he said quietly.

She dropped the curtain and whirled about.

She couldn't quite manage to get her guard up in time and he saw what was beneath her reserve: a sort of wild joy and heat.

He couldn't help it: he moved toward it as he would toward a chink of light in a cell.

He was grateful he'd gotten that one glove off, because the next moments were filled with shocking little pleasures: her satiny cheek against his bare hand, the warmth of her head tipping into his palm, the silk of her hair as he threaded his fingers through it and tugged gently back. She was rigid with surprise for about a heartbeat.

In the next he saw her eyes go hazy and dark just before they closed, just before his mouth touched hers.

Oh God. That first taste of her hit his bloodstream like opium and his breath left him. The

give of her lips opening beneath his, the sweetness and satiny heat, the hunger the equal of his,
the soft surrender of her body melting against
his. He groaned low in his throat.

Her arms looped around him and he rotated
the two of them until her back was at the wall
and they fell against it. He slid his hands down
to cup her arse and pressed her up against his
hardening cock, and the sound she made in her
throat, a tiny cracked, nearly stunned moan of
pleasure, made him wild. She shifted to move
against him; she threaded her fingers up through
his hair, and just like that, for moments or drug-
ging, glorious eons, that kiss went dangerously
carnal.

He kissed her as though her bare legs were already hooked over his shoulders and a mattress
was squeaking beneath them. He was tempted to
furl her dress and yank open his trouser buttons,
and he thought for an instant, *Yes, yes, we can do
this in twenty seconds. So what if someone comes
upon us.*

It needed to stop.

And as if she'd had the same thought at the
same time, somehow, tacitly, through some effort of will he didn't know he possessed, stop was
what they did. He lifted his mouth from hers.
It felt like a sundering. His senses were furious
at the end of this riot of pleasure. His every cell
seemed to protest.

He was torn between leaving his eyes closed,

just to linger in the spinning world of that kiss, and opening them to see what kissing him had done to her.

He opened them.

She cleared her throat.

"You should not have done that."

For an instant the words almost didn't register. For it seemed the only logical sentence after that kiss was "My room or yours?"

Her voice was frayed velvet. Her tone was even. Almost regretful.

She looked up at him. Warily. Curiously. Perhaps wondering what her kiss had done to him. Her eyes were still hazy.

He hesitated. He wasn't quite certain what he wanted to do with those words.

"But it was good." He said it carefully. It was both a statement and a question. He was startled to hear his own voice was husky. As if he was waking from a long, long sleep. A wholly inadequate word. "Good."

There was a little silence.

She slipped out of his arms and away from him to a distance just beyond reach.

It was fairly clear there was no safe distance for either of them.

At last she drew in a long, shuddering breath. Which was gratifying answer enough. But then her chin dipped twice in a rueful nod. And that was even better.

"Nevertheless."

And it was all she said.

"Nevertheless" was not a reason.

"If you've . . . misgivings . . . about an involvement . . . neither of us is a virgin, Mrs. Breedlove. Or terribly young. We are at liberty to take pleasure where we find it, so we may as well."

Her eyes flared wide.

And then her jaw swung open.

She was staring at him in something akin to wonderment.

And then she coughed an astounded laugh, as if she could hardly decide between hilarity or outrage. "Oh, *do* say more romantic things to me just like that."

He was instantly wary. "I was just . . . Surely you don't want . . . don't you think . . . That is, courtship and that rot is for . . ."

Bloody hell. When was the last time anything had made him *stammer*?

He stopped. Pressed his lips together.

"Virgins?" She was all icy, ironic amusement.

How she must have made her charges sweat when she was a governess. His palms had actually gone cold and it was safe to say his erection would soon be nothing but a fond memory.

Had he misread her entirely? Would he now find himself facing the mythical Captain Hardy over pistols at dawn for the besmirching of her honor? Would he be forced to wed her at pistol point?

No. He wasn't wrong. And he would go down

fighting because apparently going down fighting was his destiny.

"I apologize if I was graceless. But in my experience, every kiss tells a story. This kiss told me at once that you know precisely what kisses lead to, and that not only did you welcome it, you'd been thinking about it, too. You kissed me as though you suspected just how good it would be between us once we found a bed."

Her eyes flared and her features seemed to tighten against some sudden onslaught of emotion. Her hand went up, briefly, oddly, as if to cover her face.

Angelique Breedlove clearly found it safer when she could not be easily read.

She brought the hand down again.

She was silent.

"Fair enough," she said quietly. Finally. Wryly.

He closed his eyes briefly and released the breath he hadn't been certain he was holding.

"I truly meant no insult. Forgive me if you took it as one. I merely meant that as we are no longer children we can speak as adults, a man and a woman who desire each other, and we needn't indulge in the sort of games and ritual that—"

"Lord Bolt."

Her voice was quiet and firm. Amused. And now a little exasperated.

"You may cease the self-flagellation. I knew precisely what you meant. You may rest yourself that I'm not interested in a *courtship*, of all things, either. Courtships in my experience are a means to an end that benefits the man involved but never me. Even if there have been some . . . compensations . . . during."

Lucien went still. He was particularly mesmerized by the plurals: courtships. Compensations. He was not known for his reticence, but oddly, he dared asked none of the thousands of questions that suddenly buffeted him. The answers would unspool stories about other men. Suddenly the specter of unknown men was unwelcome indeed.

And up to the very second before he'd kissed Mrs. Breedlove he could not recall caring very much.

Who courted you? Who failed to win you, or disappointed you? Was it your husband?

"Compensations, is it?" he repeated at last, thoughtfully. "Now who's the romantic?"

Improbably a reluctant smile began at one corner of her mouth and spread slowly to the other.

Imagine a woman who could shorten his breath and blank his mind with just one curve of her lips.

"From now on, when I hear the word 'compensations,' I shall feel aroused, Mrs. Breedlove."

"You may consider that my gift to you, Lord Bolt."

He smiled faintly.

A tiny awkward silence fell.

He cleared his throat.

"May I ask, is it because . . . are your . . . er, affections now otherwise engaged?" he said stiffly, feeling absurd. And oddly raw. In other words, like any other poor sap who had ever needed to question his powers of attraction.

He regretted saying it the moment it emerged from his mouth.

She stared at him.

"No," she said, sounding almost mystified. And a little exasperated again. As if he'd failed to grasp a critical concept.

He was perilously close to blushing.

He supposed "no" was better than "yes."

Or was it?

It didn't mean it was true. He thought about that American Cassidy, all rugged politeness and teeth.

"So is it just the general *notion* of . . ." oh, devil take it ". . . vigorous sex . . ."

"Not even your considerable charms are inducement enough to threaten my hard-won contentment."

He suspected the compliment was meant to distract him. The way one might throw a beef bone to an annoying dog. But he was arrested instead by that word—"hard-won." Because this was the closest thing he'd ever heard to her uttering a complaint. And yet it was less a complaint than a sudden window into her.

"Well, clearly my charms are not nearly as formidable as I thought they were," he said, finally. "I shall proceed to get drunk and brood."

"A time-honored way to ease shattering disappointment, I'm given to understand."

That she should go on being beautiful, and go on saying things like that, things that delighted him even as she thoroughly rejected him, seemed too cruel.

But then it got worse.

"I should like it if we could be friends, Lord Bolt."

She sounded appallingly sincere.

A silence spread like a stain.

"Friends?" he managed finally, on something like a croak, as though she'd extended a silver platter upon which rested his own testicles.

"Oh, come now," she said mildly. "No need to be dramatic. It strikes me that you could use a friend or two. Even if it's a woman." This last word was rich with irony.

"I could use the sort of friend who would rush to my defense with a pistol, Mrs. Breedlove. The sort who will stand at my elbow in gaming hells and at the racetrack and goad me on. Talk me out of duels, should the impulse take me. That sort of friend."

"I should imagine I'd make an excellent second, should a duel be imminent."

Somehow he *could* easily imagine her coolly inspecting and loading a pistol and handing it to him.

"*Can* you shoot a pistol?"

"I can, as it so happens. Captain Hardy insisted we learn."

This somehow didn't surprise him, either.

"Even Dot?" It had to be asked.

"Even Dot."

He paused a moment, imagining.

"That's all well and good, but I need the sort of friend who will intervene if I should ever consider anything so mad as matrimony. Or offer romantic advice. What then?" he countered.

He regretted saying this almost at once. Mainly, oddly, because he thought it might have hurt her.

"As your friend, I shall stand ready to advise you," she said evenly. Softly.

He narrowed his eyes. "Know a good deal about romance then, do you?"

"Precisely enough, I should think."

"I imagine you're as good at being a friend as you are at . . . everything else . . . Mrs. Breedlove."

He wasn't above stealing a glance at her mouth. Of all the injustices life had visited upon him, the notion that he may never kiss it again ranked very near the top.

"In truth, I am learning how to be a good friend. And if *I* can do that, then you can. You do like me, after all."

"You're tolerable."

Her smile was swift, wholly confident, and genuinely pleased with him.

Hell's teeth.

He *did* like her.

Perhaps this should not be quite the epiphany that it was. "Like" had always struck him as a sort of neutered word. He realized now that the word was comprised of particulars: He looked forward to hearing the words that came out of her mouth. He enjoyed being surprised by her reactions to things. Her opinion mattered to him. Being in a room that contained her was better than being in a room that did not contain her.

It was just that until this moment, all of his encounters with women had felt like . . . transactions. Burdened by strategy or ritual or suffocated under the weight of expectation.

All at once he felt, absurdly, a little shy. And intrigued. As though he was new and she was new and everything was new.

It wasn't at all what he'd wanted from her. If it was the only thing on offer, it would be churlish to refuse.

"Then we are decided. We are friends," she prompted brightly.

The word "friends" still had a bit of a funereal knell. But Lucien found he could not equivocate when those soft hazel beams were aimed at him.

He sighed. "Very well. We are friends."

She at once looked relieved. Which did nothing at all to balm his pride. And there she stood, a flush lingering in her cheeks. He'd put it there with his hands and his mouth and his body. The sun was giving her a halo she probably didn't quite deserve. His stomach contracted against an onslaught of sensations, unfamiliar, warring. A restless, hungry desire and a curiosity that bordered on want, assailed him.

"Shall we shake hands on it?" he added, idly.

Her eyes fell to his outstretched hand. And for a moment she seemed unable to look up.

He would have given three guineas all over again to know what she was thinking.

Touch me and then tell me I feel like a friend, Angelique.

At last she shifted her shoulders resolutely. Then gave him her hand with every evidence of confidence.

He did not expect to be moved. Her hand felt unconscionably small and cool in his, too easily crushable. Rather like the trust she was giving.

He clasped it gently. And released it.

"Well, then," he said heartily. "What do friends such as we do, if we aren't to passionately make love?"

"We shall chat pleasantly in the parlor at night, as I do with my other friends. I shall read aloud from a book, perhaps, and you shall read aloud, in your turn. Perhaps you'll join in one of the musicales, or hold my yarn when I knit." Her eyes flashed mischief.

"*Hold* your—I regret my decision to be your friend immediately. I'd like to rescind."

"But we shook on it, Lord Bolt, and rumor has it you're a gentleman, momentary lapses notwithstanding."

"Momentary Lapse. Perhaps that will be my pet name for you."

"I'll be happy to answer to Mrs. Breedlove in company. Perhaps as the years wear on I'll allow you to call me Angelique."

"And yet you called me Lucien outright a moment ago. Is that what you call me in your private thoughts? 'I wonder what Lucien is doing right now. I wonder what he looks like in the bath.'"

She regarded him with a slight head tilt.

"Silly," she said almost tenderly. "I don't think of you at all."

He'd never had a more baffling exchange with a woman. Or a more excruciating one.

Or one, perversely, he'd enjoyed more.

Silence again. A frustrating and fascinating one.

"But I can chat in the parlor with *Delacorte*," he said finally.

She laughed. "If you can do that with Delacorte, then I'm afraid you have more than one friend, Lord Bolt. And doesn't that make you a rich man, indeed?"

She backed away swiftly and gracefully, and trailing a glance alight with mischief and a hand raised in farewell as she moved out of the light, and down into the busy heart of the house, away from him.

He stared down at his hand, bemused. He thought perhaps he would not forget holding hers.

Chapter Eight

❧

"WHAT IS it? Do tell," Delilah urged on a bright hush. And elbowed Angelique playfully.

"What?" Angelique was startled.

Dinner was over and they were in the parlor alone, apart from Dot. This seldom happened, and while they loved it when it was full of happy people, it was rather nice to have the big room to themselves for a bit of a change. They'd brought down the basket of mending they usually saved for the upstairs sitting room, shifts and shirts and that sort of thing.

"You look as though you've a lovely secret or are preparing a pleasant surprise for someone. Your face is like a lamp. You've a very nice glow. And you've sewn yourself to Mr. Delacorte's shirt."

"Oh!" Angelique lifted her arm. Mr. Delacorte's vast shirt did indeed come up with it, as though she were raising a mainsail.

Mr. Delacorte was hard on his shirts but they appreciated the challenge of keeping the rents from showing and the buttons all firmly in place.

Dot had once sewn her entire sleeve to a sampler that said Bless This Home, and they'd been hours extricating her.

"Allow me." Delilah reached over and snipped the thread, and she was free.

Would that it was just that easy to free herself from thoughts of Lord Bolt. One snip and voila! A return to peace of mind.

"I suppose . . ." Angelique attempted by way of explanation. "I'm just grateful we've a house full of happy guests who seem to be enjoying each other. And I'm grateful for the quiet."

Mainly because it was *anything* but quiet inside her head. Things were an uproar in there.

It was indeed a rare evening where nearly everyone was availing themselves of what London had to offer: Mrs. Pariseau had gone to the theater with a friend; Mr. Delacorte had taken Mr. Cassidy to some race involving animals that weren't horses, perhaps donkeys?—she'd stopped listening because she frankly did not want to know—and Lord Bolt was off some place, too, and she didn't particularly want to know about that, either. Odds were she'd read about it in the newspapers in due time.

But she felt his presence so powerfully he might as well be sitting in the chair across from her, long legs outstretched, eyes fixed on her as though she were the first sign of land after months at sea.

Honestly. She considered it a triumph of fortitude akin to surviving a shipwreck, perhaps, that she had managed to stop kissing him at all.

He had gathered her into his body as though she belonged to him. As though he already knew the fit and feel of her. And she had gone with the ease of a concubine reporting to a sheik, but with perhaps considerably more enthusiasm. This shocked her. She'd thought sincerely that no part of her was beyond her control, and yet there she was. Not after the lessons she'd learned about men, every one of them the hard way.

But doubtless every woman who kissed him felt that same sense of destiny. Because of a certainty everything about him seemed expressly designed to get a woman to go boneless with surrender, from those green eyes to his long, hard body to the way he smelled—which, if she'd been asked to describe it in a single word, would best be described as "need" for how it made her feel.

Perhaps she should view him as something a daring woman ought to treat herself to just once in life—but just a very little, like a sip of absinthe. He dazzled; he impressed. He was even admirable. But there was nothing about him to suggest he was more than a man of appetites.

So perhaps it was good to get the kiss over with, because the wondering about it could stop. She could confirm to herself: yes, it was very good. And yes, it would be insanity to be naked with this man, because she'd never be the same again. What a relief to know that.

But the way he had touched her.

She had only to revisit it for the quicksilver shiver of pleasure to pour down her spine. The wonder. Tenderness, shot through with demand. Possession.

And hard slam of his heart against hers.

All for her. All for her.

Why did it seem, in the immediate aftermath, that things like that kiss were the entire point of life and everything else sort of just milled around it?

It was all an illusion, of course. The kind designed to perpetuate the species. It did not mean more beyond that moment. He was right. She did know the pleasures that could be had. And he was probably right that it would be outrageously good between them.

She could also, thankfully, recognize heartbreak on two legs.

She would sleep easier knowing she'd done the right thing.

Wouldn't she?

Hadn't she?

"Quiet's over," Delilah murmured.

Mrs. Pariseau had returned, followed by Delacorte and Cassidy, all dutifully in well before curfew. All filing in to speak with Delilah and Angelique first, because they wanted to, because they were happy here. And this was a good life, a fine life, and she was happy knowing it could go on as always.

"You MIGHT HAVE to resort to duplicity, sir." Exeter sat on one side of his desk in his offices on Garland Street, near Bond, and Lucien occupied a chair opposite. Exeter had yet to offer him tea, because he was a cheap bastard even though his services came dear.

Lucien rather admired this, actually.

"You mean, make an appointment, lie about who I am to get in. Or sneak into the place, like a thief, corner him in his library, that sort of thing."

"You've a fine grasp of the word 'duplicity,' sir."

Lucien scowled at Exeter but without conviction. Time spent with the man was a bit like spending time with sand down one's trousers. His loyalty was as unwavering as his benign contempt, which Lucien suspected was more after the fashion of affection. Somewhere between them had grown a begrudging respect, much the way grit irritates an oyster into forming a pearl. They each had their strengths and knew it. Their relationship dated back to before Lucien had been hurled into the Thames.

They both knew Lucien had too much pride to attempt to trick his father into seeing him.

It was a matter of getting the duke alone for a few minutes of his time, because there were things he needed to say. A request he needed to make.

But the Duke of Brexford was seldom alone. He traveled with a phalanx of servants when he was on horseback; otherwise he rode about in some enclosed carriage. His pursuits and hobbies seemed to involve crowds of people—the theater, his clubs—presumably so he could enjoy a ceaseless warm bath of admiration and awe. He was conservative in his revelries, however; unlike his son, he did nothing to excess.

Other than that he was at home, at least for the season, and home was St. James Square.

"What if . . . What if, Exeter, you send a note over, with a card, telling him that the head of a successful importer would like to discuss business opportunities with him. Send him round a copy of our profits and losses and projected earnings. Tell him that a representative of the company will be in in London for only a short time but hoped to discuss it with him in particular, as he is known to be canny indeed about where he troubles to invest."

"Tell him . . . the *truth*, sir?"

"The truth."

"Unorthodox."

Lucien snorted.

"Without giving my name. Simply the company's name. Triton Importers."

"I'd say the odds are slim of responding to something so vague."

"The duke likes money. And flattery."

"Very well, sir. Perhaps you will advise as to the content of the letter?"

"Naturally. I take it you have more faith in my ability to charm than your own?"

"We all have our strengths, sir." Exeter's tone implied that he scarcely considered charm a strength.

"I expect you'll be in touch if you've had a response."

"Straightaway, sir."

"Meanwhile, you can find me at The Grand Palace on the Thames, making marks on the wall with a burnt stick."

"Something tells me, sir, that you hardly find the accommodations intolerable."

"Oh?"

"You look well-fed and you've a certain bemused air."

"And I don't normally have this air, is this what you're trying to tell me, Exeter?"

"You've no air at all, sir. No air at all."

Lucien snorted again.

WHEN CAPTAIN HARDY had first arrived at The Grand Palace on the Thames a few months ago he'd taken to occupying a table in the corner of the drawing room while trying to read *Robinson Crusoe*. His was a Rock of Gibraltar sort of presence. Not a motion or word wasted.

Lord Bolt occupied the little table, fingers drumming in a little tympani of boredom, eyes hooded yet alert as he looked out over the room

the way he would eye a hand of poker, deciding
how he would bear the evening. He couldn't do
what he wanted to do, which was to stare at
Mrs. Breedlove unabashedly. Perhaps even yearningly. Perhaps accusingly.

He relived the kiss often, because what man
wouldn't? The ceiling of his admittedly comfortable room, the best room in the house, was a convenient scrim for reflection.

But he found himself thinking less about her
lips and body than her words. Odd to realize that
the elegant reserve overlaying what was clearly
a passionate nature—very like a beautiful glaze
over fine porcelain—was both part of her allure
and . . . a sort of accommodation.

For some reason, Mrs. Breedlove did not wish
to be fully known.

He'd decided he was going to be the best
damned friend Mrs. Breedlove ever had.

Delacorte and Cassidy were at the chessboard
again, and Mrs. Pariseau was trying to talk Delilah and Dot into a game of Whist, and Lucien
thought he might as well jump in to being a friend
with both feet.

"What are you knitting, Mrs. Breedlove?" he
asked.

Everyone pivoted their heads in shock and, it
seemed, concern. One would have thought he'd
burst out with something in Turkish.

Mr. Delacorte looked seconds away from offering him some tonic from his little Case of Horrors,

which was what Lucien had christened the leather satchel after Delacorte offered him a peek inside.

He ignored all of them.

"A . . . coverlet?" she said cautiously.

"Ah." He imbued this syllable with fascination.

There was another little silence.

"Winter is coming. Shouldn't like any of our guests to shiver even a little," she expounded politely.

"Yes. Winter is always an eventuality," he contributed. Somberly.

She fixed him with dry, baleful amusement, eyebrows raised. She could not have said "You can do better, Lord Bolt" any more plainly if she'd said it aloud.

He smiled slowly at that.

Mrs. Pariseau had persuaded Delilah and Dot to join her in a game of Whist over in the corner and they were all arranging their chairs happily around the table. Dot hadn't yet learned how to play Whist, which ought to make the game last a lot longer than it normally did.

He stood and wandered, nonchalantly, over to where Angelique sat, and pulled out a little chair, a Chippendale copy. He had misgivings about it bearing his weight, and about how he looked perched on it. Probably a bit like a spider perched on the head of a pin.

She eyed him, bemused and wary.

"Your yarn is looking a bit tangled," he said.

"Because it is. Gordon got into it the other day

and had unrolled it all the way down the stairs. It was rather hastily recovered from his clutches. It has not been the same since."

"Shall I untangle it for you?"

She flicked her gaze up, amused but cautious. A little pleat of concern appeared between her eyes.

"If you like," she allowed magnanimously, finally, like the gracious hostess she was supposed to be.

"Anything to help a friend."

The expression flashed sort of cautious optimism and pleasure jabbed him ever so slightly in the solar plexus with its sweetness, even as it did nothing at all for his pride. Clearly she hoped he was taking friendship seriously.

He shifted his chair across to the settee where she sat, then picked up the yarn and inspected it critically, as if looking for a way in.

The Whist had rapidly become lively, from the sound of things. Under cover of domestic cheer, he could speak to her.

And yet for a time, neither he nor Angelique said a word. It was oddly less torturous than he would have expected, sitting in silence unraveling a ball of yarn simply because, like the proverbial prisoner in a cell marking off days with a bit of charred stick, it was all there was to do.

"I untangled a lot of nets and ropes and the like when I worked on a ship. It was all I was fit for at the time, both physically and in terms of skills. It's rewarding work."

She looked up, surprised and clearly fascinated. He was encouraged.

"Bastard lords don't get a lot of training in useful things, apart from riding and shooting and fencing, all of which are surprisingly much more useful on the high seas than in London. Shall I put a pence in the jar for the 'bastard'?"

"A donation wouldn't go amiss. But now it's *two* pence."

"I see why you are now turning a profit here at The Grand Palace on the Thames."

She smiled, but abstractedly. "Hence the gambling?"

"And believe it or not, they in fact tried to teach me to knit—most sailors can—and I can, after a fashion. I haven't your gift for precision." He thought he might as well flatter her. As a friend.

"Maybe it's because my father was a surgeon."

"Ah. Perhaps that is also where you get your *very* precise way with a cutting word."

She smiled. "Probably. What do you suppose you got from your father, Lord Bolt?"

Ah ha! He'd found a place to begin unraveling the knot. He proceeded to follow it methodically.

"A signet ring. A gold watch. Height. Arrogance. Devastating good looks. A gift for making piles of money."

She was clearly amused by this list. "And yet you haven't bought that building."

"Very well, Mrs. Breedlove, I will tell you. The greater portion of my piles of money are currently invested in piles of cargo that I will then convert into piles of money when they return to shore. The ship is a trifle behind schedule, which on occasion occurs. Nothing to be concerned about," he said evenly. "I shall enjoy being your neighbor, Mrs. Breedlove. Perhaps you'll come to love gambling. Now it's your turn to tell me why you haven't yet bought the building."

"We can't afford it," she said simply.

"If you're a gambling woman, I know how you can attempt to—"

She cut him off with an amused warning glare. "I suppose merchants abound here by the docks. Did you know Captain Hardy, Delilah's husband, bought a ship not too long ago? He's engaged in a similar business."

"Delacorte did indeed mention this. When do I meet this Captain Hardy?"

She looked faintly, wryly troubled for an instant, and he wondered why. "In a week or so, I believe. If you're still here. There was some problem with his crew or captain or some such that he had to see to straightaway."

They worked in oddly companionable silence for a time.

"What did you inherit from your mother, Lord Bolt?"

"Her eyes. An appreciation for finding beauty in surprising places."

Angelique's gaze flickered.

Doubtless she'd heard compliments from those

men in her life who had—how had she put it?—courted her, and left her convinced not one of them were worth the trouble, apparently.

But it was only the truth. And he did love to watch her face change when he said something to surprise her.

"And from whom did you get the relentless impulse to flirt?"

He laughed. "From my mother as well, I suppose. But I only speak truth when I flirt, Mrs. Breedlove. And my mother would also have stared at a patch of dirt and seen a garden, as you did. She had a talent for making things beautiful. She'd bring branches of blossoms into our house when the apple trees began to bloom. It's what she missed the most when . . ."

He stopped suddenly, surprised at the rapid unraveling of his own story. He was accustomed to the *ton* at large knowing at least the outlines of his life. As Delacorte had pointed out, it hadn't been easy for everyone to know his business. But it occurred to him that he hadn't the sort of people in his life to whom he'd say these things offhandedly. To whom his own interpretation of these stories mattered.

She waited patiently. Eyes warm.

". . . when he married and had no further use for us." He said that shortly.

He quirked the corner of his mouth wryly at the raw truth.

Angelique had stilled. Her thumb and her

forefinger rubbed softly together. She did that, he'd noticed, when she was troubled about something. As though she, too, were smoothing out a knot.

She resumed knitting more slowly than before, as though the weight of her thoughts controlled the speed of her work. She seemed to be deciding what to say.

And in the quiet he reflected on how odd the significance little things took on now that she'd made it clear they would not be passionately riding each other. The pale, soft skin of her throat, the curve of her ear, the flash of creamy flesh when she moved and her shawl slipped, just a little, and showed a shadow of cleavage. All the eloquent shapes of her.

"She would have liked you, I think," he said. "But then, she was generous spirited."

Angelique gave a short, delighted laugh at that.

This was more reason to like her. She laughed at things like that, because she knew her own worth. And yet he suspected this knowledge was another thing she might have learned the hard way.

She flicked her eyes up at him. They were still troubled and soft.

He'd put that particular expression on her face. That unguarded concern. This notion, for some reason, shortened his breath. As surely as if she'd slipped her hand into his surreptitiously.

He crowed with quiet triumph as he freed yet another long portion of yarn.

She knit a few more stitches, then stopped abruptly.

"Do you mind if I ask . . . Lord Bolt . . . how did you . . . This is, it is difficult for me to imagine how it must have been for you and your mother, and how . . . that is, what became of . . . if it's not a presumptuous question."

But she *was* imagining it. And it was clear it was causing her distress. He found he wasn't eager to expound on it. But he did want to take that worried expression from her eyes.

He gave the ball of yarn a three-quarter turn in order to free a strand from where it was twisted about three others.

"Is there such a thing as presumption between friends, Mrs. Breedlove?"

She flashed him a wry look.

"Well, the new duchess-to-be, was, shall we say, ill pleased with our very existence when she learned of it. Seems a condition of her marriage to the duke was a severing of his ties to us. Her blood was blue and she could provide a legitimate heir, which of course they set about doing with alacrity. We lived in a little house on his property in Sussex that the duke would come to visit—that's where the apple orchards were—and overnight we were removed to a squalid flat in London. I was seventeen years old. And I . . ."

Maybe it was because he hadn't ever said these words aloud in this precise order. Or maybe it was the hazel eyes on him, soft as pillows. But unspooling his story was more difficult than he'd anticipated. It felt a bit, in fact, like unraveling something that would leave him exposed, and this was a revelation. ". . . I set about making certain that the Duchess of Brexford understood how difficult it would be to forget me."

He said this lightly.

Good God. He hadn't anticipated that this friendship thing was a tricky business.

She was studying him with those eyes that gave the illusion that one could see right into her soul if only one got close enough.

He had been so close, once. So close.

He thought maybe she could see into his and was momentarily desperately curious to hear her conclusion.

"I struggle to think of a circumstance in which you would be forgettable, Lord Bolt."

She said it dryly. But she lowered her eyes almost immediately. Her hands lay awkwardly. And it seemed for a moment she had entirely forgotten how to knit.

His exultation was quiet but deep. For a moment he simply couldn't speak. He looked at the fine bones of her hand. He imagined pressing his lips against the pale blue veins in her wrist, long enough to feel her pulse speed.

His head went as light as if he were jerked to the top of a mountain.

"Oh, of a certainty I leave an indelible impression. But I thought it best to race high flyers up

Bond Street and make wagers, anyway. As I said before, I am nothing if not thorough."

She smiled at him slowly.

As if to give voice to his own pent frustration, a long groan erupted behind him. Mr. Cassidy had rather melodramatically dropped his head into his hands.

"Bolt," he moaned. "Come and play a chess game with Delacorte. He has unmanned me yet again and I cannot bear it. I am going to play Whist with the ladies, which is only what I deserve."

The ladies would be only too happy to accommodate Mr. Cassidy, of course.

"We will unman you, too, Mr. Cassidy," Mrs. Pariseau said placidly. "I hope you've a pocketful of pence. Dot is rather ruthless, as it turns out."

Lucien looked down at his lapful of blue yarn, startled as if from a daydream. He suddenly wondered if being Mrs. Breedlove's friend would ultimately unman *him*.

And yet, for a mad, mad moment, if time had stopped and left him sitting here forever, watching her knit, he might not have objected.

He stood up quickly, almost as though to prove to himself that he still could. This was quite enough friendship for the evening.

"I've nearly untangled your yarn. I best go humble Delacorte."

"Ha!" Delacorte was amused. "I'd like to see you try, Bolt."

"CHECKMATE," LUCIEN SAID lazily.

Delacorte stared blankly at the chessboard for a full two seconds.

Then up at Bolt.

His expression called to mind that of a man who had been struck cross the head with a plank.

It was the third time in five days out of five games Lucien had won.

"Ha!" Delacorte muttered weakly, finally.

Then he rallied. "Well, then! Ha. Ho. Good for you. You must be some sort of sorcerer, Bolt, that's what it is." He gave his fingers a little drum. If Delacorte possessed slightly worse manners, he'd likely be upending the chessboard by now.

"No. Just good at chess." Lucien idly inspected his fingernails. Knowing this would madden Delacorte, who was very, very good at chess. But not at all good at losing. Perversely this amused him. But he also admired it. Lucien hated to lose, too.

And at least Delacorte fought hard for his wins.

He lifted his eyes reflexively, wondering if there was any point in fighting for something else he wanted.

Angelique was leaning toward Delilah, her face alive with mischief, and Delilah's eyes were laughing. They were exchanging some joke known only to the two of them. He returned to this view again and again because it was really the only available option from his little cage of friendship.

He told himself he had no choice but to endure this odd little purgatory. He was still waiting: for his ship to arrive so he could convert all those silks and spices into money again, so he could buy a building, so he could build a gaming hell. For a message from his father that might never come. Though, of course, if that message didn't come, he'd try another way, and another way.

His days passed eventfully enough. He put Exeter on the job of researching likely candidates for running his gaming hell. He revisited his favorite places in London, reliving his youth. He found that he still savored every filthy, shambling, beautiful corner of the city, its spires and bridges and gargoyles and columns and the Thames churning on through. He was fiercely glad to be back, a feeling that did not diminish as the days passed.

From the perspective of the man he'd become, he understood that his life in London after the duke had abandoned them followed by his mother's death, had been like a cut suspension bridge thrashing in a windstorm. He wasn't entirely certain that bridge had come to rest yet. But how different that rudderless man seemed from the one he was now. The one possessed of a preternatural patience.

Because deprived of innuendo and other overt tools of seduction and bound by the rules here at The Grand Palace on the Thames, Lucien had expected to die a slow death of tedium. He'd amused himself by remembering a man in Canton who claimed he'd once been held prisoner in a Turkish jail. He'd found a pebble and had made a game of rolling it from one end of the cell to the other. That was it. The entire game. One tiny pebble was all that separated him from madness.

Instead Lucien was reminded of the day he'd strolled along the beach in Brighton with his mother, collecting seashells. Each one unique, a fresh surprise, and he'd begun to horde them in his cap. Until his mother touched his arm and pointed up the beach. The bright specks of little shells scattered over the sand went on for yards, possibly miles. There was no end to the riches. He'd felt joy and panic simultaneously. He wanted to discover them all.

This was what it was like talking to Mrs. Breedlove.

And all the talking could lead nowhere except farther up those miles of beach, metaphorically speaking, he supposed.

And yet he could walk those miles.

It was a delicate business, this wanting to know. He could not go about it like a Bow Street runner and interrogate her, because Mrs. Breedlove was open in some ways, and very careful in others. He approached it strategically. Strategy often began with Delacorte, who could be counted on to enthusiastically run a topic into the ground, or spread it around the room like cholera.

Angelique had taken up her knitting again. A

game of Whist was being negotiated on one side of the room. Mrs. Pariseau had recruited Delilah and Dot thus far. Lucien needed to move quickly before Mrs. Breedlove was swept into it, too.

Lucien stifled a little yawn. "Say, from where do you hail, Delacorte? I knew a chap who deployed a similar chess strategy. Came from a town in Scotland."

"You don't say. Northumberland border, originally. What about you?"

"I grew up mostly in Derbyshire, I suppose. Country house there."

"Mrs. Pariseau, from where do *you* hail?" Delacorte was predictably infected with curiosity.

"Grew up in County Clare, married a rich man, and had a right grand time traveling thither and on, when he died, rest his soul, and now I'm abiding with *you* characters."

Everyone laughed.

"New York," Mr. Cassidy reiterated. "But you all know that. Mrs. Hardy?"

"I was raised in the country, too. Sussex."

"You're up, Cassidy, if you want to take your chance with Delacorte." And with that, Lucien rose from the chessboard, strolling idly across the room to sit down, with studied nonchalance, across from Mrs. Breedlove. He picked up her yarn again, turned it about in his hands like a crystal ball.

She looked up at him. Then returned her eyes to her knitting, a little smile on her lips.

"How about you, Mrs. Breedlove? From where do you hail?"

She eyed him a moment, with a little smile.

"Devonshire," she said shortly.

"The country."

"Yes."

She said it in a way that made the word sound like a bolt sliding into a lock. Click.

"With your father the surgeon."

"With my father the surgeon."

"And . . . your mother as well? Were there more in your family?" he asked idly. He'd found another place to begin untangling the yarn. "I've a half brother I've never met, which seems odd."

"Yes. Well, I was the only child. My mother died when I was fifteen years old. Her heart was never quite strong, and then fever weakened it more, and . . ."

She looked up at him, her mouth quirked ruefully.

"I am very sorry to hear it." He'd lowered his voice. "It's a difficult thing."

He meant it. He knew at once what that must have been like for a girl her age with a father who wasn't gentry. And she knew that he knew what it was like to lose a parent when one was young.

The moment—that exchange of silent sympathy, tacit understanding—was entirely new to his experience of women, at least ones he also desired. And all at once it made him feel a little uncertain, unfamiliar with how to navigate it, which he did and did not like. The past few years had tempered him like steel, or so he thought. Now he'd begun to suspect he was made of steel save perhaps one golden-haired, hazel-eyed, Achilles' heel whose creamy throat made him long to draw a finger softly down, down, down until it vanished into the shadow between her breasts.

But even he knew that one did not stroke the breasts of one's friends.

"And do you miss your mother still, Mrs. Breedlove? What was she like?"

She paused and gave a little self-conscious laugh. "Oh, well. She was kind and funny and beautiful. Every now and then I talk to her a little bit, where no one can hear, so no one will think me mad."

He paused, hopelessly charmed and touched in a way so unexpected it made him nearly irritable.

He paused in turning the now less tangled yarn. He didn't think he was quite ready to tell her that he occasionally talked to his own.

"Would your mother like me?"

"I think you would shock her to her toes."

He laughed.

"So . . . is that when you became a governess? When your mother died."

"Yes. Well. That is, I became a governess to support my father and myself after he became ill. He believed in educating women and my *five* languages were a useful commodity."

His eyebrows shot up and he gave a low whistle.

"There weren't any gaming hells in Devonshire, so my options for income were limited."

He smiled at that. But it struck him that she'd been orphaned, then, at a rather vulnerable age, and absurdly, though surely that was about a decade ago at least, he felt uneasy on her behalf, a little restless, as though he wished he could go back and protect her from all these losses and their consequences. Was that when she'd married?

Unlike Mrs. Pariseau, she wasn't one to lightly toss the fact of her widowhood into conversation. There was a story of some sort there, he suspected.

For some reason he found himself reluctant to ask. He did not want to bring another man into the conversation.

"Lord Bolt." Mrs. Pariseau's ears pricked up at the words "gaming hell." "Dot here thinks it might be amusing to appear in the gossip in the newspapers."

Angelique's head swiveled sharply. "Dot! I thought we discussed that," she said, imbuing this with a thousand shades of reproach. Delilah supported her by adding a reproachful stare of her own.

Dot hung her head. "I'm sorry, Mrs. Breedlove. I didn't really mean it. I was joking with Mrs. Pariseau, you see. A *joke*," she reiterated, half-accusingly, to Mrs. Pariseau.

"Nonetheless," Mrs. Pariseau persisted breezily. "We wondered what *you* had to say on the subject, Lord Bolt. Given your experience."

And suddenly all eyes were on Lucien.

He considered saying something glib, which would have been the fun thing to do. And indeed, it was right on the tip of his tongue.

But he was aware of Angelique's gaze on him.

Hell's teeth. He would need to give it some proper thought before answering.

"I would say it isn't something to aspire to, for it adds little value to your life, all in all, Dot. But if the things written about you are true, you should be unafraid to face them with your head held high."

He was aware of Angelique studying him as though he was a Latin text.

"Well, that is very sagely put, Lord Bolt," Mrs. Pariseau enthused.

"Your approval means the world to me, Mrs. Pariseau."

Mrs. Pariseau shot him a droll look. "What about you, Mrs. Breedlove? Wouldn't you want to appear in the broadsheets?"

He pivoted his head back toward Angelique. For some reason, his breath was held.

"Oh, good heavens. Never. Firstly it would hardly be good for business, would it? And I feel life at The Grand Palace on the Thames is quite operatic enough. An ordinary, quiet respectable life is quite a fine thing and it is everything I want. And life here with all of you is as entertaining as a musicale, which almost makes musicales redundant, wouldn't you say?"

It was Delilah's turn to aim a dry look at Angelique.

An ordinary, quiet life. Beautiful women were seldom allowed to have those sorts of lives. They were objects of fascination, envy, lust. Men would be fools for them. Or brutes.

Had life buffeted her so thoroughly—life, largely meaning whatever men had courted her—that peace was her sole ambition?

Clever woman that she was, no doubt she knew no encounter of the naked kind between the two of *them* would be entirely peaceful.

But neither were oceans or skies. And they were spectacularly beautiful.

His mood grayed a little as he freed another strand of yarn from where it was hopelessly tangled about other strands, and thought about how sex always changed things between people, a bit the way an earthquake shifts a landscape. After the delightful sweating and grappling, came the need to pick their way through the new terrain, confronting new qualities churned up, like possessiveness or jealousy or temper. His various associations with willing widows and mistresses often ended with recriminations and vases being thrown across the room. But then he supposed those women had been volatile reflections of the man he'd been then. Temperamental, selfish, restless.

That man would have been shocked to learn that the man he apparently was now found the notion of anything, even magnificent sex, bringing to an end these moments of quiet confidences, these evenings of ease, with Mrs. Breedlove was unsettling.

"Mrs. Breedlove, will you join us at Whist?" Mrs. Pariseau called.

Mrs. Breedlove, it seemed, would.

She tucked away her knitting, stood and left him with one of those smiles that pierced like an arrow shot by a cherub.

"Perhaps you'd consent to read aloud, Lord Bolt, while we play?" she called over her shoulder.

"Anything for a friend," he said.

Bloody hell. He was beginning to think that was true.

Chapter Nine

❧

"I DON'T KNOW why we're doing this to ourselves," Delilah said wistfully.

The estate agent had handed them the key with his usual laconic "watch out for rats and falling timbers," and Angelique and Delilah had gone to view the building for sale near them one more time. "Thought it might be a location for a thriving whorehouse, until you came along and ruined the street with your respectable business," he called after them. He always eyed them with a certain wondering reproach.

"Why, thank you." Angelique and Delilah were touched.

Change was difficult for everybody.

The Grand Palace on the Thames did indeed glow like a jewel, which rather highlighted the dinginess of their neighbors. Keeping its white stone facade clean was a near Sisyphean task here at the docks, subject as it was to the winds off the sea scouring it, then racing through London, collecting as much smut as possible, and depositing it right back on the buildings by the docks. But by virtue of *their* efforts a few businesses nearby had made similar attempts to keep things a little cleaner, and within a decade or so they could probably anticipate that no men would feel free to piss anywhere beneath the windows of The Grand Palace on the Thames.

And this building—they had begun to refer to it rather grandly as "the Annex"—needed everything The Grand Palace on the Thames had needed before they opened for business: new wallpaper and carpets and curtains, hammer and nails and lots of scrubbing and polishing and perhaps its own cat to chase away rodents. And furniture.

It hadn't a grand chandelier in its foyer, but the floors were marble. It hadn't a vast cozy kitchen with the kind of stove that Helga presided over like a symphony conductor, but the suites were much larger and not too drafty. There were fewer rooms for staff, but they were a little larger, so any families who wished to stay there could house their servants.

And then there was the ballroom.

It was currently decorated courtesy of spiders, and the afternoon light glinted from webs. There were rodent droppings in the corners instead of courting couples or gossiping friends. But if they squinted, they could envision bunting instead of webs, and hear the music, and see the jewel-colored gowns flashing beneath a chandelier as couples rotated about to the sound of a fine orchestra. And for an instant she indulged in a fantasy of twirling around that room in the arms of Lord Bolt.

Certainly deciding that she and Lord Bolt would be friends had made him a little safer.

In the way that putting a tiger in a cage made one a *little* safer.

He was, in fact, all that was respectful.

But she hadn't anticipated that their exchanges of confidences would act as a sort of loom. He threw a thread, she threw a thread. And suddenly she felt as though they were like Delacorte's shirt and her sleeve: unexpectedly bound. Her favorite color (green), the name of the first horse he'd ever ridden (Bunny), the story about his first fencing master (who'd run off with one of his father's maids).

But that's what friendship was, wasn't it?

Until the first thing she did when she walked into a room was to look about for him, as if he were the warmest seat by the fire.

To discover that his eyes were already on her, like the beacon she ought to follow.

Ironically the Lord Bolt who lived in the broadsheets, who fought duels and brawled and made outlandish bets, seemed infinitely safer than the one in the drawing room who held her yarn and mined her secrets. She did not want to know the *reasons* for him, and yet it was too late. She saw his youthful recklessness as a result of wounds. She saw his intelligence and strength and resilience and wit.

She liked his arrogance, because she was perverse.

Sometimes when she looked at his long, beautiful hands, a rush of blood to her head nearly stopped her breathing and she needed to move across the room, away from him, because that was the safe thing to do. One needed to breathe in order to survive, after all.

And he had not once touched her since he'd kissed her. Not even surreptitiously, and most men certainly would try.

Which was all for the best. She was relieved, was she not?

Because the closer they became, the more they knew of each other, the more dangerous any ensuing kiss would be. Things that are bound together make terrible ripping noises when torn asunder. She wanted no more pain, and no more sundering.

"I thought we could build a little covered walkway between the two buildings, for inclement weather, so our guests could somehow go to and fro," she said abstractedly to Delilah.

"And we'll definitely need to hire footmen to answer doors and carry messages to and fro. Our maids are busy enough as it is."

"And perhaps a coach and four to ferry all of our guests to the opera and to promenade on Rotten Row."

Delilah turned to Angelique, eyebrows upraised wryly.

"Since we're dreaming," Angelique clarified.

Once upon a time it had been Delilah persuading a reluctant Angelique to dream.

"Footmen will cause riots with our maids and double our food budget. And yet I think we do need to hire them," Delilah mused.

"It might be an adventure," Angelique allowed. "Has Lord Bolt said anything more about wanting to purchase this building?"

"Not to me. We can only hope he's exploring all of his other options throughout the city, if that's his ambition."

Delilah sighed. "Well, at least we'll be prepared with a plan should a miracle occur and we muster the funds needed for our first payment."

"Precisely. And since it hasn't the modestly sized gargoyles that our building has, perhaps window boxes with flowers."

"I wonder if the tunnels that run beneath our building pass beneath this one. Wouldn't that be interesting?"

And they continued spinning dreams. Angelique cast a glance over her shoulder and thought she could almost see herself laughing up into the face of a tall green-eyed man as they spun round and round the room.

EVERYONE AT THE Grand Palace on the Thames was a little nervous but hopeful about introducing Captain Hardy to Lord Bolt, the way one might be about introducing a new puppy to the family cat. There was no real hope they would become friends or even rub along, but perhaps they wouldn't be tempted to kill each other and could safely be given cushions on opposite sides of the fire. This trepidation was mainly because it seemed the qualities the two men had in common—arrogance, a certain inflexibility, an alleged way with swords and guns, the kind of height that enabled them to reach the sconces without standing on a ladder—were not necessarily the sort of qualities that meshed people into friends. Then there was the fact that Captain Hardy's guiding principle for the entirety of his life had been duty and the rule of law.

Whereas Lord Bolt wanted to open a gaming hell.

Both had spent a little time in the newspapers, for very different reasons. So there was that.

When word spread throughout The Grand Palace on the Thames that Captain Hardy had returned from his trip and would be joining them in the drawing room that night, the atmosphere had changed to the sort of breathless anticipation that preceded a boxing match.

All the guests and hostesses were gathered in the drawing room when Captain Hardy stepped into it that evening, looking like a man who had finally found land after a long trip at sea, but then, The Grand Palace on the Thames always felt like a harbor to him even when he was away for a few hours.

Everyone stood to greet him, but the greetings were rather hushed and subdued.

They were waiting for Captain Hardy and Lord Bolt to formally exchange words.

Lucien had stood with the usual slow elegance that somehow managed to convey arrogance, danger, and command.

Captain Hardy stood there doing something rather similar.

They'd regarded each other for an appraising second of silence.

"I think you both have killed pirates!" Delacorte finally blurted. He liked both of them and was eager to get the bonding underway.

Captain Hardy and Lord Bolt turned as one to Delacorte, each sporting twin expressions of bemusement. There was one thing they had in common, at least.

"A pleasure to meet you at last, Captain Hardy," Lord Bolt said. He bowed, beautifully. "I've heard your praises sung for some time."

Captain Hardy returned the bow in kind. "Likewise, Lord Bolt. I do hope you're enjoying your stay here at The Grand Palace on the Thames. I apologize for needing to rush out so soon after your arrival, but I've just purchased a ship and there was a spot of trouble with the crew up the coast."

Lucien's eyebrows rose. "Do you captain your own ship?"

"I hired my own captain, but it seems he's going to need a little help hiring a crew that isn't shiftless."

Lucien gave a short laugh. "I'm an importer myself. The Triton Group. Captain Douglas Fleming is sailing. Silks and spices. Before I returned to London I spent some years learning the business in the East Indies."

"You don't say. You wouldn't happen to know a Captain Janssen, would you?"

"I sailed with him, in fact. Taught me most of what I know."

And on and on they went.

The talk turned to quays and customs and warehouses and cutters and so forth.

It was *very* disappointing.

Also, riveting.

And then a little boring.

Angelique and Delilah had been watching with held breath, Delilah prepared to leap in to mediate her husband's impatience. She sat warily back down.

"Bolt's bound to say something to annoy Tristan eventually. Everybody does," she murmured to Angelique.

"And Bolt will say something meant to provoke a little mischief. He can't seem to help it."

They watched and listened for a time.

"I think it's entirely possible they are more similar than different, which seems an extraordinary thing to say," Delilah mused. Puzzled.

Angelique instantly fell quiet. Because why on earth should she feel . . . *proud*?

Perhaps it was a general kind of pride: everyone

under her roof was enjoying each other. But watching Lucien in this context—informed, confident, relaxed, unguarded, thoroughly enjoying himself discussing something so . . . well, very nearly *boring* . . . was entirely new. She respected Captain Hardy perhaps more than any other man. Who would have thought that one of Lucien Durand's more dazzling facets would be the ability to hold an ordinary conversation?

Soon a circle of chairs had formed about Lucien and Captain Hardy, who had taken chairs and stretched out their legs. Everyone had a glass of something in hand, brandy or sherry, including Mrs. Pariseau and Dot and Angelique and Delilah. Delacorte was pulled into the conversation about the import trade, then Mr. Cassidy was impressed to give his opinion about cotton and sugarcane, and then the talk got around to guns on ships and then pirates.

"Tell us about that pirate attack, Bolt," Delacorte demanded, somewhat predictably.

"Well . . ." He demurred at first. More out of a sense of showmanship than true reluctance.

"Tell us!" everyone echoed.

"Very well, then. I'll indulge you, Delacorte. Picture this: It was a brilliantly sunny day, hot as the blazes, and we could see the flag of their ship coming, and we knew we couldn't escape it. We would have to fight. I had survived near drowning, I had survived a fever, and I would be damned, I say, if I would be killed by a pirate that day."

He reached into his pocket, and with a deft flick of his wrist, hurtled a pence into the jar, and a soft "oooh!" rose from the ladies.

"We could see them coming over the sides, like spiders they were . . . We were badly outnumbered. But we had the courage. The battle went on for *hours*."

Delacorte was enthralled. "Show us! Show us, Bolt! You and Hardy! Show us how it went!"

Lucien turned to Captain Hardy and raised a brow, eyes glinting.

"I'll be the pirate trying to kill you," Hardy volunteered rather magnanimously. Given that Lord Bolt was the guest.

"Huzzah!" Delacorte cried.

Angelique and Delilah exchanged a stunned glance. Was it possible Captain Hardy was about to be *playful*?

Angelique could not yet decide whether Bolt was a good influence or bad in this regard. But Captain Hardy had gotten to his feet along with Lucien.

"All right, then," Lucien said briskly. "To set the scene convincingly, we shall need *all* of you to be pirates. Everyone stand up and make a good deal of frightening noise."

Dot leaped immediately to her feet and bellowed, "BRAAAAAAAAAAK!"

Poor Delacorte jerked violently as though poked by a hot iron, badly startled. He'd been standing right next to her.

A stunned silence followed. Lots of hands were clapped over lots of hearts.

Fierce, indignant glares were aimed at Dot.

"It was the most frightening noise I could think of," she explained, meekly.

After a long moment of regarding her with a sort of gleeful wonderment, Bolt said:

"Perhaps I should have been more specific."

He sought Angelique's eyes to share his wicked delight. She was struggling mightily not to laugh. "Something along the lines of 'Grrr, prepare to die!' or 'Taste my steel, scallywag' would suit."

Much murmured practicing of growling and "Taste my steel, scallywag" ensued.

"You will *also* all need a sword," he proclaimed, dramatically.

And with a skill any mime would envy, he slowly unsheathed and hefted an imaginary blade aloft. So convincing was it that Mrs. Pariseau actually gasped, though nearly everyone could imagine they saw it glinting. He turned it this way and that, so they could admire its craftsmanship.

"Captain Hardy?" Bolt said.

And to everyone's astonishment, the dignified to a fault Captain Hardy similarly unsheathed a terrifying invisible sword.

Somehow he didn't look at all whimsical doing it, either.

A prickling thrill traced the spines of all the observers.

The two of them, rather than looking silly, looked truly dangerous.

Angelique had a sudden, captivating vision of the two of them as little boys, roughhousing and bonking away at each other with sticks, and her heart gave a little squeeze, as though wringing its hands in pleasure.

Caught up in the drama, every last one of them— Delilah and Angelique included—unsheathed invisible swords and made great show of testing the blades with their fingertips.

Lucien and Captain Hardy faced each other and adopted a fencing stance.

All was riveted silence.

And Captain Hardy lunged at Lucien.

Pandemonium ensued.

"DIE, SCALLYWAG!" Mrs. Pariseau roared and feinted at Dot, who slashed back with a two-armed swing of the invisible scimitar she'd decided she was wielding. Delilah was holding off Mr. Delacorte with her own sword. Mr. Cassidy shouted, "FIRE!" and mimed lighting a cannon, displaying a talent for improvisation.

And then suddenly Angelique froze, riveted.

Lucien and Captain Hardy had locked invisible swords in the air.

Suddenly it was almost too real. Men with actual blades that could pierce and slice had once rushed at Lucien and he had not died. Thank God, thank God, he had not died.

The absurd miracle of him standing in this

room right now, captivating a little audience, persuading even her into pretending to be a pirate, struck her dumb with a gratitude so enormous it felt nearly holy. And an absurd impulse took her to bellow "Braaak!" and go at Captain Hardy with her pantomime sword.

But she was still for too long.

Mr. Delacorte lunged at her with his invisible sword just as Delilah accidentally trod on her shoe, and in her attempt to dodge Angelique stumbled and began to topple to the ground.

"Oh, no! You've killed Mrs. Breedlove!" Dot shouted.

In the spirit of things, Angelique crumpled prettily to the floor, closed her eyes, and obligingly lay still.

She gave a start when something immediately landed with a thud next to her head.

She opened her eyes to see Lucien's face, white and stricken.

That thud had been him dropping to his knees.

They stared at each other a moment. He was breathing quickly.

"I was play-acting," she said gently. "I was not really killed by a make-believe sword."

He blinked. His face went utterly blank.

He momentarily looked rather like Delacorte after he'd been beaten in chess. As though someone had taken the flat of a board and swung it like a cricket bat at his head.

He sat back hard on his heels and frowned blackly down at her.

Then rose to his feet and, after a peculiar little pause, during which he eyed her the way a sailor might have eyed a siren, knowing his fate was predestined and unable to avoid it, he extended his hand to her.

It was the moment of hesitation between the time he extended his hand and the time she finally took it that told them perhaps more than either of them wanted to know.

And then her skin was against his skin. Again. At last.

His hand closed around hers, gently.

Angelique was tempted to close her eyes against the soft rush of pleasure that stood the fine hairs on her neck on end.

Everyone was watching this, smiling.

No one seemed shocked.

Because it was not quite the eternity it had seemed to Lucien and Angelique. One brief grip of the hand did not betray their passionate kiss in the hall, or the fact that she knew precisely what it was like to be pressed up against Lord Bolt's erection and that she had liked it.

He pulled her to her feet and released her hand at once as though she were made of flame.

Delilah helped Angelique smooth her skirt.

And then Angelique offered a smile to the crowd at large. "I live to fight another day," she said.

"Hurrah!" everyone cried, amid laughter.

But Lord Bolt absently sheathed his invisible sword. Then he pivoted and left the room without another word.

He did not return to the drawing room for the rest of the night.

Chapter Ten

❦

LUCIEN WAS dressed and out of The Grand Palace on the Thames just after dawn, feeling martyred and irritable. A man would have to be mad to turn his back on the seductive smells of eggs and sausage and kippers rising from the kitchen.

Perhaps he was.

He thought perhaps a good walk in a stiff ocean breeze on a foggy London day was the "get a hold of yourself, man!" kind of face slap he needed.

Last night—at least about three seconds of it—was purely an embarrassment.

It was also an epiphany.

This was what troubled him the most.

When he'd turned and seen Angelique on the carpet two profound events had crowded themselves into a fraction of a second, stomaching their way beneath his solid foundation of good sense.

His heart had stopped and the world—almost literally—went black. Snuffed right out, like a candle. It had dropped him to the ground.

And he'd knelt there like . . . like some *looby*

seconds away from rending his garment and howling his grief to the heavens. Something had him in its grip and it had naught to do with sense. Without his knowing, without his *permission*, his life—thoughts and feelings and all that rot—had reshaped itself around her.

If she were to be plucked out of it . . . well, what was left behind closely resembled a void.

A moment later her voice had returned him to his senses, but she'd seen his expression, in all its raw, exposed glory. Of that he was certain.

Because he'd seen the impact on her own. She'd been stunned.

Bloody hell.

It had felt like a calling, for a mad moment: simply helping her up. It occurred to him that whatever she needed, no matter what it was, he'd be too happy to provide. Holding her hand had seemed *absurdly* profound. Laughably so. It brought home to him that something about her had indeed stripped him down to a strange, raw newness. As if he was once again a green boy quivering at the very thought of the touch of a female. His thoughts careened between resentment and bemused wonderment, but came to rest on one certainty: even if he never experienced the glory of touching the rest of her, he'd still rush to help her up if she should ever stumble. If she should ever need him. No matter when. No matter where.

Even if he wasn't the sort of man she'd dreamed

of, with his ignominious history indelibly recorded in newspapers and in the memories of the people he'd fought, raced, or wagered with.

This seemed like a terrible weakness and an epiphany, but he wasn't quite sure why.

But perhaps this was merely the definition of friendship.

How he wished now he hadn't agreed to be her friend.

He wasn't a morning drinker, so a morning walk it was. He'd walk all the way to Exeter's office.

But as he walked, he found himself heading for Bond Street.

He slipped his watch from his pocket. The winding mechanism had needed looking at for some time. He hefted it, thoughtfully.

He pondered what he was about to do and why and for whom he really wanted to do it, and somehow it felt riskier and more foolhardy than any wager he'd ever made.

What he wanted had more than he cared to admit with who he wanted.

It drove his decision. Once on Bond Street he strolled nonchalantly, like a gentleman of the *ton*, nodding at passersby when their eyes met.

Some of them did indeed whip their heads about for a swift second look.

When that happened, he smiled benignly. Pleasantly. As though he was delighted to see them even if they couldn't quite place him.

Finally he stopped in front of the jeweler, Sylvester & Sons, from whom his father had purchased his gold watch. From whom most men of his father's station purchased watches, in fact.

He hesitated.

And then he pushed open the door, to the jangle of bells.

The shop was artfully lamplit; fine gold and silver watches, rings, and fobs twinkled and gleamed on little beds of velvet residing in cases, meant to tempt men with money to surrender to impulse.

The skinny and bespectacled young man behind the counter looked up, smile at the ready. He took in what sort of customer Lucien happened to be with a swift, educated glimpse. He was instantly all deference.

"Good afternoon, sir. How may I be of service?"

"Will you kindly tell Mr. Sylvester that Lord Bolt would like to speak to him about my watch?" His tone was polite, edging toward jocular.

A flicker of recognition passed over the boy's face, but Lucien could tell his name rang only faint bells of recognition.

"Of course, sir. One moment, sir."

He disappeared into the back of the shop while Lucien inspected the gleaming things in cases and listened with a little smile to the muttered conversation. He could not quite make out all the words, but the intonation was unmistakable: disbelief.

Finally Mr. Sylvester emerged briskly, wiping his hands on his apron, clearly prepared to make short work of the imposter or interloper who had the nerve to claim to be a long-dead viscount.

He froze, hands tangled in his apron.

"Lord . . . Bolt . . . ?"

"How are you, Mr. Sylvester? I'm so delighted to find your shop still thriving."

"But . . . sir . . . Lord Bolt . . . that is . . . you are . . ."

Poor Mr. Sylvester's face had gone as white as his hair.

Clearly he was too polite to come right out and say, "But aren't you dead?" Perhaps in case Lucien didn't know himself. Perhaps if Lucien was a ghost.

"Ah, Mr. Sylvester!" he said at once, all soothing, amused concern, a tone that instantly removed at least one furrow from the poor man's brow. "I see you haven't yet heard. You see, I've only lately heard the nonsense about my dying in the Thames, though I suppose the confusion is understandable, as I *did* fall into the river. As you can see for yourself, I emerged soundly. You know how incorrigible gossip can be, and how it so often gets everything very wrong for the sake of selling newspapers."

"Incorrigible," Mr. Sylvester repeated faintly. But the color that had retreated from his complexion was advancing once more. He ventured a smile.

"I've been off making my fortune across the world, Mr. Sylvester, and I've only just returned to London. I've had the most fascinating decade. I've been to many places, I've seen beautiful things, but I've never met a finer purveyor of watches than you. I would never let another man touch my timepiece, and a busy man needs a working watch, wouldn't you say?"

And Mr. Sylvester glowed as Lucien handed over his watch, that unmistakable signet ring glinting in the lamplight.

"Lord Bolt, what a *pleasure* to know both you and your beautiful watch have survived. I fear I did indeed fall prey to the gossip."

"I shall not hold it against you, Mr. Sylvester, as anyone would have been persuaded by such a story. I've a job ahead of me making sure the truth is known."

Mr. Sylvester was a little abstracted now, inspecting the proffered watch as though it were a long-lost love. "Lord Fawnleigh left a similar timepiece with me the other day for repair, but I daresay yours is finer, Lord Bolt."

"Ah, Fawnleigh. Do give him my regards when he returns, will you? Perhaps I'll see him at White's. And do feel free to share the news of my"—he winked—"resurrection."

Mr. Sylvester beamed. "I shall be happy to assist you in that regard, sir."

It was a beginning.

Lucien hoped the news—*his* version of the

news—would spread gradually, like moss on the side of buildings after rain.

And little by little it would seem as if he'd never been gone, and little by little he would come to seem—what were the words she'd used?—well, "ordinary" and "quite respectable." Not the sort of man who would ever again appear in gossip columns.

EXETER HAD A surprise for him when he arrived.

Mutely he pushed a sheet of foolscap over to him. He hadn't broken the seal, but Lucien recognized it. He stared down a moment, stunned.

Then slid a finger to break it and unfolded it to read.

> *A representative from Triton Importers may call upon His Grace, the Duke of Brexford from two o'clock to two thirty this afternoon.*

His already beleaguered heart jolted.

He sat while the news reverberated through him.

He could not quite decide whether the knot in his gut was trepidation or excitement. But he had learned the hard way that imagination could just as easily torture as it could entertain. It was something that needed to be done. He was ready.

"Well," Lucien said finally. "I suppose it's a good thing I shaved this morning."

HE'D BEEN INSIDE the London townhouse twice when he was very small, about three years old. He remembered how everything gleamed, the marble floors like a glassy sea, the chandelier in the foyer hovering like a planet. His feet had clattered and echoed, whereas running across the floorboards of their country cottage resulted in a satisfying dull thunk, like a deer running on grass. He'd wanted desperately to slide down the gold banister and skate across the floor in his stocking feet. He had been forbidden to touch anything, of course. His father had gone up the stairs with his mother while a kind housekeeper had given Lucien a biscuit.

He was admitted by a butler whose expression was admirably as fixed as the statue of Apollo inside the doorway, but whose eyebrows could not be restrained. They twitched upward.

No doubt because he'd noticed how Lucien could have stepped right out of those portraits lining the staircase, the ones of ancestors done in oils. One after the other as he walked on up. He saw his eyebrows on one dour fellow. His long, chiseled chin buried in Elizabethan ruff on another. The beat of his heart echoed in his ears, as if it, too, were being slammed down on marble, like his boots. It was cold inside his chest. His hands were hot.

He paused in the library doorway.

The man standing behind the desk gazing out the window was tall, portly, and his hairline had inched back until it began in about the middle of his head. What hair he had left was gray. Lucien's hand curled reflexively. He remembered once grabbing fistfuls of it when he'd been hurled up onto his father's shoulders when he was three, so he could reach a branch of blossom for his mother.

Lucien understood, with a blinding epiphany, then that he had loved this man, with a child's inability to discriminate.

And this was why he could not reconcile one man with another. It was not so much fury as love. And fury had been easier to sustain than grief and pain.

The duke turned around with a start.

He froze, his face blanked in fear. And squinted. "What the *devil* . . ."

His voice was a rasp. The duke was still a handsome man. No signs of dissipation. He had no proclivities toward excess, like his son. Some other ancestor must have bequeathed that particular impulse to Lucien.

The duke shoved a pair of spectacles up onto his face.

Lucien, of course accustomed to stares, waited it out.

"Lucien?" The duke's tone, while frayed, wondering, even dumbstruck, could not be precisely described as "joyous."

His eyebrows were fluffy gray tufts now. Lucien suspected he was looking at his own eyebrow future.

"You're neither hallucinating nor suffering dementia, Father. It is I." He kept it light. Ironic. His own voice was steady enough. But it echoed strangely in his ears. He felt a bit as though he were witnessing this moment from somewhere up near the ceiling, rather than participating in it. He couldn't quite feel his arms.

But he managed to bow low.

The duke didn't move so much as a hair. When Lucien was upright again, his father continued staring, mouth parted slightly. Then he seemed to rally, as though he'd administered a mental slap to his own face

"So . . . the broadsheet nonsense wasn't nonsense," he said finally. Sounding somewhat ironic himself. His voice was still faint. Lucien half-admired the fact that he wasn't letting the bad shock he'd sustained show.

"No."

"Upset the duchess terribly every time you were mentioned."

That was my plan. "I can imagine it did" was all he said. The poor, poor duchess who'd paid Cuttweiler to facilitate his drowning death. Perhaps he ought to bitterly say, "Just like your letter upset my mother."

But this spotless grand office in this gleaming house . . . Somehow he knew that something about the sterile marble and gleam of it all would leech every sentence of emotion, sterilize it, turn it into a statue about emotions.

His heart was still beating harder than he pre-ferred.

Jingle bang jingle bang jingle bang hi ho. Rather in that rhythm. Bloody Delacorte.

"She told me some years ago that she'd written to you to ask you whether you'd consider more decorous behavior, for our son's sake."

Our son. His half brother. The future Duke of Brexford.

"She did." It seemed unnecessary to say more than that.

The silence rang almost shrilly.

"You've got my height," the duke said. With the ghost of a smile. He was wary, a bit uncertain, but he didn't look a bit like a man suffering from guilt or regret.

It's my *height now*, Lucien felt like saying, absurdly.

He said nothing. He was waiting to feel something definitive. Fury or heartbreak or bitter-ness, some echo of the love or affection he'd once felt, something he could use as a lever to settle scores, get answers, form powerful sen-tences the duke would never forget. And per-haps it would come after the shock of the first moments of meeting. But somehow he doubted it.

Something had changed. And that something was him. He'd been fitted with a new lens.

The duke cleared his throat. "Well. Er. Would you like to sit down?" He gestured to the leather wing chair in front of his vast oak desk.

Another surface in which the duke could see his reflection.

Lucien sat. They regarded each other in silence.

"Forgot you had your mother's eyes. Unusual color. Unsettling, sometimes. You're like your mother in the way she could seem to look right through you."

"I've used it to my advantage once or twice," Lucien said pleasantly. Ironically.

The duke pressed his lips together, uncertain what to do with this statement.

He seemed not quite able to hold Lucien's gaze, and that was, in fact, the power of Lucien's gaze. The whole of his personality shone through it.

Did the duke feel guilty?

Did Lucien even want him to anymore? Suddenly he didn't know.

And then the bastard turned toward the clock as though there was something, anything he'd rather be doing than talking to his bastard son, returned from the dead.

Lucien's lips curved in a small, hard smile.

"So . . . we thought you drowned. Cuttweiler reported what happened and it was upsetting indeed."

"I didn't drown. I was rescued by a ship sailing to China."

"Ah. Well. That's a good thing, then. I paid for your funeral. Quite the turnout. Drinking and brawls. Women bawling. For God's sake. I wonder who we buried? Wouldn't it be amusing if I paid good coin to bury some rummy who rolled into the river? Of course, we all rather thought that's what happened to you. Seemed inevitable, the way you carried on. I imagined you'd be knifed by a gambler or run over by a carriage." Those last words had an edge to them.

"Amusing," Lucien repeated slowly. Carefully. After a moment.

He could not recall the last time he'd been so astounded by a mere word. Perhaps when Delacorte had pumped his fist in the Gentleman's Room.

There passed another silence.

"Were you upset, Father?"

"I beg your pardon?"

"Were. You. Upset. You hadn't said a word to me for six years. Were you truly upset?"

The duke's eyebrows dove irritably. "Of course, Lucien. One doesn't wish drowning upon anyone."

Lucien almost laughed. "I suppose you rent your garments, that sort of thing?"

The duke glared at him as if he'd been insolent.

And it was odd, but Lucien felt a distant amusement. It was abundantly clear there was nothing in this man before him that felt like the man Lucien remembered. The man who'd once lifted him on his shoulders so he could pick apple blossoms for his mother. Who'd laughed and chucked him under his chin and was indulgent. He understood now that he hadn't really known that man at all; he'd interpreted that man based on a few moments. The sensation was akin to standing in a house while the walls collapsed. It had seemed like shelter, once, those memories. But suddenly the view was infinitely more expansive. Suddenly there was more air to breathe.

"The last we spoke, Father, was a few days before you sent a letter to my mother explaining why her services were no longer needed."

Finally. The duke's features spasmed in discomfort, perhaps distaste. Maybe even a hint of fear. His finger traced the edge of his desk nervously. Back and forth. Back and forth. The duke was not a man accustomed to being called to account for anything. Perhaps it was only now occurring to him that a boy he'd entirely abandoned might hold a little bit of a grudge.

The duke sighed finally, heavily. "You were a charming little boy, Lucien, and I liked having you about when I saw you. But one needs a legitimate heir when one is a duke, and a legitimate wife; and the proper wife for me, the current duchess, would not tolerate having a mistress and an illegitimate son hanging about. I'm certain you understand. You're intelligent and I made certain you received a fine education. I decided I'd given you the tools to get on with life and that what you did with them was up to you. And as much as I enjoyed your mother . . ."

The little smile the duke produced here made Lucien want to run him through with a sword.

"Oh, yes, Christine was *so* lovely . . ." His father turned to the window, where, presumably, memories resided.

Lucien said very slowly, "Her name was Helene."

The duke lifted his hand. "Oh, of course, of course. I used to love the way she said my name. *Robairrrr*," he said mistily. "*Robairrrr*. Ah, youth."

Lucien's teeth clamped down hard.

And in another blinding epiphany Lucien realized that his memories and the duke's memories were inverse images. Not reflections at all. The grand themes of Lucien's life—love and loss and heartbreak, betrayal and fury, his own and his mother's—were not a part of the duke's story. Helene and Lucien had been features in his life, something that made it a little more pleasurable, like hunting dogs or a good horse. It had amused him to indulge them. And it had probably been easy for him to stop.

The muscles across his stomach tensed as finally emotion pierced: it was unbearable to think his mother's life had been of so little consequence to the duke, when she had given so much of her heart to this man. But it was a choice his mother had made, for reasons of her own.

Still, for an instant, Lucien struggled to take a breath.

The duke would be baffled if Lucien said to him, "You broke my mother's heart." It would be like so much shouting into the wind. Like hysteria without context. The contents of his mother's heart had probably never concerned the duke. He had taken her devotion for granted, because he'd paid for it.

He considered how it would sound if he said it now: *your wife, the duchess, arranged to kill me, so embarrassed, annoyed, threatened was she by my very existence.*

This, too, would have sounded like so much delusional ranting.

And of course, he couldn't prove it at all.

And now he realized he would simply never say it. His mother was dead. Lucien understood definitively that he wanted nothing from the duke.

And gloriously he realized he needed nothing from the duke. Not explanation or answers or absolution or apologies or money. Nothing.

Well, perhaps one thing.

"Is this a pretense, then, Lucien?" His father waved at the correspondence from the Triton Group. "A ruse to come and see me and ask for money? I cannot think of what you want from me. I gave you a fine education. You've a title you weren't born into, thanks to me and the rare generosity of the king. It's up to you now to make a life of it."

"It's not a farce. I'm well-off. I don't want or need your money. I thought you might like to see for yourself the results of your generosity," Lucien said gravely. "And I thank you for it."

He said all of these things quite neutrally. He didn't want to give this man anything more of himself than he'd already given him. No emotion, no details, no clues to things he'd endured and learned to become the man he was now.

The duke nodded gravely, accepting the gratitude as his due. Interest flickered in the duke's eyes. "Well. Success is a fine thing. Alas, I cannot possibly invest in your endeavors, because the duchess wouldn't allow it, anyway."

"Well, one must always do what the duchess says."

The duke smiled. Oddly he had no facility for detecting irony, because he had no need for it. The spoiled and comfortable seldom did.

"There's still a sad bit of land in Northumberland entailed to your title. You might as well claim it."

This was useful information.

Lucien nodded.

"All right, then. I'm glad for your sake that you're not dead," the duke said briskly. After the manner of a person drawing a meeting to a close.

"Actually, Father, I did hope you'd indulge me in one modest request. I wondered if I might have the music box you gave to my mother. It's ormolu, set with amber and carnelian, and it plays a tune by Mozart. I have nothing else of hers and it's something she loved. I should like it to remember her by."

Some instinctive caution prevented him from mentioning the false bottom that hid locks of hair, his own and his mother's. He could not conceive now of exposing such sentimentality to the duke.

The duke gave his desk a little drum with his fingers. "Oh, yes. I know the box of which you speak. Alas, the duchess is quite attached to it and she keeps it in her bedchamber. But I can give you the name of a jeweler who made it, and perhaps you can get one made for yourself."

And with this he looked pointedly at the clock.

LUCIEN PLACED HIS feet carefully on each of the stairs as he moved down, down; his head felt light and tight. Above him swung the chandelier with seeming infinite layers of crystals, one perhaps, for every anticipated generation of the dukes of Brexford. Everything, peculiarly, seemed new, as though he were seeing it for the first time. Nearly everything in his life he'd once formed a judgment about now seemed to require recasting, because things could only be understood by contrast with other things, the way light and shade need each other.

He paused to draw a breath up through a raw, scraped sensation that had settled in his chest. He knew what it was: the very last vestiges of a misguided love excised, like that last bit of shrapnel removed. It was all to the good. It was glorious that it was gone. He was free. And he knew what to do with pain. Breathe through it. Walk it off. Wait it out. Drink.

Think of Angelique, which he did now. Because somehow she was both anodyne and ache.

The questions she skirted, as if to confront

them would jar an old wound . . . the things she left unsaid about those courtships and compensations. He suspected the stories centered around men just like his father.

How he wished he could change Angelique's story.

He got out the door, and was just cramming on his hat when he heard the hard slam of boots coming up behind him on the cobblestones.

He pivoted sharply, hand on his pistol inside his coat.

Something of the ferocity in his expression must have stopped his pursuer cold.

It was a boy. Standing about ten feet away. He was nearly all legs; his feet and eyes were enormous, and his cheeks were rosy. About fourteen if Lucien had to guess. He was dressed like a lord, but he'd managed to get some sort of stain, mustard from the looks of it, on his cravat. It was glaringly apparent in the sunlight.

They stared at each other. Lucien's senses were all a little amplified. Perhaps that accounted for the peculiar vertigo he felt as he looked at this boy. As though his own past was chasing him down.

"Sorry. Sorry. To shout. It's just . . ."

Lucien arched his eyebrows aggressively.

"Would you be L-Lucien, then? Lord Bolt?"

"Who wants to know?" Lucien said coldly.

The boy blushed scarlet to the line of his hair. "I'm R-Robert, sir. "

Lucien stared at him, frowning enough to make Robert fidget a little, fussing with the buttons on his waistcoat.

And then as though he'd given a spyglass a quarter turn to bring it into focus, he realized his vertigo was because he might as well be looking in the mirror at his fourteen-year-old self.

But Robert had his mother's dark eyes and straight brows.

And of course, his father's name, just as he would one day have his title.

"I'm your brother. Well, half brother," Robert, the future Duke of Brexford, said shyly. "We haven't met, I don't think, unless I was a baby and then I wouldn't remember, now, would I? Ha."

He looked up at him hopefully.

And Lucien could not speak through the thousand emotions pulling him in a dozen different directions, as though he were stretched on a Catherine wheel.

"I always wanted a brother," Robert confessed. "Don't think I'll get one now, ha ha, parents are a bit old."

He blushed freshly. Searching hopefully for some spark of humor in Lucien's face.

"Don't underestimate the caprices of your father, Robert," he said ironically.

There might be dozens *of us*, he was tempted to add. *If he could so blithely throw me away, surely he has extras.*

Robert looked a little uncertain.

Lucien felt as though he'd kicked a puppy.

"You're a legend, you are!" Robert enthused. "The duels, the races, the g-g-girls, the—"

"Robert." He was firm but kind.

Robert stopped at once.

"As your brother I forbid you to emulate me." He kept the tone stern. But he hoped a little lightness shone in his eyes.

Robert searched his face for what to believe.

After a moment or two he furrowed his brow and said, "You're not suggesting I emulate *Father*?"

And his eyes were lit with wicked humor.

Bloody hell.

He did not want to like this child, this future duke, current marquess, who was cherished because his mother had the right pedigree. Who, unbeknownst to him, was part of the reason the duchess had decided to try to drown her stepson—so that not one thorn, not one complication, would snag this boy's ankles on his path to adulthood and glory as a duke. Lucien did not even want to *know* this person.

And yet here he was. Smiling shyly up at him.

Finally Lucien smiled. Faintly.

Oh, but it cost him. It seemed grossly unfair to need to do this now, in this moment.

Robert glowed, prepared to worship his exotic bastard brother.

His *brother*. Odd to think he did indeed share blood with this person. And probably so much more. Tastes, inclinations. Humor. What would it have been like to grow up with a brother? Would he have wound up careening about the world if he'd someone to look after or someone to look after him?

Would he have wound up in a boarding house on the docks yearning after his "friend," Angelique Breedlove? A woman who might want him, but who certainly didn't *need* him.

Did *anyone* need him? It was as maudlin and bleak a thought as he'd ever had. And an indulgence, surely. He didn't have *time* for those kinds of thoughts.

Surely Exeter's world would be significantly less bright without him.

"I don't think either your father or your mother would like knowing that you spoke to me, Robert. You strike me as an intelligent person, so I'm certain you understand why."

"But . . . that's a big part of the reason I wanted to do it."

Damned if he wasn't tempted to smile at his brother again.

Experiencing Robert as a real person was inconvenient. Lucien remembered far too well what a delicate time the age of fourteen had been for him. How every feeling was new and outsized and confusing. How one could be so easily steered this way and that, given someone to admire.

He looked down at that still-innocent face and wondered how Robert's expression would change when he learned his brother had opened a gaming hell called the Duchess of Brexford's Den of Iniquity. What it would do to his innocence.

"Our father has some fine qualities," Lucien said.

That wasn't easy to say, either. The need to be magnanimous in this moment, on the heels of the conversation with his father, seemed grossly unfair. But then, life had never concerned itself with fairness.

He did it for the boy, who would need to believe in somebody.

He wasn't at all certain it ought to be him.

Mordantly, he congratulated himself, *Just look at the person I apparently am. That was downright noble. I'm not nearly as horrible as I wish to be.*

And suddenly, for the first time in his life, he could picture it. If he'd had a son, Lucien knew of a certainty he wouldn't ruin him at all. He knew precisely what he'd teach him. He knew precisely how to love him.

"Mother is a bit much, but she can be all right, sometimes," Robert added, with the touching eagerness of a child to share his own life. Just to see approval, or some other sort of judgment or information, on the face of another. Which was how a young person went about understanding or learning about his world.

Was she ever all right? Did she treat this boy decently? Or was every boy inclined to give his mother the benefit of the doubt, because any other truth could not be borne?

Robert was too young to need to bear it.

And Lucien, God help him, wanted to protect him in the way he could not have protected himself.

"Shouldn't you be in school, Robert?"

"Oh, I'm here just for Mother's birthday." He waved an arm. "They talk about you at Eton, you know," Robert said. "I cannot quite measure up in cricket but I daresay my marks are as good as yours were."

Lucien struggled not to smile. But he wanted to be alone.

He did not want anyone to *need* something from him in the moment.

"I told them I don't care if he's a bastard because he had naught to do with it," Robert said fiercely. "Sorry if you don't like to hear 'bastard' but it's what they say."

How could two such objectively dreadful people as the duke and the duchess produce this decent one?

Robert had not yet been ruined by wealth and privilege and by the awful people who were his parents. This ruin seemed inevitable.

It made Lucien feel regretful. Even a little despairing.

He was desperate to end the conversation. And yet he found himself saying, because it needed to be said.

"I don't mind. One should never mind the truth. One should never be afraid to live and face one's own truth. You'll find life is unbearable otherwise."

It was the first bit of wisdom he could recall sharing with a child. It seemed a worthwhile use of his life to date: to be able to produce that sort of wisdom. Robert couldn't possibly understand that yet. But he could see him absorbing this as if it were gospel.

"Robert, we may not see each other again. Best of luck to you." He bowed, because he wanted his brother to remember, if nothing else, that his bastard elder sibling possessed grace.

He left him staring after him.

Chapter Eleven

❧

"THE SWORD fight was regrettable. They're going to want to do it all the time now," Delilah murmured to Angelique that evening.

"We should have a sword fight every night!" Delacorte enthused from over at the chessboard, where Mr. Cassidy's hand had hovered over his knight for a good five minutes now. He was staring at Delacorte, trying to gauge whether this would be wise or not.

Delilah gave Angelique a "do you see?" eyebrow raise.

"Maybe just once a year, like waltzing, Mr. Delacorte," Angelique countered sweetly. "We wouldn't want it to lose its novelty."

"Mr. Cassidy killed a bear once," Mr. Delacorte added. "Perhaps we can do that instead."

Mr. Cassidy shot a swift, wry sidelong look at Delilah and Angelique.

"How long do you think Delacorte will be *with* us?" Angelique murmured to Delilah.

"He's ours forever, I think, like Dot."

Ours forever.

In some ways, it was the loveliest thought. Finally, finally her life had a forever of *some* kind. It was one she'd always thought she could live happily with.

Until she'd looked up from the carpet last night into Lucien's stricken face.

And then he had disappeared for the night.

Their hands hovering in the air between the two of them, as though they knew something irrevocable would happen if they touched. A sword-from-the-stone kind of moment.

She had held these images in her mind all day, breathlessly, as though they were a new and exquisite object she would shatter if mishandled.

And her day had been wonderfully full: apple tarts, wrangling over the budget for the following month, firing a maid and hiring a new one, and she looked forward to dinner. Lamb in mint with peas.

But Lucien did not appear for dinner.

Very well. This was not shocking, she supposed. He was entitled to dine elsewhere now and again, though even the finest restaurants would struggle to match Helga's skill.

And surely he would be in the drawing room tonight to read *Rob Roy* aloud, as he'd promised Mrs. Pariseau, and enact all the voices.

But he wasn't.

And as everyone wandered up to bed, he was still nowhere to be seen.

As the night wore on, her worry amplified. In a way that made the backs of her hands cold and her heart feel small and shard-like instead of featherlight, the way it had earlier today.

By ten thirty in the evening, the house was quiet. Everyone had gone up to bed, and Angelique and Delilah and all the servants had performed the ritual of tucking in the house for the night—candles snuffed, doors locked, and so forth.

Angelique brushed her hair and plaited it and climbed into bed.

It quickly became clear that she would not be sleeping anytime soon.

She sometimes, restlessly, did one more round of the house to make sure the fires and candles were doused, and just to savor the silence and the pure pleasure of knowing that all of this was hers. Hers and Delilah's. She decided to do that tonight.

At least that's the reason she told herself for shoving her arms into her night robe and creeping quietly downstairs.

She paused on the landing of the floor where Lucien's room was located. She heard nothing. No stirring, no breathing. Then again, no one could hear anything, really, over the sound of Delacorte snoring below.

She wasn't quite so mad as to aim the candle at his keyhole.

She followed the stairs all the way down. Captain Hardy usually rather obsessively made certain the front door was locked by curfew, but surely it wouldn't hurt to look one more time. Or to touch it to see whether it perhaps felt warm, as though a dangerously compelling man had whisked through and on up to bed.

She paused in the foyer beneath the chandelier that had so enchanted her and Delilah and Dot and stopped. Something made her turn her head.

Her heart leaped.

"Lord Bolt?" she said softly.

He was sitting on the long brown settee, his feet on the little table, his arms stretched over the back of it. He'd flung his coat somewhere; his rolled white shirtsleeves were brilliant in the dark.

His stillness unnerved her.

And his expression, exposed in three-quarter profile, was hunted.

"Lucien."

Finally he looked up.

She felt the bleakness in his eyes as surely as if ice had rolled down her spine. She realized she'd gotten accustomed to searching for that familiar spark—irony, humor, the something in which she realized she basked whenever he looked at her. Perhaps she'd gotten to need it.

And his eyes did gain light when they met hers. As if he simply couldn't help himself.

"Well. Angelique," he murmured. "That is your name and you are my friend and tonight I believe I shall use it." He said this with faint belligerence.

"Very well. I shall allow it," she said lightly.

"I was inside by curfew by just this much." He held up this thumb and forefinger so that no light shown through them. "I see that you are in your night robe. But will you come keep company with me? I shall be a gentleman."

She found she could not refuse that request. He was hurting, that much was clear, and her stomach contracted with something akin to panic. Something akin to what had shown on his face when he had bent over her the night before.

She ventured deeper in and sat across from him.

After a moment he said, "You smell delicious, Mrs. Breedlove, if I may be so bold."

"Well, we did make apple tarts this afternoon."

"Ah, yes. That's precisely the smell."

"*You* smell a bit like brandy."

"More than a bit, I should think," he said equably.

She gave a soft laugh.

"Why are you sitting here in the dark, Lucien?"

"It seemed the appropriate lighting for my mood. I am feeling bleak. Bleak indeed."

"I'm sorry to hear it."

"Also, a trifle drunk."

"You don't say."

He gave a short laugh at that. Then sighed. But it was apparent even in the way he sat that something hurt, and she would warrant it wasn't a physical injury.

"Perhaps you should tell me what is troubling you."

He was silent for some time, moving the brandy

snifter between his fingers idly, like a magician about to perform sleight of hand.

"Angelique, my friend . . . I do not think people use the word 'love' correctly."

Her breath left her.

She didn't think anything he said could have shocked her more.

For a moment she couldn't speak.

"No?" It seemed the safest response.

"They abuse the word, you see. Treat it frivolously. Bandy it about. Even now *I* would not be using the word if I were not *un peu* foxed. It's not the done thing, is it? In casual company, that is."

Suddenly his gaze was a little too direct.

"I suppose it's not," she said carefully. "A bit like cursing in the parlor. One feels one ought to put a pence in the jar if they say the word."

"Or rather like Delacorte's gastric emissions after a rich meal. It rather irrevocably alters the mood and the course of conversation."

"Perhaps in salons," she suggested. "In an intellectual fashion, such a thing is discussed."

"Oh, *salons*," he said darkly, as though he had a whole silo full of grudges against them.

She covered a laugh with her hand.

It hurt to laugh because here was clearly something he couldn't quite accommodate, could not squelch with irony or defuse with humor. She knew full well that some wounds could not be vanquished. Some old wounds never did heal and you just learned to adjust them, the way you would adjust a burden on a long journey.

"It's a lens," he said.

"What is a lens, pray tell?"

"Love is. You see everything through it, and then when you learn it is false, you are forced to recast everything in your life in a new light. Everything."

She didn't know how to navigate this mood. He was the one who was good at untangling things. She was good at waiting.

And so she waited.

"I saw my father today," he said finally.

"Ah. The duke."

"Oh, yes. The duke." Every letter of that word was literally forged in irony.

"Well, from the state of you I'm going to guess it went very well."

He looked up at her and his smile flashed in the near dark like a shooting star.

"I *spoke* to him, too. I did not merely gaze upon him from afar."

"Well."

She thought it best to let him tell her about it, a bit at a time.

"Angelique, my friend. I am going to say the word again, because I've had just enough brandy for it. Do you know what it is to love someone . . . and to believe that they love you, too . . . but then learn that this love never existed?"

Her breath left her.

Of all the things he could have said. It was a bit like taking a scythe to the knees.

If she hadn't already been sitting, she might have been forced to sink melodramatically to the settee. She curled her fist beneath her for balance.

She breathed in.

Breathed out.

Why should one word, so honest and raw, frighten her so? If she said "yes," she'd open a door, and he would shoulder his way through. But he was hurting, and what he needed was to know she understood.

"Yes."

His head slowly turned toward her. He regarded her with less surprise than she'd expected. With a warmth, an intensity, that she almost turned away from because she could feel it penetrate the gauze of her reserve right into the raw heart of her.

And then he shocked her again.

"I am so sorry that you knew pain, Angelique."

She went utterly still, as if attempting to hide in the dark. She could not, for a moment, speak at all.

She lifted and let fall a shoulder. "What makes you think I felt any pain at all?"

She was sorry now she'd been truthful. She was not accustomed to anyone else having a rummage about in her soul.

"Because . . ." He leaned forward, so that she could smell both the brandy and the delicious

warm scent of him, like something freshly
toasted. "I've had all manner of experiences and
known all manner of people . . . I believe I can
say with some authority that people become who
they are more because of the pain they experience than the pleasure. And you, my friend, I do
believe you carry about your pain the way you
might carry eggs in your apron."

Her breath left her on a little stunned sound.
She was perversely hopelessly charmed by the
analogy. Even as it stripped her bare. She was
stunned that he had seen it.

It made her instantly understand why he'd felt
like running away last night.

"People are who they are because of the kind-
nesses in their lives, too." Her voice had gone
faint. She said it more because she wanted to believe it.

"Do not attempt to divert me from my sulk
with sense, if you please." His voice was stern and
amused.

"Oh, *do* forgive me."

But she had diverted him from his sulk.

He suddenly looked nearly entirely sober and
his eyes were fixed on her as if she were a rare
plant that bloomed only once every decade and
would do it any second.

The fire crackled and popped. It occurred to
her that it would be wise to say good-night and
leave.

"Who was this person, Angelique?"

She waved his question away. "I'm much more interested in what your father had to say to you."

"Who was this person—or persons—who was unworthy of your love?" He said this as though she hadn't said a word.

"Oh, Lucien. That is quite the way to put it."

"I should think you'd expect that sort of thing from me by now. My expensive education, as my father put it, is stamped all over me and there's naught I can do about it now."

"I don't suppose it's important."

"It was once important to you, so it's important to me. If there were a list of rules for friendship, the telling of details would be among them. If I feel I am not alone in my betrayal, if you will, perhaps my mood will"—he snapped his fingers—"drift away like so much London fog."

"What an artful way to dress up your rank curiosity."

"Curiosity is not against the rules here at The Grand Palace on the Thames. I have memorized them."

She gave a soft laugh, which tapered into a long sigh.

"There was . . . the heir to an earl. Very handsome and charming and very persistent. I worked as a seamstress and he was a customer. He led me to believe he was smitten. *I* certainly was. He took me off to Scotland." Somehow in this almost-dark room it was easier to talk of things, using adjectives and emotions. Somehow things that once loomed large seemed dimmer, less significant, in his dazzling, singular presence. "And there he told me he was marrying someone more appropriate and I was a bit of fun."

Lucien was absolutely silent. He's gone expressionless.

"And there was . . . there was one other. The father of my charges when I was a governess. It was an old-fashioned seduction. I was naive and a virgin . . . and it did rather quite put paid to my chances at being a governess anywhere else. And my relatives disowned me."

She didn't mention the Earl of Derring, who had naught to do with her heart. He had not caused her pain. Only terror when he died and left her penniless.

Lucien was silent for a time.

"I shall need their names."

"Why?"

"So I can kill them for you."

She gave a startled, wry laugh. "Men."

"Such fools who do not recognize the true wonder of you should not still roam the earth freely, Angelique. It cannot be safe for anyone."

The wonder of her. He was teasing a very little again. But his eyes were serious.

"That is . . . so very kind of you, Lucien. I am quite touched by your offer of murder."

"I don't suppose I am a kind man. I try to be a truthful man."

"Perhaps those men weren't altogether terrible

people. Perhaps they did care for me after a fashion. Perhaps they were merely careless in the way of most men. Men often blithely do terrible things to women without realizing it all. Because they, like your father, don't need to care."

"But how could anyone who . . ." he began.

And then realization dawned on him.

"How could someone who loves you so thoughtlessly hurt you," he said slowly. "Ah. Aren't you clever, Angelique. You led me to that, did you not. It is a good question and I take your point. Because people are not perfect, I expect is the correct answer. Present company excepted, of course. People are weak and riddled with flaws and still go about loving people like a toddler with a rifle. They do not know the damage they do."

"No one would ever love anyone at all if perfection were a requirement first."

"Perhaps we don't love as well until we have lost a good deal," he suggested. "Perhaps one takes love for granted if everything else is easy, too."

"Perhaps."

"And when people loom very large in our lives, we forget that we might, in fact, not be so very consequential to them. That . . . they are the mountain, and we are just one of many trees at the base of the mountain." He added, with rich irony, "And mountains, of course, must consort only with other mountains."

He'd turned toward the fire, and she thought this might be a sensible time for her to leave.

"My mother was a good person." He said this swiftly, rather gruffly. In the way that people do when they speak of things closest to their hearts.

"What was she like?"

"You would have liked her, Angelique. She loved music and singing so much the duke bought a music box for her, made of ormolu with tiny insets of amber and carnelian." He held up his hands a few inches apart. "A pretty thing, about this big and not terribly expensive, but it played a tune by Mozart. It enchanted her. It had a false bottom and in it she kept locks of my hair and hers, entwined. Today I asked my father if he would give it back to me. And he said . . . he said the duchess is quite fond of it and would never part with it."

Angelique remained silent. But she took this like a blow.

She felt her stomach contract from the hatefulness of it.

"She is a dreadful person. The Duchess of Brexford."

He paused, as though he were about to say something, then thought better of it. "Yes.

"My father . . . the esteemed Duke of Brexford . . . wrote a *letter* to my mother to tell her he could no longer see us or speak to us because he was getting married. He would provide a small settlement only and we were to leave straightaway."

She was stricken silent.

"Good God," Angelique breathed.

"I will never forget my mother's expression that day. The . . . confusion . . . as she read the letter. She thought perhaps at first it was a joke. Then the realization that he did not, in fact, love her or me, had never actually loved her any more than he might have loved a favorite plaything. I watched this dawn on her face and you do not want to see such a thing. This . . . what it did to her, Angelique . . . another woman might have been furious. Sometimes strength and clarity can be found in fury. But it merely broke her heart. I stood there and watched the moment he broke her heart. She was never the same and she died knowing she had loved a man who had never loved her." His voice didn't quite break. But the pain made his voice hoarse and Angelique could very nearly not bear it.

"But she loved *you*, too, Lucien."

"Of course she did. How could she not? Behold this remarkable creature. They all cried when I emerged from the womb."

Angelique couldn't smile.

It was difficult to breathe; she could feel his pain as surely as if it were her own.

"But he'd been her lens, you see. She saw the world through her love for him. And the fact that he put that expression on her face . . . that he made my mother feel like *nothing* shortly before she died . . ." His voice raised a little. He took a breath. "It's that I can't seem to forgive. And perhaps in order to bear it I must make him and his evil blue-blooded wife gravely uncomfortable for the rest of their lives."

"Lucien . . ."

"You're about to say something wise to make me think again, aren't you? I forbid it. You have already contorted me into a somewhat better person."

"But it's a burden, don't you think? To carry around these wrongs that can never quite be undone?"

There was a silence. He breathed in.

Breathed out.

"You are not wrong. It is indeed a burden. It just . . ." He gave a bleak laugh. "It just seems intolerable to live in a world where my mother's life was treated as though it were of no consequence. I do not yet know how to bear that burden."

He looked up at her. Rueful in his pain; sorry to burden her with it.

It cut her in two.

And she laid her hand gently against his cheek. It was an instinct, a reflex, to take away or share his pain. In that moment, it was intolerable he should suffer alone when she had comfort to give.

His hand came up and covered hers. Gently.

The silence was different now. Wary. Velvety. Fraught.

Their fingers, like flowers blooming in reverse, curled, then turned, then laced. Eyes averted, together they savored the meeting of their skin. She could feel her heart beating in her wrist.

Time seemed to elongate like honey dripped from a spoon.

He turned her hand over gently and pressed his lips to her palm.

She exhaled a shuddering breath. He turned his head to find she was there to meet him, and as his lips found hers she freed her hand and threaded it up through his hair to hold him.

It was hesitant at first, the kiss. Gentle. Tentative. As though they were kissing someone new. As though, somehow, if they were furtive they could claim no responsibility for what their lips were getting up to.

But as she laced her hand up through his hair, as their tongues met, and twined, she could feel his desperate, savage relief, a sound of pure want, hum in his throat; it was very nearly a sound of pain. He was shaking with a surfeit of need, or she was; she could not be certain. Perhaps they both were. *We can't we shouldn't I musn't.* Her good sense wasn't entirely mute but her senses were anarchists: her senses were greedy for him, and they were deaf to reason. The pleasure of kissing him—it seemed in the moment inconceivable she had ever denied herself the pleasure of this man. And as her head fell back into his hand he transformed the kiss into something so tenderly carnal and demanding. She felt it in the very soles of her feet, in every corner of her soul, until, when their lips parted for a moment for a breath, that breath she took was staccato.

Her eyes were still closed when Lucien's hands lighted on her shoulders; he pushed the night robe from her so gently, so leisurely, that she could, at this point, pretend to herself that this wasn't happening. And then unhurriedly, as if they weren't doing this in the parlor of The Grand Palace on the Thames where anyone could conceivably come along at any time, so unhurriedly she could have at any point put a hand on his and said "no, stop," he drew the ribbon at the throat of her night rail loose; she felt the cool air against her skin as it sagged loose.

And she opened her eyes when he tugged the soft linen down, down, down. She wanted to see his face now.

His exhale in a gust of wondering, pained pleasure. He buried his lips beneath her ear and filled his hands with her breasts, stroking with clever, delicate fingers, dragging thumbs over her nipples as hard as beads, and she heard her own breath as a roar. She didn't dare say a word. His breath and tongue in her ear sent jagged filaments of bliss through her and she nearly sobbed from the pleasure. *We can't we shouldn't I mustn't.* Anyone could come upon them at any time. They both knew it. The prospect ought to be mortifying. *"Angelique,"* he whispered right into her ear, turning every syllable into a rueful caress that banked her lust, her name a word synonymous with need, his voice shaking with desire, as if she'd bewitched him. As if only she could free him. Oh God oh God.

She reached for his trouser buttons.

They fell open with a tug or two. She reached in and closed her hand over his hard cock and stroked him, once, twice. He ducked his forehead into her throat, his breathing jagged, the tendons of his neck taut. She did it again and his head fell back hard with a stifled hiss of pleasure. She moved into his reaching arms until she was astride his thighs, and he grasped, with shaking, desperate hands, the hem of her night rail and furled it up and up, and slipped a hand between her legs, and she choked back a sob of pleasure. She may have whispered, half choked, "Please."

And then she rose up so he could guide his cock into her. Her breath snagged on a moan in her throat.

"Christ . . . oh Christ . . ." he breathed.

The exquisite torture of moving slowly, slowly together. So as not to rock the chaise, which would likely sound like a goat trapped in a stall. The exquisite torture of this needing to be over quickly, because anyone could conceivably discover them at it. Staring awestruck down at him staring up at her, his eyes black with desire, hot, then as she moved over him, closed to endure the pleasure, the tendons of his neck taut. Her release was already bearing down on her, pressing at the seams of her very being, like a shivery river of sparks. Her breath came in swift ragged sobs as he gripped her hips and arched up to meet her, and she bit her lip hard to keep an animal keen of pleasure from escaping. He bucked his hips up to meet her as she came down hard. And in an instant, it was impossible to pace. She clung to his shirt with her fists as he gripped her hips as they collided, their skin slapping, and when his hand reached to stroke her hard where their bodies joined, her release was on her like a cataclysm. She arched backward as it struck and left her in smithereens of bliss. Wave after untenable wave of bliss shook her and she tipped forward, her face against his shoulder to smother her scream. She may have bit him.

His arms tightened on her to keep her from toppling and to drive himself to his release. He went rigid and somehow had the extraordinary presence of mind to pull from her as his release slammed into his body, and she covered his mouth with her forearm.

All was silent, apart from the soft gusts of breathing.

He buried his head against her breasts, heaving; he kissed one softly. She rested a hand on the back of his soft head, damp with sweat. They sat, for just a minute, like that, breathing in time, their bodies rising and falling, as though they'd been tossed onto the surface of a sea.

They did not yet look at each other.

It was a moment before Lucien's senses could

reassemble. For it quite felt like that: as though he'd been taken apart and reassembled, into a better, newer, freer, infinitely more sated Lucien Durand. His mood was transcendent. Making love to this woman was clearly why he'd been born. He was a little drunk on both brandy and sex, but it didn't strike him as an unreasonable reason for living.

And just as he lifted his head to see in her eyes how the lovemaking had changed her, she staggered to her feet and backed away.

She dropped her face into her hands, her shoulders still heaving for breath.

"Angelique?"

She stood for seconds just like that.

And then seized her robe and yanked her night rail up over her shoulders, and turned, and it could quite fairly be said that she fled.

Chapter Twelve

❧❧❧

SLEEP WAS elusive and fitful, mainly because Angelique had fought it off. She wanted to re-live each moment while Lucien was still fresh on her skin. Her lips were hot and kiss swollen; her cheeks were scraped from the start of his beard; her mouth still tasted of him, of brandy and musky sweetness.

She didn't wash. Her body still smelled like him, of sweat and sex and desperate want. She seized a fistful of her hair and dragged it across her face, and there he was, too.

Her heart yearned to soar. She could feel it surge toward the light. But she'd tethered it like a falcon. She trembled with the magnitude of what she'd done. She didn't know sex could be like that, something that launched you from your body and nearly made you sob from the unbearable pleasure, and it had terrified her. Sex that *she* had chosen, that *she* had wanted. And that was part of both the terror and pleasure of it, too.

All that talk of love and so forth. *I am sorry that you knew pain.* How did he know? Because the two of them, courtesy of the events of their lives, had been fitted with similar lenses. He could see her in ways that others could not. And on the one hand, it was a luxury that made her want to surrender to him utterly, everything in her mind and heart. And on the other hand, it left her raw and exposed; it was so much easier, safer, more comfortable, to go on as she'd been.

Memories of his expression when she walked away without another word also kept her awake. Betrayal and hurt.

She was not prepared for what might follow, for Lucien, doubtless, would not let it lie. And while she knew that it was so much better to be the one who left than the one who was left, she also knew leaving like that, no matter how overwhelmed she'd felt, was cowardice.

And she was ashamed.

Because Lucien Durand was a lot of things, but he was not a coward.

All of this was why she was all but tiptoeing down the stairs to the kitchen the following morning, hoping Lucien was snoring away in a sex stupor. After all, he'd paid for the best room and there was no reason he should get up before he wanted to.

She froze on the landing.

Lucien was just turning the key in the lock on his room.

He went still when he saw her.

They paused to study each other.

She wondered if her expression was as wonderstruck as his. Her knees, already tired, nearly melted beneath her when his eyes met hers.

But the wonder in his was fleeting. Something cooler set in.

"Good morning, Mrs. Breedlove."

"Good morning, Lord Bolt."

Motionless, they regarded each other.

"Well. Aren't you going to tear away at the very sight of me?" he asked finally. Their voices were low.

"Perhaps not just yet."

There was a little pause.

"I have witnessed a good many things in my day, Mrs. Breedlove. I can't say I've seen a woman just get up, cast her face into her palms in despair, and drift away like a wraith in a horrid novel after I've made love with her."

"My goodness. Perhaps *you* ought to try your hand at a horrid novel."

He didn't smile.

There was another little silence.

"You should not have simply left like that, Angelique." He said this evenly.

"Why? Isn't it the done thing? You ought to know how I feel about the word 'should' by now, Lucien."

He pressed his lips together. "I won't ask if it was any good for you. I literally saw stars, and you bit me. Given those two things, it seems rather evident that it was very, very good."

She was silent. Then:

"Stars?" she whispered.

"I nearly lost consciousness," he confirmed tersely. Almost accusingly. "White lights burst in my head. I believe I may have briefly met God, which will likely be both the first and last time I do. He sends His regards. Angels did not sing, unless one considers that little sighing sound you made when my tongue was in your ear. I have *never* . . . felt such pleasure." Every bit of this sounded so much like an indictment that she nearly smiled.

"I suppose I did bite you a little. Are you very injured?"

"My shoulder is not injured." He said this in a way that implied that, nevertheless, he was not entirely unscathed by the encounter.

He cleared his throat and lowered his voice. "About that . . . is . . . biting something you enjoy or . . ."

"I believe it's the first time I've done such a thing. It's just that otherwise I might have screamed as I . . . when I, and so I . . ."

His eyes widened. And then he closed them slowly, and squeezed them a bit, looking like a man in agony.

"What," he said hoarsely, "are you trying to do to me, Angelique?"

"It's . . . unwise, Lucien. What we did. We can't. We just can't."

"What on earth does *wisdom* have to do with what we did last night? I do not bet on horse races for the *wisdom* of it. One does not eat blancmange for the *wisdom* of it. Wisdom is the very opposite of pleasure."

"Actually—"

He was exasperated. "Indulge me. You take my point."

"Tell me, should you never make love to me again, can you imagine making love to other women?"

The question clearly startled and unnerved him.

"Of course. In the same way that if I'm denied a roast goose I shall inevitably eat hardtack if it's the only sustenance available."

"H-hardtack, is it? Sustenance, is it? Sweet Mary mother of . . ." Her voice had gone faint.

She gave her head a shake.

"What on earth did you expect me to say, Angelique? I am the last person to join a monastery."

"Appetites are fleeting, Lucien. One endures them until they pass. You've endured greater trials. You'll endure this one, trust me."

"What if I told you I knew untold ways to give pleasure, and all I want to do is show you all of them?"

"Oh, honestly. Untold?"

"It's very difficult to seduce a woman who refuses to admire my hyperbole. And it took me years to perfect it."

"And I imagine dozens of women to hone it once it was perfected."

He was still. "For God's—not *dozens*. What do

you take me for?" And now he sounded surprised, bordering on genuinely angry, which surprised *her*.

And he was clearly hurt. Which made her
stomach knot.

"Lucien . . ." She lowered her voice to a more
reasonable pitch. "I'm capable of saying no to
things that are delicious but unwise. This is
something every woman learns the hard way.
The consequences for us are *always* graver. And
men never consider that at all because they *don't
have to.*"

This brought him up short.

A silence, gentler now. He stepped toward her.

"Angelique . . . I will not hurt you. I give you
my word."

"No. I refuse to hold you to a promise that may
be impossible for you to keep."

And now they were both breathing as though
they'd ridden each other hard again.

"I cannot think of a woman . . . I have . . . I have
liked more." He'd gone quite pale. The words
seemed to cost him.

"I believe what you *like*, Lucien, is my elusive-
ness."

He frowned. "Was it a strategy, then? The
leaving? Did you want me to pursue you?"

"No!" She was despairing now.

"Then . . ." He was clearly maddened with frustration. "Why?"

She brought her hands up to her face again. "I just . . . I can't . . . if you'll please just let me pass, Lucien. *Please*."

He hesitated, stubbornly. Planting himself in front of her.

She stared him down.

And finally he stepped aside. Resigned.

She turned and had taken two steps when his voice rose. "Angelique."

She stopped. And turned.

"Is it something about me? Or do you feel as though you can treat all men as though what we feel is of no consequence?"

She sucked in a sharp breath.

He stood, waiting for that question to sink in. But he didn't wait for an answer. He turned on his heel and was gone.

MRS. LETITIA LOCKSLEY'S eyelashes were sable fluffs. Glossy dark tendrils lay like little filigrees against her ivory cheeks. The ribbon trim on her bodice and sleeves and bonnet had been chosen to match her eyes: all were the color of bluebells. Perched on the rose brocade settee, she was equal parts appealing demureness and straight-spined resolve.

Dot had admitted her to The Grand Palace on the Thames fifteen minutes ago and had dashed upstairs at once to fetch Angelique and Delilah. "Oh, she's quite, quite nice, Mrs. Hardy, Mrs. Breedlove. We *must* have her. Oh, do say we can!"

"It sounds like you're referring to a cocker spaniel, Dot, and I think our cat would object."

Gordon, their plump striped cat and Head Rodent Catcher, stretched out all of his toes in his basket near the fire then curled them into his body, dreaming of giving a dog a good swat on its snout, perhaps.

"Mrs. Locksley is a woman and she reminds me of you, Mrs. Breedlove!"

"Well. We must meet this paragon at once, then."

She and Delilah smoothed their hair and untied their aprons and went downstairs.

Within minutes of sitting and chatting with Mrs. Locksley, Delilah and Angelique could picture her joining them in their own little sitting room at the top of the stairs, taking turns reading from their book of Greek myths, doing the mending, laughing about the day, and planning the next one. Just like them!

"I've heard from my cousin Mrs. Andrew Farraday that the proprietresses of The Grand Palace on the Thames were kind and genteel and might have a room to let for a fortnight or so. I've a place to live, you see—I'm so much more fortunate than many others. It's just that my aunt's townhouse is undergoing some renovations and she's been waylaid in Brighton for a time and she cannot get home just yet but . . . oh! Now that I've met the two of you I think I'm glad she can't get back yet!"

They all laughed merrily.

"I can see that your guests are fortunate indeed. My goodness, you've made the place so charming." She turned her head this way and that in wondering delight.

If they had put their heads together to invent the ideal guest, they would not have come up with one quite so perfect as Mrs. Locksley.

"We're so glad you think so. We want everyone who stays with us, no matter how long, to feel as though it's a real home," Angelique told her.

"I think I shall be fortunate if I am able to make my new home half this charming. I hope you will advise me on the choice of colors for the little sitting room off my bedroom. The rose color just glows in the light, doesn't it?"

"We decided it was best to use colors that please us rather than allow fashion to dictate our choices."

Limited funds had, in fact, dictated their choices, but Angelique and Delilah were pleased to be able to frame it in this new light.

"How *bold*," Mrs. Locksley exclaimed with pleasure.

"Will your husband be joining us, too, Mrs. Locksley?" Delilah asked delicately.

She paused. "I'm afraid my husband died nearly two years ago."

"Oh. We are so sorry for your loss," Delilah said, after a second or so worth of appropriately somber silence.

"Thank you," Mrs. Locksley said with great

dignity. "I miss him greatly, but I have decided that I shall get on with things and try to live a happy life as he would have wished me to do. My aunt has invited me to live with her in London. She is quite lively and we shall go about and enjoy what it has to offer in the way of diversions and . . ."

She paused.

And then, astonishingly, a rosy blush traveled from Mrs. Locksley's collar to her hairline.

Angelique stared at it, fascinated. She couldn't recall the last time she'd blushed.

Flushed, of a certainty. Every time Lucien so much as looked at her.

He hadn't looked at her at all over the past several days. When he couldn't avoid it, he had on occasion aimed a vague, polite smile more or less in her direction over the top of her head in the sitting room. But they had not exchanged a single word.

And during that time he had sat dutifully in the sitting room with the others. He beat Delacorte in chess. He had gone out and come back in by curfew three nights out of the week, by all accounts sober, because if he hadn't been, the maids who lit the fires and brought up morning tea would certainly gossip. Many recalled working for drunk lords who mistook their shoes for chamber pots or snarled oaths when the curtains were drawn back to let the sun shine on their drink-soaked morning-after faces.

". . . men?" Angelique suggested, delicately. Completing Mrs. Locksley's dangling sentence.

Mrs. Locksley laughed. "Well, it's just . . . I should not object to being wed again. And one does enjoy a little romance, isn't that so? Even when we're married?" she said earnestly, her eyes dancing between Delilah's and Angelique's faces and back again. "Flowers, a poem, a stroll in a country lane? My husband did excel at that. Do you know, when he proposed, he got down on bended knee before my family at a gathering and asked for my hand," she said dreamily.

"*So* romantic," Delilah agreed. Who had been proposed to on a dock.

"Mmm," Angelique agreed. Who had never once been proposed to.

Angelique sardonically wondered whether Lucien would think of Mrs. Locksley as hardtack or roast goose.

And at once there flashed before her an image of Lucien's white, taut face the day she'd left him in the hallway. Not for the first time today.

And her heart felt like a lead fist.

He was hurt. And angry. She could scarcely breathe knowing she was the cause. She thought she understood why but she didn't dare to look at the reasons too closely, because they frightened her, too.

No one knew better than she did the lengths required to accommodate pain so that one could just get through the day. So that no one, *no one*, ever saw it. She didn't wish any more pain on him.

And if only she could make him understand the lengths that she would go to in order to avoid hurting again. But perhaps he already knew and had made his peace with that.

Lucien would leave, eventually.

She supposed she would exhale then.

And then suffer quietly and without comment. She knew how to do that very well.

"Well, we've a number of gentlemen staying with us," Delilah confided. "In fact, one of our guests is a viscount."

"A *viscount*!" Mrs. Locksley was dazzled.

Angelique went rigid.

"How exciting! Is he young?"

"He is not old. He is, in fact . . ." Delilah lowered her voice to a whisper ". . . rather handsome."

She left out the "notorious" bit.

"You must be *thrilled* to have him here," Mrs. Locksley breathed.

"Indeed," Angelique said.

In a tone that made Delilah slowly turn to stare at her.

But Angelique kept her own smiling face aimed in the direction of Mrs. Locksley. Who hadn't seemed to notice anything odd.

"We were raised to be ladies," Delilah continued, "and therefore we ensure that everything here is proper as can be. All of our guests currently present have *exquisite* manners, but our rather gentle rules are designed to ensure everyone enjoys each other and remains on their best behavior."

The "exquisite manners" bit was a trifle exaggerated, but Mr. Delacorte considered it an aspiration, and it one day might be true.

"How very pleasant. I miss my own family, but they are so far away in Northumberland and they all agree my aunt could use the company. But one gets to wanting a family of her own, you see."

"Oh, I know how you feel, Mrs. Locksley. I've only lately remarried," Delilah said. "My husband, Captain Hardy, is away for a bit of business at the moment but he'll return before a fortnight's passed. You shall likely meet him."

"Oh, that should be lovely. How exciting! A captain. He must be so brave."

Which was the precise right thing to say to Delilah if Mrs. Locksley wanted a friend for life.

What would Mrs. Locksley think of Lucien? With his complicated gaze and lean body and a voice one felt at the base of the spine. A voice that could ignite desire with one whisper. Or was that just her?

Mrs. Locksley turned an expectant bright-eyed gaze to Angelique. Because this was where she was to volunteer something about her own husband, because it was what women did when they formed bonds with one another.

That was when Angelique realized with clarity how wrong Dot was. Angelique wasn't a thing like Mrs. Locksley.

She wasn't, in fact, like anyone, really.

For some peculiar reason her throat was thick. The benign lies she usually so smoothly offered could not get past. She'd never been a "Mrs." of any kind. Before she'd arrived here she'd been the Earl of Derring's mistress and he had died, leaving her destitute. Although she supposed it could be said that he'd indirectly bequeathed his widow, who was now her dearest friend, a way of life she desperately cherished.

She could never say these things to Mrs. Locksley. Somehow, as she'd once wanted to protect Delilah from various sordid truths about men and love, she wanted Mrs. Locksley to go on being innocent, so there was at least some proof walking about that life could be kind.

Odd how she had gone so long without realizing her past was, indeed, ballast. She'd once advised Delilah to abandon the guilt she felt over not loving her first husband. She'd advise Lucien of the same thing.

Angelique understood that all she'd done with her own past was to hide it, and it was as cumbersome as if she were smuggling a wheel of cheese out of the cheese shop under her dress.

"Mrs. Breedlove is also a widow," Delilah said finally. Gently.

Angelique knew Delilah had said it so Angelique wouldn't feel responsible for the lie. And the gentleness was because she'd gleaned a bit of Angelique's mood.

"Oh, I *knew* we all had so much in common," Mrs. Locksley said warmly. And she gently touched Angelique's arm.

THEY BROUGHT MRS. Locksley, who'd enjoyed a light repast in her bedroom, into the parlor after dinner to introduce her. All the guests sprang politely to their feet at once.

"Mrs. Locksley is a widow, and she will be staying in London with her aunt, but we'll have the pleasure of her company for a few weeks at least," Delilah told them warmly.

There was brief little silence, interrupted only by the faintest most peculiar sound.

"What *is* that?" Delilah whispered to Angelique.

"I think it was the sound of the men in the room sucking in his stomach a little bit," Angelique whispered. "Trousers rustling, buttons squeaking. That sort of thing."

Everyone beamed at Mrs. Locksley with pleasure.

Lucien was conspicuously absent from the gathering. Over the past week or so he had taken himself off on evenings when he was not required to sit in the parlor, in accordance with the rules of The Grand Palace on the Thames, getting up to whatever pleasures London had to offer, she supposed. He'd always returned by curfew. She found her eyes going to where he normally sat, over and over, the way one's tongue seeks out a hole where a tooth once was.

"Oh, please do sit down, everyone. It will make me feel right at home. I'm so sorry I wasn't able to join you for dinner." Mrs. Locksley was, charmingly, a little shy. "I found I needed a bit of a nap. But I cannot wait to sample the cooking tomorrow. I hear it's beyond compare."

Mr. Cassidy said gravely, "Beyond compare, indeed." His face was glowing with admiration.

She smiled at him as though the words were all for her.

Mr. Delacorte lunged to seize a chair and brought it closer to the fire.

"Why don't you have a seat here, Mrs. Locksley." He gave it a pat. "It's the warmest seat in the house!"

It was also very close to the chessboard Mr. Delacorte usually presided over.

"Very kind of you, Mr. Delacorte. But I am not so delicate as that!" She laughed merrily and everyone laughed with her, though it wasn't clear that anything was funny. It was born of a sort of general delight, the kind inspired by spring days and gamboling baby animals. "Perhaps we should draw straws to see who may sit next to the fire."

"Straws!" He laughed giddily. "I ask you, isn't that a clever idea?" he said to the crowd at large.

"Clever, clever indeed." Everyone agreed on a happy murmur.

Introducing people was always a grand experiment, Angelique thought, and it was one of the mischievous pleasures of being a proprietress. Like altering the ingredients in a cake, one never knew whether the result would be something marvelous or something that would upset everyone's digestion.

"Why don't you settle there tonight, Mrs. Locksley," Angelique suggested. "You may find it becomes your favorite place. And if you'd like to knit with us, we'll make room on the seat for you here."

"I'd be delighted to, thank you, Mrs. Breedlove. You are too good to me." She'd brought downstairs with her a little blue ball of yarn she hoped to make into a muffler for one of her nephews and she clutched it between her hands.

She settled in and gathered her pretty knit shawl snugly about her. The firelight picked little red glints from her dark hair and lashes.

There was a contented hush as everyone beamed at their new addition with great pleasure and she beamed back at them. Every one of them got an equal portion of her attention for a moment.

"What we usually do of evenings is listen to someone read aloud, while we knit, or chat about our days, or play chess or whatnot. And sometimes there are musicales," Delilah said suddenly.

Angelique shot her a startled, quelling, side-long look.

"We've had one musicale so far," Angelique added quickly. *"One."*

"We once even waltzed!" Mr. Delacorte exclaimed.

"Now see what you've done to Delacorte," she muttered under her breath to Delilah.

"Do you play pianoforte, Mrs. Locksley?" Mr. Cassidy asked.

Mrs. Locksley smiled a trifle uncertainly to the crowd at large. "I do play pianoforte. Not splendidly."

One got the sense that she did not want to do it tonight, either.

Mrs. Pariseau, who'd been studying Mrs. Locksley with those dark eyes of hers that seemed to see right through a person without judging them at all, saved her. "I could read your cards for you, my dear. Unless you've notions about that sort of thing being wicked."

Mrs. Locksley gasped in delight. "On the contrary, I think I shall find that rather thrilling! I'd always longed to visit the gypsy encampment near our home in Northumberland, but my parents forbade it."

The crowd present had varying degrees of faith in Mrs. Pariseau's ability to tell the future—Mr. Cassidy was perhaps the greatest skeptic, being aggressively practical—but they liked her and they were very much in favor of anything that pleased Mrs. Locksley. So off Mrs. Pariseau went upstairs to fetch her cards.

They gathered around a little table as Mrs. Pariseau shuffled and cut and Mrs. Locksley peered with what was apparently bated breath.

"Oh, my! Would you look at that! We've pulled 'The Sun'! Why, it means good fortune and happiness is shining all around you!"

This surprised no one at all. It was met by "ooohs" and murmurs of approval.

The next card required very little interpretation; it involved an illustration of a man and woman beneath a florid angel.

"Oh, my goodness, my dears, it's the 'Lovers!' My dear, I would suggest this means your sojourn to London could prove more interesting than you an-*tic*-i-pated . . ." She sang this teasingly.

Mrs. Locksley's lashes lowered as gazes ricocheted around the room.

Mrs. Pariseau was matter-of-fact. "Let's just take a look to see who you might keep an eye out for . . ."

She pulled a card featuring a tall, lean, stern-looking, regal man.

"The 'King of Swords!' Oh, my goodness, you are *in* for a time. I would look for tall, very dark, very handsome, mysterious and powerful, a bit unyielding, full of himself, a force to be reckoned with indeed."

"Oh, my," Mrs. Locksley breathed, as anyone

understandably might after news like that, and her hand reflexively rose to her heart, and she lost her grip on her ball of yarn.

It bounced off her knee, then rolled merrily and speedily across the room as if making a yearned-for break for it. It was nearly out to the foyer by the time Mrs. Locksley was able to leap to her feet to give chase.

And then all at once there appeared in the doorway the shining toe of a boot.

Which gently and firmly, with a tap, halted the speeding yarn.

A hush fell as, slowly, gracefully, the entire man came into view in the doorway.

Then gracefully, casually bent to retrieve the yarn.

Mrs. Locksley remained frozen in place. Her fingers were curled into her shawl, and her eyes were enormous. She seemed mesmerized.

Then Lucien took three slow steps into the room and held out the ball of yarn as if he were handing Mrs. Locksley the world.

"Does this belong to you?" he said gently.

For a long moment she seemed unable to speak.

"Mewp." This little sound was apparently all she could manage after a second or so of being held in Lucien's gaze.

And then before everyone's eyes Mrs. Locksley turned scarlet to her hairline, gradually, dramatically, and inexorably as though she been dipped in dye like a bit of wool.

Lucien looked about the room, getting a sense of what everyone was doing.

And his gaze, as usual, passed just above Angelique's head.

Though she'd been transfixed with cold horror for the duration of his exchange with Mrs. Locksley.

And then his gaze returned, as though to safe harbor, once again to Mrs. Locksley's enthralled, upturned blue eyes.

He smiled.

"I intended to go out again this evening," he mused, "but now I think I will like to linger a while."

Chapter Thirteen

❧᷒᷒᷒᷒᷒᷒᷒❧

*H*ER FATHER—a surgeon, well-read, and curious about the world—had kept a small but cherished library of books, all of which he'd encouraged her to read. Which was how Angelique knew all about Dante's *Inferno* and the nine circles of Hell.

If she were to write her own epic poem about Purgatory, one of those circles of Hell would involve doing nothing but watching Lucien Durand docilely hold a ball of yarn for Mrs. Locksley while she knitted and prated happily, and other guests stopped by at intervals to whisper to Angelique and Delilah things like "what a fetching creature!" (Mr. Delacorte) and, horribly, "the 'King of Swords!'" (Mrs. Pariseau, with a wink.)

The gradations of emotion visited upon her were a shocking revelation.

Misery made an icy, windswept tundra of her gut. While the corrosive envy was more like a fever; her head fair throbbed with it. Watching the guileless, trusting Mrs. Locksley effortlessly charm and perhaps effortlessly find happiness again in an eyeblink churned that windswept misery tundra into a cyclone. *She* was not plagued

with doubt and fear and a history full of bad
choices and unsavory twists and turns. None
of that nonsense shaped any of Mrs. Locksley's
choices. And who wouldn't want this simple creature? What could be more soothing to a man like
Lucien?

And there were oh, so many reasons to loathe
herself: She loathed herself for the envy, which
Mrs. Locksley did not deserve. For her own weakness, when she'd thought she was so very beyond
any of that.

That was the other revelation: that she could
so thoroughly, thoroughly fool herself about what
she wanted and what she felt. She who was so
clever.

Enough was enough.

"I've a *mal de tête*," she whispered to Delilah,
finally. "Will you extend my apologies to the
guests?"

She slipped from the room under cover of
happy chatter.

She got as far as the sitting room at the top of
the stairs.

And then she'd sunk onto their little worn settee and dropped her face into her hands. Gordon
the cat rubbed her shins a few times but she could
not seem to move even to scratch his back. So he
returned to his basket.

She was uncertain how long she'd sat just like
this. She was dimly aware of the house growing
quieter. And then she heard Delilah's footsteps on

the stairs. Even then, she couldn't seem to raise her head again.

"Well, everyone has gone up to their rooms. What a pleasant even . . . Angelique . . . oh, my goodness . . . you are . . . you look . . . Do you need a tisane?"

Delilah sounded deeply concerned.

Angelique shook her head rapidly but she did not yet lift it because it was still the weight of a cannonball, suddenly.

She heard Dot's light, quick step on the stairs, and her voice came with it. "Wasn't that fun, Mrs. Hardy, Mrs. Breedlove? She's so fetching and so sweet, Mrs. Locks—"

"Dot, Mrs. Breedlove's dinner isn't agreeing with her. Would you go and get her a tisane from the kitchen please? Something for . . . indigestion. And . . . ask Helga to brew a brand-new one."

"But that will take a long time, Mrs.—"

"It's just what Mrs. Breedlove needs."

This was all Dot needed to hear.

She was off at a canter down the stairs. She likely would be gone for some time, which was the point. Neither one of them could bear to drink Helga's tisanes.

Angelique felt Delilah's hand settle gently on her arm. "Angelique. Do you want to tell me what is troubling you?"

Angelique took a long breath.

And then her mouth opened. To her horror, what emerged was:

"I do not want to feel feelings."

It was the unadulterated truth in the moment, anyway. If not completely accurate. The feelings she *was* feeling now were causing her great suffering.

She fanned open the little screen of hands to discover Delilah regarding her with alarm. As well she should after a statement like that.

"Apart from the things I feel now, mind you," Angelique added more reasonably. She sighed at great length, which seemed to release some of the terrible weight sitting on her chest, and put her hands back into her lap to take up her mending. "I feel pleased when our rooms are filled with satisfied guests and we are making a profit. I am pleased that we will soon be hiring footmen, and I'm even a little pleased at imagining the uproar this will cause among the maids. I will be beyond pleased if I feel safe and certain here every day, and I shouldn't like to feel anything more than that. Ever."

Delilah took this in with a complicated expression.

"Well," she said carefully, "I'm not certain 'pleased' counts as an emotion. I've always thought of emotions as things that buffet you a bit, like the wind makes a full carriage sway. It requires a little . . . finesse . . . to steer through them. Even the happy emotions. They always require a bit of adjustment and balance. Or like walking along a fence rail. It's what keeps life interesting."

Angelique half smiled. "I did that as a girl. Walked a fence rail."

"So did I."

"That was before we did only what we were supposed to do."

"*And* we can more or less do what we like now," Delilah said pointedly.

Rather *too* pointedly.

As though she knew precisely what Angelique wanted to do and with whom she wanted to do it.

Or was letting Angelique know that what she got up to was entirely her prerogative.

"Everyone went up to bed a few minutes ago," she said. "Except for Lord Bolt. He left the house about two minutes after you did."

Angelique felt marginally better hearing that, which was probably inadvisable.

The trouble with good friends was that they knew one rather too well. Which was also the brilliant thing about good friends.

"It's just . . . Delilah, for the past several months, I have felt safer and more at peace than I have since I was a girl, when both my parents were alive."

"I'm glad. So do I, oddly."

"I do not want anything to change that. Or interrupt it. I want to go on feeling safe and happy in one smooth trajectory until I die in my sleep as a dashing old woman."

Delilah pressed her lips together. The temptation, obviously, was to smile, and Angelique hardly blamed her.

"While that is indeed an admirable ambition . . ."

Delilah's careful dryness made Angelique laugh.

". . . I would like to submit that safety is not quite the same as happiness. And happiness is . . . Well, do you remember when Helga accidentally left salt from the stew . . ."

Delilah was very careful with her own joy in loving and being loved by Captain Hardy. Mainly she radiated it, and shared as kindness and gentleness, as if she had great fresh new stores of it to spare. She was too wise to assume that everyone would be blessed with that kind of joy; it still felt a bit like a miracle. But she wished it on everyone. Most particularly Angelique.

"But the potential for misery is precisely equivalent to whatever happiness you might feel," Angelique said.

Delilah took a breath and reached for a shirt needing mending.

She thought for a moment. Without being explicitly told, she knew Angelique had reasons to distrust.

"You see, that is all the difference now. You are safe to feel anything you please, because if those emotions should knock you off course, why, everyone who lives here will right you again. You can *skip* along that fence rail if you wish, and we will catch you should you fall, and we will make sure you're able to get on with things even if that fall is bruising."

Angelique smiled at her. "Thank you, Delilah."

"Peh," Delilah said, and waved a hand.

They both gave a start when a thud signaled the arrival of Dot and the tisane, which arced through the air and splashed on the floor when Dot tripped on the last step.

WHEN DELILAH AND Dot went to bed and she was alone again, Angelique sat on the edge of her bed with its charming quilted counterpane and realized she couldn't yet even contemplate sleeping. Her comfortable little room seemed much too small to contain all of her still-roiling feelings.

She decided to take a candle downstairs to make herself a cup of tea. She would sit by the lowering fire and maybe finish the embroidery work Dot had left behind. She'd suggest to Dot that fairies had sneaked in to do it, which might be amusing.

The candle lit only a few feet in any direction. But the dark didn't bother her and the sounds of the big house—the little creaks and groans and sighs, as if it, too, were snuggling down for the night, like Gordon in his basket—she'd come to find comforting. She could hear Delacorte snoring as she crept down the stairs. She tried not to think of Lucien in his room alone.

She'd just settled down onto the settee when she heard a key turn in the front door.

Her heart shot into her throat.

It opened and closed noiselessly.

They lovingly cared for every knob, latch and hinge here at The Grand Palace on the Thames.

For some reason the fact that he put his booted feet down softly touched her untenably.

He paused.

She would not be surprised if it was because he heard her heart beating.

He'd toyed with the rhythm of it since they met. He ought to know it the way a violinist knows his own instrument.

He peered into the room.

His hat was in his hand. As was his coat.

For a long moment they merely studied each other, somewhat warily. "I was at White's," he said finally.

"Ah. Were you?" she said quietly.

He glanced back over his shoulder at the stairs, probably thinking that's where he ought to go.

Then he sighed.

"Is aught troubling you, Mrs. Breedlove?"

"Of course not. It's a fine evening. Everyone is well-fed, tucked in, and safely inside by curfew. What could possibly trouble me when all is well at The Grand Palace on the Thames?"

"*What* indeed," he said equably.

After a long moment of studying her.

He enunciated and elongated all of those consonants.

She said nothing.

He didn't turn to leave, though he ought.

"You are a good liar," he said thoughtfully, almost lightly, as though she'd asked for his opinion on the matter. He was loosening his cravat as he spoke. "But not nearly as good as some of the thieves and scoundrels I've met in my day. You'd want a bit more practice on someone with even less of a conscience than me."

She dropped her jaw.

Their eyes collided.

His gaze flickered and became something more soft, as though he simply couldn't help it.

Then his expression went neutral.

He turned halfway to leave.

Then turned back to her and said, irritably, his words rushed, "Did you know, Angelique . . . you rub your thumb and forefinger together, as if there's an invisible coin, or something very soft and smooth between them, when you are troubled by something? It's quite subtle. Still, I wouldn't gamble if I were you. A clever or unscrupulous person will always know what you are thinking."

Her fingers stopped moving at once.

She stared at them.

"And sometimes a little dent—like so—appears here when you are ever so concerned."

"Ah. So gratifying to know that you're noting my nascent wrinkles."

"I said *dent*. Rather like a dimple. Makes one want to drag a finger across it, to smooth it away." His voice had gone almost lulled. Almost diffident.

The breath went out of her.

He said this remarkable thing as though it was nothing at all. And yet he was always saying remarkable things.

She looked up at him with a short, stunned laugh. She could not stop a tremulous smile from forming.

She had not lied to him before.

She liked him so terribly much.

He remained there at the threshold.

He sighed. "Angelique. Are we still friends?"

"I don't see why not."

"May I sit down beside you, then? I shall dispense wisdom and solace. I suspect you need some."

"While I don't question that you may have some philosophy to impart, Lucien, the sitting beside you bit strikes me as inadvisable."

He shrugged with one shoulder, then settled himself indolently into the little chair across from her, stretching his long legs with a sigh. He lowered his coat and lay his hat atop it.

He was destined to look magnificent in firelight the whole of his life, she thought.

She wished very much she didn't know what his neck smelled like, because what she wanted right now was to bury her face in it and breathe in. To feel his breath shuddering against her skin. And the weight of his hands on her waist, sliding down to cup her arse.

"Our new guest is pleasant," he began.

Throwing a bath of icy water over her sexual reverie.

She couldn't move for a moment from dread.

She lifted her head and studied him carefully. "Mrs. Locksley."

It wasn't a question. Oddly she'd made the name sound like an accusation.

"Fetching creature," Lucien said at once, with great warmth.

"Oh, yes. That does seem to be the consensus. Everyone here has trotted out the word, as if their brains have taken a great blow and it's the only word they know now. I'm certain it's what her mother said when she emerged from the womb. Behold this fetching creature! And don't you think her eyes are a beautiful shade of blue, Lucien? Like bluebells."

She said this last benign-sounding thing so acidly he blinked.

Interesting, but confusing. He paused.

"The *temerity* of her to go about with blue eyes."

She flicked her eyes up at him then, briefly. Wryly.

But the way she held her body suggested some profound and possibly dramatic misery and it made him as restless as her beauty.

Another little silence fell.

"Has Mrs. Locksley committed a transgression? Tell me, has she a sailor's vocabulary? Oh God, please let it be so. That would be funnier than Delacorte pretending to be a good loser in chess."

She performed that almost-smile again. "You should be kinder to Mr. Delacorte."

"I am as kind to him as I am to anyone. He is a man, you know, and a sturdy one, with worth and intelligence and pride. He is not a bird with a broken wing. He doesn't need you to protect him from me. He can survive without the coddling."

"Yes, but he likes it, and we like caring for him."

He studied her.

"I know you do," he said after a moment. Softly.

Lucien might have been tempted to tease her if he wasn't certain she was indeed feeling genuinely, volatilely wretched. His vanity hoped that had something to do with him, because lately he absurdly wished that all of her thoughts circled back to him. But he could not be sure, and ultimately it didn't matter.

All that mattered was that she was suffering and all he wanted was to do anything necessary to make it stop. Even though for the past several days all he had done, it seemed, was suffer, and mainly because of her.

She closed her eyes and drew in a long, long breath, which she blew out resignedly.

"Mrs. Locksley is all that is fine and lovely. She is intelligent, amusing, and kind as well as quite pleasant to gaze upon, and if we could stock The Grand Palace on the Thames with such people, I should sleep easily for the rest of my days. I like her very much. And that is the truth."

"Instead you are saddled with the likes of me."

"Yes." She said this glumly, almost absently, and with not one shred of irony.

Which normally would have made Lucien grin. But it was clear that she was indeed in a state.

"Do you know, she told us her late husband proposed on bended knee, like Galahad, before a gathering of friends?"

Lucien winced. "Oof. Poor sod. Begging and that sort of thing is not a good look on a man, that."

Angelique eyed him balefully.

She put her needle through her embroidery once. Then again. Without looking at him she said, "It struck me that she's precisely the sort of woman a man takes as a wife. Everything is just right about her—her appearance and breeding and sweetness."

Usually Lucien dodged words like "propose" and "wife" the way he would a drunk man waving a knife in a pub. But Lucien was baffled by the misery with which she said these things. And Lucien had begun to envision another kind of future entirely.

"Oh, certainly, I suppose. When one gets tired of enjoying life one gets a wife like that and retires to the country to replicate the species, as the good Lord intended."

She did almost smile at that, perverse creature that she was.

Good God, he did like her.

"Perhaps she'll fall in love with Delacorte," he suggested. "He has lovely eyes, too. They can make loud, lovely-eyed children."

But she was so muffled in her mood that not

even that could fully penetrate. And surely it deserved a laugh.

"Of a certainty your husband provided something of ceremony when he proposed."

She went still. Needle poised.

She opened her mouth to say something.

Then closed it again.

"Lucien." She gave a short sigh and squared her shoulders. "I have never been married."

Well.

"So the Mrs. is . . ."

"The Mrs. is just to make me sound . . . respectable." That last word was imbued with great irony.

She let that word ring as she sat in what was clearly silent misery.

He was still a moment. His first two emotions, in surprisingly swift succession, were a helpless spike of fury that these men in Angelique's life had so disappointed her. That neither had seen her for the rare treasure she was, or seen fit to honor her with their name. And this was followed by an entirely irrational, perhaps unworthy satisfaction that no other man had ever been able to claim her as his own.

She was so clearly meant for him.

"Well, obviously your stratagem has worked, for here you are presiding over a fine inn with a list of rules, an epithet jar, and a viscount beneath your roof. And what could be more respectable than that."

This won him a ghost of a wry smile.

But something was still troubling her.

He tried not to frown. Somewhere between that doubtlessly difficult admission and the baffling rumination over Mrs. Locksley lay the answer to the cause of her mood tonight. He suddenly felt a bit like he was searching for shrapnel in a wound, which he had indeed once done—his own.

He had not, however, ever before, had this kind of conversation with a woman.

He did not know what she needed.

He would feel his way in the dark. He would steer with his heart.

"Do you know, Angelique," he said conversationally, "when I first noticed your eyes . . . I was sitting on the little settee in your reception room, and the light was behind you. I was reminded of . . . well, it was a bit like looking out the window of my father's country house as the sun was just rising. The sun seemed to touch one leaf at a time on its way up. Green and gilt. It made one restless and hopeful. As though anything wonderful could happen."

Her head slowly lifted.

She stared at him. She in fact looked very nearly stricken.

"Doubtless you find that absurd," he added hurriedly, somewhat panicked. Because he *felt* absurd. It wasn't the sort of thing he would have shared with another soul.

She shook her head slowly to and fro. Still wordless.

His relief was short-lived, however. She pressed her knuckles to her lips. And that's when he saw that her eyes, to his horror, were shining.

"If not, then dear God, why are you weeping?"

"Weeping?" she muttered scornfully. "Now who's being absurd?" She ducked her head and sneaked one knuckle toward the corner of her eye.

He sighed, stood, and resettled himself down next to her on the little settee at a genteel distance. He retrieved a handkerchief from his pocket and held it out.

She took it wordlessly and pressed it once to each eye. "Dust," she muttered. "I'll have a word with those shiftless maids."

Never mind every speck of dust that dared enter The Grand Palace on the Thames was evicted before it could even settle, let alone in the finest suite in the building, and that the maids might be a little flighty but they were ever-so-slightly more afraid of Mrs. Breedlove than of Mrs. Hardy. They both knew it.

She handed the handkerchief back to him with great conviction, as if to say: *that is the last time I shall ever weep*.

He tucked it back from whence it came.

Silence, unlike dust, did settle. For quite some time.

He didn't try to disturb it.

Mainly because he hadn't the faintest idea what to say. But sitting here with her was as interesting and fine a thing as he could imagine doing, whether or not anyone ever said a word again and the silence went on so long that her words rang like a bell when she said them quietly.

"I do not want to want you."

She'd said these astonishing words almost lightly, ending the long silence as though they were in the midst of a conversation.

In truth, they were. They always were. A silent conversation that had begun the moment they'd laid eyes upon each other and had not ended.

The breath stilled in his lungs. Those words coursed through him as a rush of heat and ice. He thought he understood now the source of her anguish tonight.

And his heart pounded.

His every muscle was at once taut, imagining her wanting him. The way he wanted her.

"One of the grand tragedies in life is that we cannot have everything we want." His voice was low, amused. His eyes were burning.

Her smile was just a wry lift of the corner of her mouth. She pressed her lips together.

"If this desire is causing you to suffer . . . I cannot claim to fully understand why, but I would take the suffering from you, if I could, and leave only the pleasure of anticipation. Believe me. But God help me, in this instance, I cannot regret your wanting. It seems only fair, you see. Because the nights alone in my bed—by curfew, naturally . . . Angelique . . . are haunted by you."

He heard the little catch in her breathing.

He knew her heart had skipped.

And his soared.

She was absolutely motionless. She seemed enthralled.

"And it's a funny thing," he continued. "Lately, now and again, when I see my hand . . ." He turned his palm up, then down. "So mundane and familiar, going about its business splashing water on my face or lifting a drink or scratching my bum or moving a chess piece . . . suddenly I stop. And marvel at the fact that it knows what it is to touch your skin. That it holds that magic, that memory. And when I remember . . ." He gave a short humorless laugh. "I cannot breathe for lust. It slashes like a sword."

Her face suffused with a dazzling, fleeting radiance. He could all but see the light rush the surface of her skin.

Her hand went up as if to shade her eyes again. He was beginning to realize it was because it was an unconscious gesture, a protection against the glare of some emotion too brilliant to bear. She brought it down again.

"Lucien." She managed to make his name an ache, a regret, an accusation, a hosanna. As if there were a million things she wanted to say, but his name was synonymous with all of them.

He smiled faintly. But unapologetically.

"There is but one cure for wanting, after all." It was a struggle to keep all of his words light. He felt anything but light. His every cell seemed to pulse.

His heart beat against his rib cage as if armed with a truncheon. Every part of him wanted her, wanted her. But every part of him wanted her to choose this for herself.

"What you're thinking is hardly a cure." She said this dryly. She sounded more like herself.

"Very well, then. Then it's a . . . momentary forgetting. And surely it's surcease for something that has no cure? Which is I suppose the best we can hope for."

The following moments were wordless. But his senses were so raw even the silence abraded him, like sharp cold air.

He knew he could seduce her with the slightest touch right now. To stroke a strand of hair behind her ear. To take her face in his hands.

And even in the wordless sitting he was somehow happier than he could remember being.

Finally she spoke.

"Lucien . . . do you still feel hopeful about things?"

He was stunned.

He could truthfully say he hadn't been expecting that particular question at all.

There was something tentative about the way she asked it. Something that started an ache inside him. In it he saw a glimmer of the girl she must have been when he was a boy staring out the window of his father's house, scarcely daring to believe his luck at the turn life had taken. And then life had of course taken other turns for both of them.

He wanted to give that girl a proper answer. Not an ironic one.

And yet he realized the answer was fraught.

"For many years . . . I did not indulge in anything so frivolous as hope. I had no use for the word. I lived day to day, you see. And now I find that the word . . . might be of some use to me again."

Oh, the language of irony. How useful the two of them found it. It was the shield they held up to circle whatever had long been simmering between them, as if it were an animal with fangs or quills instead of something new and possibly miraculous.

He could run a man through with a sword with precision, if necessary. And he would, if necessary. And yet nothing seemed riskier than saying what he felt right now. He could not imagine ever laying down his pride the way he might lay down his weapons. Surely it was pride, not fear, that kept him from saying anything more ardent.

"The reason I was at White's tonight," he began, slowly, hesitantly, "and the reason I've gone there on other days and nights these past few weeks . . . is because I am renewing acquaintances. Making amends. To those with whom I may have quarreled when I was young and hot of head. I want them to come to know the man I am now. Because, Angelique, I do not want a gaming hell. I want an extraordinary, ordinary, respectable, operatic life and to never be a source of gossip again."

She stared at him.

Wonderstruck.

Then she smiled. Slowly, radiantly, and fully.

And he could feel that smile in his chest, like a sun rising. He could nearly taste the portent, the way one could feel the salt air before one's first glimpse of the sea. And the moment was like a wire strung between cliffs separated by raging waters. *All* of the possibilities seemed exhilarating: a triumphant crossing. A stumble and plummet, followed by the chilly plunge.

And so. He might as well.

"Angelique . . ." he said on a whisper.

She met his eyes.

"You do want me?"

A perilous second of silence or two ticked past, during which he tried to read the answer in her eyes. He saw only himself in the great, soft, black mirror of her pupils.

"God. Yes." The last word was cracked with rueful yearning.

"Good. Because I intend to take you."

Chapter Fourteen

⟨⟨⟨◦⟩⟩⟩

She would not think as his hands reached behind her to loosen the laces of her dress, slowly, deliberately, gently as he would unwrap a breakable gift. She would not think as his lips pressed against the pulse in her throat, or his teeth, so delicately, closed over her earlobe, sending a shock of pleasure arcing like lightning through her, or when he traced his tongue beneath her ear. She only sought and took pleasure, and moaned softly and arched for more, more.

She would not think as he settled his palms on her shoulders and pushed her dress down, down, and she definitely wouldn't think about the little shrug she gave to help him slide it to her waist so he could, with the soft groan of a man suffering a surfeit of pleasure, fill his hands with her breasts. And then their lips met, caressed and clashed, and their tongues twined. She felt the confines of the world drop away and she could not have said which way was up or down, as though she were caught in a rogue wave and tumbled heedlessly out to sea.

It was this thoroughly surrendered person Lucien gathered in his arms and carried up the stairs with a grace and silence that belied the fact that she was no feather.

And he lay her on his bed, and set about divesting her of her clothes, and she submitted, raising her arms for her dress to be lifted away over her head. His fingers skimming her breasts as he unlaced her stays. The unfurling of the petticoat. The peeling of her stockings. Each one an act of sensuality that banked the fires of lust.

And when she was entirely nude on his bed, he partook as though she was a feast, with astonishing, relentless, carnal competence. With his lips and tongue and hands he savored her. The hollow of her throat where her pulse beat. The bones at the base of her neck. He filled his hands with her breasts, traced her nipples with his tongue, and in an inspired moment gently bit them, sending bolts of pleasure through her. His mission, it seemed, was to ignite her every cell with pleasure, to demonstrate to her that her entire body could be an instrument of bliss if she surrendered, rippling and arching, and when his fingers slid between the tender skin of her thighs and took their time sliding to where she wanted them to go, she was pulsing and wet.

Her moan was low, an anguish of begging. "Lucien . . ."

He muttered something in French, some hybrid of oath and endearment. His clever, clever fingers delved and stroked and slid teasingly into her. She heard her own breath sawing like a storm; she swore and whimpered, moving her hips in time with his hands, her own fingers curling into the counterpane as if she knew any minute she would be flung from her body skyward. And when he put his mouth and tongue where his fingers had been and stroked, it broke over her, whipped her upward with a silent scream, her every cell incandescent with pleasure.

And then he was over her, trousers down to his hips, eyes burning down at her, arms bridging her body. She locked her legs around him and pulled him to her, bowed up, rubbing against him to tease herself before he guided himself in.

"Angelique . . . my love . . . dear God . . ." he murmured near her ear, dipping to kiss her. Then to lick her nipple, as he paced his thrusts, slowly, slowly, so she could feel every inch of him until, miraculously, she felt yet another release building.

She held on to him while he shook in the throes of his own release.

And then he tipped from her to stretch out alongside her, and he gathered her gently against his body. For a time Angelique, inebriated with pleasure, listened to the music of their breathing, the sway of his chest against hers, as his hand moved softly, softly, to stroke her hair. She felt lulled and safer, somehow, than she'd ever felt in her life, even as she was completely nude and he was still dressed. Who would have guessed that the secret of safety was surrender to this man?

A few moments later she eased from his arms and began to undress him, slowly, gently, and he submitted, amused. Pulling his shirt over his head, gently, to fold and lay aside. Pulling his boots from his feet, lining them next to the bed. She dragged his trousers from his hips, down his long legs. Until he was gloriously nude, magnificent in the moonlight peeping in through the window. She took his beauty like a blow to the head. Elegantly faceted with muscles, from the planes of his chest to the cut of his calves, furred over his chest and thighs. Lean and spare as a rifle, built for pleasure, and, she supposed, to kill a pirate if necessary.

The rush of gratitude and awe were nearly unsustainable. Her breath stopped.

He smiled slowly, wickedly, savoring her expression.

"Much better," she managed. Softly. "Now we match."

"Birthday suits," he muttered drowsily.

She settled back down alongside him and sighed, and they lay skin touching hot, damp skin.

Lucien turned to kiss her, very softly; her lips were tender. But the kiss was like a flame touched to a fuse. It deepened, and seduced. Their muscles tensed and lust surged like a river at flood tide. She wanted to devour and be devoured. To taste and discover every corner, hollow, shadow of him. To learn his scars, smells, and textures. To wantonly bask in the burning, greedy, awestruck heat of his gaze.

It was like being unleashed in a new, beautiful country. She traced her tongue down the little gully dividing his ribs, followed with her nails, softly, and her breath and teeth, the roads between the muscles on his chest, tickled the little ferny trail that led right to his alert and swelling cock. She reveled in the catch of breath, the drawing up of his knees, that little thrash of his head. That soft laugh and little groan and oath as she took his cock into her mouth and traced it with her tongue. She'd never been so grateful to possess fingers and mouth and skin so she could make him groan, just like that. So she could take and receive pleasure. Lovemaking had never before been an act of confidence and joy.

A little sensual battle ensued then, comprised of demands and surrenders. Of savage kisses and skillful tongues applied to sensitive places. A delicious chafing of skin against skin. Briefly she was astride him, like a champion, and then he tricked her by tipping forward until she was on her back. He won, because she wanted him to. He won, because it seemed he wasn't lying when he'd claimed he knew untold ways to give pleasure. He won, because she needed what he had to give, and his tongue was magic between her legs and he'd gently pinned her thighs with his hands so she had no choice but to suffer that exquisite pleasure. And there was no word for it, unless it was perhaps "hosanna."

She was soon begging with little sobbing breaths. "Please, Lucien, now, oh God, please . . ."

He gently turned her onto her stomach and pulled her hips toward him, and as he at first teased, then entered her swiftly, deeply, she came apart. And the counterpane muffled her screams of bliss this time, and he plunged again and again, driving himself toward his own release. And wave after wave of bliss washed over her, his own cry of release echoing in her ears.

Drenched and gleaming perspiration, impressed with themselves and each other and sated for now, they lay quietly breathing. She used his shoulder as a pillow; his arms looped around her. She dragged a coverlet she'd knitted half up over the two of them.

He turned to face her. To behold this miracle of a woman. Lucien drew a finger softly, softly over her lips. They were swollen and rosy from the savage kissing but he wanted to kiss her again, and he supposed that made him a savage.

Her lips pressed lightly against his tracing finger. She drew it into her mouth to suck, to scrape her teeth lightly along it, and the shiver of pleasure made him close his eyes.

A tender vixen.

"Are you all right?" he whispered.

She nodded and smiled faintly. Her eyes closed.

He drew a feather-soft finger along the outline of her lips. Of her jaw. Across her straight dark gold brows. Memorizing the lines of her. Down, down, the satiny length of throat, to the bones at the base of it. He traced them. Her lips parted.

Her breath landed softly against his. Swifter now.

His cock was stirring *again*.

"I do not know how to stop wanting you, Angelique," he murmured. Half wonder, half amused agony.

"Never stop," she whispered.

He let his hand wander, lightly, lightly, slowly, slowly. Between her breasts. Over, again and again, the soft mounds of them, circling the rosy ruche of her nipples. Down, down, along the seam between her ribs, over the curve of her belly, sliding beneath her arse, tangling in the curls between her legs, rising up again. Again, and again, drowsily, listening for her sighs, the tempo of her breath, to know when he should move his hand and let it settle between her legs to stroke, just as slowly, until she was reaching for him hungrily.

He moved to cover her, and when he was inside her they moved together languidly. Drugged and enchanted with lust and sex and joy, they gazed at each other.

He was going to sleep now, he knew.

"Angelique . . ."

"I'll stay."

He smiled drowsily.

Angelique would of course slip out of the room before the maids came. And she wouldn't sleep at all. Then again, she might never need to sleep again. He was champagne and coffee and opium and fresh air all in one and surely all she needed from now on was to breathe him.

She didn't say, "I will never really leave you again."

But somehow they both knew this was true.

EVERYTHING ACHED DELICIOUSLY: her cheeks from the start of his whiskers, her lips from endless kisses, her body from employing acrobatic and unfamiliar positions (rapidly becoming more familiar and more limber), and the soreness between her legs made her feel like the happiest wanton in the world.

And as she strolled through the market to do the shopping with Helga, Angelique was unaware that she left a trail of smiles behind her, and she hadn't done much more than walk through the crowd. Such was her new radiance that she lit everyone up as though she were a personal emissary from the sun.

How was it that the most maddening man she knew was somehow also the most soothing person she knew? She understood now that at the core of all happiness—such a dazzling word, so evocative of rainbows and lambs—was peace and trust. Very adult kinds of things.

And dear God, sex was a revelation.

The past week was covered in a bit of golden, shimmery haze, rather like those thick London fogs, only more pleasant, of course. She was going about with lavender shadows beneath her eyes and offering misty answers to questions, but she decided the lavender shadows suited her, and she didn't really feel tired at all, either. No feelings except satisfaction could seem to get through.

She attended to the business of The Grand Palace on the Thames by day, budget planning and dinner planning and maid squabbles and so forth. She ate at the dinner table and sat in the drawing room at night and was everything that was gracious and proper and expected of her as one of the proprietresses of The Grand Palace on the Thames.

And by night she crept down the stairs to join Lucien for a few hours of total impropriety.

Lucien whimsically imposed a curfew upon her. If she was even a minute after midnight, he demanded extra kisses by way of punishment. Alternately he demanded to be allowed to kiss her on the body part of her choice. His rules were more flexible than The Grand Palace on the Thames's.

"I will not impose an epithet jar, because I should bankrupt you soon. The way you go on when I do . . . *this* . . ." He idly slid his hand between her legs, and his fingers played over her. And her laugh had become a sigh, and then a moan.

How was it that she'd never before realized how very many colors the world contained? How beautiful everything was? The cobblestones. Even the man who would insist on pissing against the side of the building. Everything was new when viewed through a lens of delight.

But what surprised her most was the gratitude for everything, including all the heartbreaks, upheavals, betrayals she'd so far known. The wrong men had simply prepared her to recognize the right one. The seemingly wrong turns had led her precisely to where she wished to be.

In between bouts of lovemaking, under cover of Delacorte's snores, their murmured conversation meandered from dark topics to light topics, from the profound to the frivolous. In the dark, in his arms, nothing had power to hurt either of them, it seemed. So she filled in the emotions that went with the scaffolding of her story: of the heartbreak of being disowned by her family when she'd lost her governess job. How she missed her relatives nonetheless, though she'd never said as much aloud to anyone out of pure pride.

Lucien told her, as he would never again tell a soul, that the Duchess of Brexford had allegedly paid a friend of his to throw him into the Thames. Though no one could prove a thing, and Cutty hadn't even been certain she'd wanted him dead so much as frightened.

"She hadn't a prayer of vanquishing me," he murmured drowsily. "Then or now."

The notion of anyone attempting to harm Lucien was like an icy finger reaching through her bubble of bliss to touch, very lightly, her heart. But then, he'd fought back more frightful enemies than the Duchess of Brexford. And surely nothing could harm them here at The Grand Palace on the Thames.

But she did not tell him everything. Some parts of her past were too raw and shameful; she didn't want to introduce them into her idyll. One day, of course, she would. Because of a certainty her life would be filled with nights and days like this from now on.

Chapter Fifteen

꙯Ꙭꙮ

THIS WAS all he wanted.

To wake every morning with his arms around her, her breath falling softly on his chin. His body her pillow; his heartbeat her lullaby. To slide his arms down, and set his hands free to slowly, wonderingly roam over the eloquent, satiny curves of her. God, the untold pleasure of the learning of her, the claiming of her. To feel desire stir then, and build, and lance him breathless, but to hold it in check, to slowly, slowly seduce, to prolong these pleasures, to ramp it up, as one would pull the string on a bow back and back and back. To feel her ripple against him, her own want fierce and building. To softly, softly kiss her, their lips like feathers, teasing, languid, as their bodies moved, her ruched nipples chafing his skin, his cock hard at the soft golden curls at the crook of her. To know that she wanted him inside her, needed him inside her, and that glorious thrust into the tight velvet heat of her. To move, joined like this together, side by side, coming together in a plunge, parting, undulating like waves. To feel in her body the tension that meant her release was upon her and it was because of him. To feel his name, "Lucien," a ragged gasp against his lips. To see her eyes hot and hazy, her arms locked around him as though he was the only raft in a stormy sea. The frenzy as their bodies collided toward a release of such shattering, violent pleasure they nearly lost consciousness. And holding her as the storm of their breathing settled.

It was how he'd begun his morning, and how he wanted to start every morning for the rest of his life. Or at least as long as they were physically able.

He was going to be the man she needed and wanted. Had any man ever had such a noble ambition? He thought not.

And as part of his noble ambition, he took himself off to White's on Tuesday night.

Where he was greeted enthusiastically.

"Bolt! You've got to try this port I've sneaked in. Thick as blood but sweeter. Come and join us."

"Thank you, Beacham. I think I will. I've just one thing to attend to."

And to think three weeks ago Beacham had glared warily at Lucien as he walked through the door and reflexively gripped the edge of the table. Many years ago Lucien had gotten into fisticuffs with someone and tipped over the table with Beacham seated at it. He'd gone legs up in the air, like a turtle on its back. Naturally he had never forgotten it.

A few weeks ago Lucien had sought Beacham out and proffered a bottle of Courvoisier.

"I was an ass and a menace and I hope you'll forgive me, Beacham. Or at least accept this by way of helping drink away the memory of it."

Beacham had laughed, surprised.

And then, cautiously, after a moment's silence, he'd invited Lucien to sit.

They shared the bottle—Lucien drank but the one glass, Beacham noted and told everyone later—and spoke of mundane things, business and safe political topics and mutual acquaintances and how Lucien might like to have one of the spaniel puppies Beacham's favorite hunting dog had just whelped. Lucien explained he already had a large cat who ran up and down the halls.

And thus, after a fashion, a friendship, a new one, was born.

Every transgression he could recall—reckless racing, raucous, absurd arguments, frivolous wagers, hot-headed fights, even if he hadn't entirely been in the wrong—he addressed them, one man at a time.

And now, where once upon a time he'd walked a gauntlet of gimlet gazes into White's, now he strolled through smiles and upraised, greeting hands and invitations. He'd become such an expected and welcome and charming presence, so generally entertaining to have about, that everyone

not only took for granted that Lord Bolt was back,
they were *glad* Lord Bolt was back.

Except, no doubt, Cuttweiler.

But then, he hadn't seen Cutty at White's since
that little encounter on the bridge. Which was all
for the best. Lucien's penance did not include politely suffering Cutty's presence, and Cutty was
wise enough to know it.

He was assembling something of the life he
wanted. Of laughter, camaraderie, love, and friendship. As Angelique had put it, ordinary life was
sufficiently operatic enough.

But the vestiges of the man who had arrived in
England remained.

And tonight he had a particular mission.

He wove through the crowd, through the
smoke and the waiters bearing trays and the upraised newspapers that mercifully contained no
gossip about him.

But he was aware of the murmurs that rose
when he stopped at the betting books.

He ignored them.

He turned until he found the page he was
seeking.

It was Exeter who had managed to sneak into
White's to write the words, with his gift for being as invisible as he was visible. How that had
amused Lucien at the time.

He studied them now, bemused. It was striking
in how a few short weeks the sentiment seemed
to have been written by another man entirely.

*I wager every penny I possess I will
have revenge. —BOLT*

With a flourish, Lucien crossed them out.

And he could almost feel something like an invisible shackle fall away.

Revenge could not be had, not really, even if he still wanted it. He had no need of it, anyway. Nor did he have need of a gaming hell, when heaven could be at Number 11 Lovell Street, a white building by the docks known as The Grand Palace on the Thames.

He felt he now knew the reason he'd been born: to cherish and protect Angelique Breedlove's heart.

The way he felt . . . it was the opposite of being thrown into the Thames. Launched into the sky, perhaps. Up into the heavens, past the blue, spiraling and spiraling among the stars.

And that one final bit of business addressed, he turned around to face his future.

He blinked.

Standing right behind him—or rather, swaying right behind him—was Lord Hallworth. Drunk already, and it was scarcely two o'clock in the afternoon. His blue eyes were pink at the rims and he was scarcely thirty and sporting quite a set of jowls, also pink thanks to an excess of drink.

"BOLT!" he exclaimed joyfully. Even though they'd greeted each other in passing a week ago.

"Hallworth," he said politely. Cautiously.

"Glad ye're back, Bolt."

"Kind of you to say, Hallworth." Though Hallworth had said it once before, Lucien knew better than to point that out.

"Cutty and I were talking of your exploits not more than a month ago. Who but Lucien would be able to return from the dead like that, we said!"

"Who indeed? They don't teach resurrection at Eton, more's the pity."

"HA HA!" Hallworth was delighted, and went to give Lucien a thump on the back. He missed by a few inches and the momentum of his chummily swinging arm nearly carried him forward onto the floor. "Say, d'you remember that night at The Palace of Rogues where two brutes threw you bodily out?"

"No."

Of course he did. Not only had Cutty mentioned it some weeks ago, Lucien always remembered nearly every event of any significance, apart from those hazy feverish weeks between the time he'd been fished from the Thames and the moment he came to halfway across the world.

He did not want to think about the former Palace of Rogues at all. Unless it was to consider it the pile of manure from which a flower had sprung.

"Just one of your many exploits, eh, Bolt. I expect they all blend together," he said admiringly.

Lucien found that his wells of patience were deeper now, but hardly infinite. His jaw tightened. "I don't reflect on that sort of thing any more than I reflect wistfully on the hobby horse in my nursery. The memories are of no use to me as an adult."

Never mind that he'd never had a hobby horse.

Hallworth looked a little deflated. "Ah. It's just I heard something amusing about the place and thought you might like to hear . . . it's a sort of boarding house now, yes?"

"Yes. The king, in fact, visited it. It's a very *fine* boarding house, in fact."

"Oh ho! I wonder if the king visited for a particular reason." His eyebrows wagged up and down and up and down and it was a minute before he was able to get control of them. "Remember the Earl of Derring? Cocked up his toes right over in that chair over there?"

He pointed to a chair occupied by a young man who appeared to be doing an imitation of a barking hound, his hands up like paws. Near him, a friend was laughing riotously and clapping his hands.

One really ought to stop aristocrats from reproducing, Lucien thought wonderingly, *if they're going to go and do a thing like that*.

"I heard—mind you, it's all hearsay, heard it from a fellow who heard it from a fellow who only knew her name, naught else—that's where Derring's doxie is living now. At that boarding house."

Lucien went still.

He could practically feel the moment his blood stopped moving. Everything did, really, for that second. His heart. His lungs.

And yet somehow he managed to stare at Hallworth.

Who likely would be surprised when he looked in the mirror in the morning and discovered two singe marks.

Of a certainty Captain Hardy would be tempted to neatly impale the man in front of him if word got back to him that Delilah had ever, in the history of the world, been referred to as a "doxie."

Lucien would need to get the story straight before he delivered this regretful news to him.

But Hallworth apparently interpreted Lucien's fixed stare as fascination. "Oh, yes! I remember her well. A laugh like bells. All that golden hair. A body that made you . . . oh, you know just . . . *grrrr*!" He put his hands up like a tiger curling its claws. "It made one want to pounce upon her. D'ye know, Derring said her skin was like satin. I *burned* with envy when I saw that he'd gotten that little piece himself. Last time I saw her was at a party, the sort one can't bring a wife to, if you take my meaning"—he tried to elbow Lucien but missed him—"on Glover Street, tried to slide a few fingers into her bodice when I thought everyone was well into their cups."

Lucien's skin had turned to ice. A little screen of red dropped before his eyes.

"Ho, but I can still feel the sting of her hand

on my skin even now. I always did wonder if Angelique was her real name. Couldn't be, right? It's a doxie's name. I s'pose winding up at the old palace of the rogues is full circle for a whor—"

Lucien's hands lashed forward like a snake and hooked into Hallworth's cravat, pivoted, and hurled him up against the nearest wall.

The crash of the table and the tinkle of glasses and shocked gasps rose.

"If you value your life, Hallworth—and I expect that you do, though only God knows why, you *worm*—you will not finish your sentence."

Hallworth dangled, legs thrashing, jowls quivering.

"Bolt."

He heard someone's voice distantly from outside the haze of fury. Lucien's blood was roaring in his ears. A caustic pain seemed everywhere in him.

"Bolt. You're hurting him."

The voice seemed to come from a mile away.

"I ever hear you speak her name again in any context—if I ever hear you mention her again to *anyone*—it will be the last word you ever speak. Do you doubt me?"

Hallworth's face was a white mask of terror. Lucien could see his own rage reflected in the man's black pupils.

"Do. You. *Doubt*. Me."

"No." Hallworth choked.

Lucien opened his hands.

Hallworth's knees buckled, and he slid down the wall to crumple on the floor. Wild-eyed, he stared at up at Lucien.

Lucien knew it was already too late. *He* was the one who'd all but ensured that everyone would know about Angelique and Derring, and there was nothing he could do to stop it.

"You may name your seconds if you feel it necessary, if you prefer to die sooner rather than later." He said it almost dully.

"I won't be doing that." Hallworth choked.

Lucien gave a short nod and turned and left.

And once again, all the eyes were a gauntlet.

LUCIEN PEELED OFF his gloves, froze in the foyer, and balled them in his fist. He paused there, momentarily stunned to find he'd already arrived at The Grand Palace on the Thames. He'd left White's blindly.

Dot was tiptoeing furtively through the foyer, ferrying an armload of dead flowers, when she encountered him standing there in the middle of it.

"Dot, where is Mrs. Breedlove?"

She stopped abruptly. She was kind, Dot was. But he had a feeling her expression was an immediate clue to how his own must look: pale and alarmed.

She cleared her throat. "Lord Bolt, is aught ami—"

"Dot." He closed his eyes. Seeking somewhere in that dark the patience, the peace. His blood still simmered. The light behind his eyelids was still red.

He opened them again to find poor Dot frozen in place like a pointer, staring at him in stark alarm.

Later she would tell the other maids, "My blood fair froze, the way he said my name. He sounded as though he was about to die."

Dot had rather a gift for hyperbole, as it so happened.

"Where is Mrs. Breedlove?" he repeated slowly.

"She's . . . up. Up . . . stairs, Lord Bolt."

"Will you tell her *at once* that I wish to speak to her in the reception room?"

But she was already running up the stairs.

Dot had forgotten she was holding an armload of drooping flowers when she ran up the stairs. They flew through the air like confetti when she tripped on the last step. Which is how Angelique, sitting on the settee, came to be covered in flowers.

"Oh, Mrs. Breedlove. I am so sorry. But something . . . it's . . . oh, my . . . goodness . . ."

And then Angelique saw Dot's genuinely panicked expression.

"Dot. Dot, my dear. What is wrong? Sit down, please. You look as though . . . Are you badly hurt?"

Some injury was bound to happen to her eventually. And yet Dot bounced back cheerfully from every trip, stumble, spill, or poke.

"No, no, it's not me. Lord Bolt would like to speak to you at once, Mrs. Breedlove. His face is . . . his voice is . . . Oh, Mrs. Breedlove, I think there is something terribly wrong and he wants to see you."

Angelique shot upright and the flower clinging to her shoulder like a fancy epaulet tumbled to the carpet.

"Lucien . . . Where is he?"

Dot's eyes widened in fascination at the "Lucien." "Downstairs. In the recept—"

Angelique was already a blur. Her skirts in her hands, her feet hammering the stairs, clattering across the marble.

And she flew to him. Heedlessly. And there he was, upright, glowing. She rested her hands on his arms, then looked up into his eyes, touched his face, as if to prove that he was whole and safe.

She saw no blood and no limbs akimbo.

She leaped back, a sob of terrifying relief caught in her throat. Astounded at what she'd done.

There was a silence between them as he took her in.

And then she saw what Dot had seen: something was clearly wrong.

He moved like a man balancing something that might burst into flame. Careful footsteps across the carpet.

To close the door.

And her heart leaped. Perhaps this was a moment she would never forget. Perhaps he was about to ask something that would change her life forever. Perhaps he was only sick with nerves.

"I wondered . . ." he said carefully ". . . if you would mind sharing how you happened to meet Mrs. Hardy. The former Lady Derring."

Her heart crashed through her body to her feet.

Whereupon it took up a pounding she could feel everywhere in her veins, like a battle drum. Her mouth went dry.

He waited. But there was nothing of surprise in his countenance. He seemed to be schooling all of his features to stillness.

"From your expression, I'm going to guess you already know," she said quietly. And somewhat ironically. Because it had traditionally been her armor, irony. That, and pride.

He gave a short nod.

There was another silence.

"You ought to have told me. I wish you had told me."

She couldn't quite read his tone. It was quiet. But shot through with what sounded like despair. A bleakness she could not quite interpret. A sick, cold ache began in the pit of her stomach.

"What difference would it have made? Precisely when do you envision me broaching the subject? Over dinners of lamb in mint? In the middle of Whist? Naked in your arms? 'That was magnificent, Lucien. So refreshing, given that the Earl of Derring made love the same way *every single time.'*"

That's when she realized this ambush—and it *felt* like an ambush—made her a little angry. Not only because of the surprise. But in large part because she could not possibly guess what came next, and really anger and fear were often very nearly the same thing.

He didn't even blink.

"Fair point," he said evenly. "And what a fool Derring must have been. Making love to you the same way every night is like going right up to the threshold of Paradise but never venturing any farther into it."

"Lucien." She was trembling now. Her hand rose; she was about to cover her face. But that was purely absurd.

He knew all there was to know and there was no hiding from herself or from him now. She brought it down.

"You ought to have told me, Angelique." Still, he sounded less furious . . . less betrayed . . . than wretched. "Because I have been honest with you. I thought you were honest with me."

She gestured impatiently. "If you'd known that . . . would you see me for myself? Or would you see me as every man before saw me, a woman defined by whatever man has the pleasure of my body? Would you assume I was willing for you if

I was willing for him? Would you assume I had a price? I am the one who *always* pays, Lucien."

"But you told me about the other men. The ones who hurt you. Why didn't you tell me about Derring?"

There was a silence. The air she drew was too hot, her heart beating too quickly. She wished she understood his mood; but there was nothing between her and the truth anymore. She had no choice at all. Her chin went up, and her tone, her armor, was irony and pride.

"Lucien, it's because . . . the other two men I told you about could be put down to youth or naivete, perhaps. But the Earl of Derring? It was the choice I made in order to survive and it's the reason I have everything I have today. I hated needing to make it, but apparently I'm the sort of woman who makes those sorts of choices. And so, no. I didn't tell you about him."

He briefly closed his eyes.

"Angelique . . . you should know by now that it would not have mattered a *damn* to me."

He said this quietly, but every word carried an equal ferocity.

She blinked. Her heart wrung with fear. Something else was happening here, and she could not yet guess what it was.

He drew in a long breath, clearly to steady his own mood.

"Did you ever see my father at the Earl of

Derring's little gatherings?" His face was taut with the struggle to keep emotion and expression at bay.

"Yes," she whispered. Frightened now.

He closed his eyes briefly. Opened them again.

"Did he . . . ever try to touch you?" His voice was a painful shred.

"No. Your father has fine manners, indeed, Lucien." She said this bitterly. "Quite reminiscent of your own."

And then her heart stopped.

Suddenly, just like that, with that question, she understood.

So she found the courage to ask the question she should have asked straightaway.

"Lucien . . . how . . . how did you know about the . . . little gatherings? Lucien, how did you know about Derring at all?"

And this was when he came forward. Closed the distance between them. Reached for her hand and threaded his fingers through hers and held her fast.

It was only then she realized how very cold she'd gone. His hand was so warm. It felt like safety and the thing that anchored her to the earth and sent her sailing like a kite.

Why, then, did the drumming of her heart make her sick with terror? He was taking so long to choose his words and she knew somehow they'd be devastating.

"Angelique. I was just at White's, speaking with Lord Hallworth."

Hallworth.

She recognized the name. And there was only one reason she would have heard of a man like that. And then she remembered precisely why.

Lucien delivered his words carefully, as if each was etched in thorns, as if speaking hurt so much their very delivery was an act of courage. "Lord Hallworth informed me that the Earl of Derring's former doxie, a woman by the name of Angelique Breedlove, was running a boarding house on the Thames. He said that he once tried to slip his fingers into your bodice and you slapped him so hard his ears rang for days."

Her mind went blank with shock and icy fear stole all sensation from her limbs.

And then through her fear a flame of fury shot through.

Because she began to understand.

"Oh God, Lucien. What did you do?" she whispered hoarsely.

He took a breath. "I pinned him against the wall. His own cravat was useful in that regard," he said with bitter irony at his own expense. "I told him that if he *ever* . . ." Now his own white-hot fury leaked through. He closed his eyes briefly, and took another breath. "If he ever spoke of you in that context again, or said your name aloud, it would be the last time he spoke to anyone."

She yanked her hand away from him.

"Were you alone? Did anyone hear?" Her words rushed out, trembling and furious.

He pressed his lips together. Closed his eyes briefly. He said nothing.

Which was all the answer she needed.

She covered her eyes with her hands. Her lungs labored to breathe. "Lucien . . . how could you . . . how *dare* you . . . don't you know what you've *done*?"

But of course he knew what would likely happen next. This was why they were here right now, having this conversation. He was here to warn her. And perhaps seek absolution.

"Angelique. Please believe me. I could not bear it. I could not bear the story. I could not bear the sound of your name in his mouth. It is not for him to say your name, *ever*. It is not for him to tell your stories, your hurts, your past to anyone as entertainment. I could not bear the notion of you being hurt again. It is not for him to be allowed to sully your name like that. It will. Not. Stand."

She was horrified.

"You didn't do it for me, Lucien! You did it for *yourself*! To assuage *your* temper and your pride. How could you be so reckless? How could you be so wretchedly, wretchedly *thoughtless*?"

His words were colder now. "There have been very few moments since we met, Angelique, that I do not think of you. And I think you know it. And I daresay you would say the same thing about me."

"But . . . how could you . . . Lucien . . . I am

ashamed of it, don't you see?" Her voice rose in frantic fury, then crested and cracked. "It's a hideous sort of shame. How my mother would have died to know what had become of me. And thanks to you, Hallworth is unlikely to *ever* forget me, or who I was, or where I am. I felt safe here. I made a new life for myself at last, and you have *ruined* it. You may have ruined everyone here! Who would rent a room from a doxie, Lucien?"

She was wild with terror.

"Do you think," he said slowly, "that you are the only one who has ever felt shame?"

He said this with a wondering sort of coolness that brought her up short. She jerked her head toward him.

"Are you perhaps acquainted with a certain bastard who knows a thing or two about shame?"

She was silent.

He took a step toward her. "Do you think, Angelique, that one can survive it?" His voice was gentler now, but still ironic; he pressed gently, relentlessly. Seeing, perhaps, a little bit of give in her. A clearing in the maelstrom of emotions.

He took another step toward her. As if he would touch her. Perhaps take her in his arms.

She stepped back from him.

For a moment she heard nothing but the hoarse saw of her own breathing in her ears.

But all of her senses were painfully raw. The air all but flogged her skin. Even the color of the carpet seemed to pulse.

"Angelique." Her name was an ache, a caress. It cracked in the middle, her name, as though she was his heart and it was breaking now.

She closed her eyes. She wished she could cover her ears. Perhaps cover her heart, so he never could have seen into it.

"All this talk of forgiveness, Angelique. And yet you have not forgiven yourself. If I could undo everything that ever hurt you, I would. I want to bear all hurts for you, fight all battles for you, because I feel that it was what I was born for. I do not know myself anymore. I am sorry. I am . . . I am at your mercy."

His voice had gone hoarse. Precisely as though he were asking for mercy now.

She measured the words out like a punishment.

"They are *not* your hurts to bear. You may have destroyed all of us here. It is not your battle to fight. And I do *not* need you."

His head went back hard, as though she'd struck him.

And then his expression went carefully blank.

The silence was hideous and echoing. It was akin to the second of realization that one has inadvertently stepped over the edge of an abyss, before the endless black plummet begins.

"Then I am afraid I can no longer be your friend, Mrs. Breedlove." He said this quietly.

She turned away from him. She could not bear to look at him. He was proof that she'd been foolish enough to participate, yet again, in her own destruction.

She heard the door open.

But she stood alone in the middle of the carpet, feeling flayed outside and numb inside, and listened until she could no longer hear his boot heels in the foyer or on the stairs.

Chapter Sixteen

◈

BOLT BLOWS!

*Lord Bolt was bound to blow and blow he did
at White's! Seems his devil's blood got stirred
when Lord Hallworth dared to reminisce about
a certain Mrs. Angelique Breedlove, dead
Derring's former mistress and current mistress
of a boarding house called The Rogue's Palace
on the Thames. Hallworth was pinned against
the wall with his own cravat for the trouble.
No duel was fought and Hallworth croaked
out an apology. But there is one doxie in the
world who can rest easy knowing Bolt will
rush to her defense. Probably because he took
Derring's place.*

Suffice it to say, no one read *that* aloud in the
kitchen.

Instead Dot read in a hush to the maids as they
all gathered in the scullery.

But only for a moment, because Helga wouldn't tolerate motionlessness for long.

"They got our name wrong," Dot said indignantly. "The Grand Palace on the Thames!" She'd been there the first moment those words were uttered. It was sacred to her.

"That's not the *only* thing they got wrong!" Helga said indignantly. "What a disgrace these gossips are! Lies!"

Privately she had her doubts. She'd never known Mrs. Breedlove until Delilah had brought them all together, but after working briefly for the Duchess of Brexford, Helga judged people on the simple criteria of whether she liked them or not, and whether she thought they were good. Not whether they'd once allowed an earl to pay their rent in exchange for the kinds of services only a woman could provide. She frankly didn't care.

She *loved* Mrs. Hardy and Mrs. Breedlove. They allowed her free rein in the kitchen. And they were wonderful friends.

She exchanged a glance with Dot. Who also had her doubts. And also did not care a whit. Her loyalty was as fixed as the stars.

"I rather like the word 'doxie.' It sounds cheerful, even if it's not a wonderful thing to be," Dot said.

The maids nodded along.

Helga snorted. "You should never believe all ye read in the broadsheets."

They did not precisely hang black bunting about the place, but the mood was mournful and uncertain. It seemed entirely possible that no decent person would want to stay at The Grand Palace on the Thames ever again after reading that a doxie was in charge of it.

It was also entirely possible that all of the wrong people would want to stay there. For all the wrong reasons.

The third possibility was that no one would care at all, which seemed unlikely, but offered a grain of hope. This was London, and gossip ran through it as surely as the River Thames. But fresh gossip flowed in to flush out the old routinely.

When she learned of what had been printed about her and Lord Bolt, Angelique took to her room for nearly an entire day, during which she remained absolutely motionless on her bed, eyes open, curtains closed. She did not appear for meals. She did not appear in the parlor. She did not appear in the kitchen to plan the week's shopping. She did not ring for assistance and when Delilah asked, politely, through the door, whether there was anything she could do, she was told, very politely and firmly, "No, thank you."

She emerged, pale and resolute and looking more or less herself, the following day.

The staff did not quite eddy around her as if she were sharp-edge flotsam, but they did speak and tread about gingerly. Some were fascinated— imagine! She'd been a *mistress*! Was it true? Why,

everyone knew even the *king* had one of those!—
others were a little uncertain. Surely a mistress
was not proper? One aspired to be a wife or nothing at all. But she was so pretty and kind and
clever, even if she were just *ever* so slightly more
strict than Mrs. Hardy.

But all were gentle.

Mainly because it was appallingly clear that
Mrs. Breedlove had a broken heart, and it broke
everyone's heart to witness her bearing it so silently and with an attempt at her usual cool
aplomb. She was a ghost of herself.

And while the walls of the house were sturdy
and thick indeed, voices carried nevertheless. The
emotion, if not the precise words. White faces told
a tale. Slammed doors and a sudden departure
did, too.

The sentimental Mr. Delacorte was in mourn-
ing, because he was quite fond of the viscount.
"Had a way with words, didn't he, though?" he
said wistfully.

Leaving a hush of sorts in the parlor at night,
where everything went on as normal, and Mr.
Cassidy and Mr. Delacorte and Mrs. Pariseau and
Mrs. Locksley still convened, but Angelique and
Delilah feared nothing would ever be normal
again.

Lord Bolt had taken the time to leave generous
gratuities for the servants, with his thanks, and
this was the thing they'd remember about him
most of all.

And to think in recent days that Mrs. Breed-love had gone about looking as though she'd been lit up like a lamp. All radiant and golden. Like some shade inside her had been drawn and all the beautiful things she truly was could finally shine.

No one but Angelique guessed she'd in all like-lihood broken her *own* heart.

As well as, clearly, Lucien's.

It was this last notion that made her nauseous. That made her tread lightly, carefully, as though she were indeed carrying inside her something broken with edges like teeth.

The idea that he was out there hurting, a man who had already borne enough hurts and betray-als bravely, and she did not know where he was sometimes proved almost more than she could bear.

It was entirely possible she'd never see him again.

And she dared not entertain this idea for very long, because it was like looking down when one was attempting to walk along the narrow perime-ter of an abyss. You kept your eyes straight ahead, and nowhere else. Lest you lose your balance and fall forever.

LATER THAT WEEK Angelique took some mend-ing up to their little sitting room at the top of the stairs—Mr. Cassidy's shirts had come undone at the shoulders, perhaps because his were vast and sturdy and bound to tax a shirt, and Mr. Delacorte's waistcoat buttons needed reinforcing. The sun was gentle at this time of day, amber and poignant.

She looked up with surprise when Dot appeared bearing a cup of tea and a plate upon which rested a slice of lemon seed cake. And stood there, clearly full of something she wished to say but not saying it.

"Yes, Dot?"

"Mrs. Breedlove?"

"Yes, Dot."

Dot cleared her throat. "I . . . we just . . ." She pressed her lips together.

"Out with it, Dot."

Her words emerged in a rush. "The staff wanted to tell you that we don't care if you're a mistress or a doxie. You are a lady to us all. We'll call you anything you'd like. We love you all the same."

Angelique was stunned.

Her hand went up to her mouth and then she lowered it into her lap. Her eyes followed it there.

It took her two or three shuddering breaths before she could look up again.

She did, and gave Dot the face she'd want to see: Mrs. Breedlove, cool, serene, in command of herself.

And she thought about what Lucien had said about not being afraid to face something difficult but true. She wanted to be brave, too.

"Dot . . . you may tell the staff that it is true that I was a mistress but I was never a doxie."

"Never a doxie," Dot repeated dutifully, as if remembering the order for the butcher.

"And you may tell them that I am *not ashamed* because at the time it seemed I had no other recourse—which means, I had no other means of survival and I do not think it is noble to suffer when one might survive and perhaps go on to do good things, like open a beautiful boarding house by the docks. It was my choice and I do not recommend it for others. Do you understand what I mean?"

"Like me, when Lady Derring kept me on. I had not another soul. I had no *recourse*." Dot was enjoying her new word.

And Angelique's heart squeezed.

How was it she had never thought about Dot in quite that light? Because one didn't normally think about servants in that light. But here at The Grand Palace on the Thames the lines between all of the people who lived here were a little blurred, and she ought to think of Dot and what her hopes and dreams might be.

"Well. I suppose that's true," Angelique said gently. "And because in time my difficult choice brought me to become friends with Mrs. Hardy, and to know all of you, and to make a true home here at The Grand Palace on the Thames. I cannot regret it. One must go forward, and learn."

And it was a subtle thing, and she realized as

she spoke it had been happening gradually, but suddenly a burden lifted from Angelique: she was no longer ashamed.

She understood, at last, what Lucien had been trying to tell her the day he left. That she ought to have told him about Derring, mainly because he knew she carried a burden, and because he, of all people, understood what it felt like to be ashamed of something one simply could not help and could not change.

Living one's truth, it seemed, was more liberating than the false safety of no emotion or no risk.

It was just so much easier to do when you knew you were loved.

And she had sent Lucien away.

She didn't think she'd ever be able to forgive herself for that.

"And Mrs. Breedlove will suffice, Dot," she said more briskly and brightly. "No need to worry about whether I'm a mistress or a doxie, as I'm neither. But I am a proprietress."

"Proprietress," Dot repeated, savoring the s's.

Angelique gestured with the plate of cake she'd finally accepted. "And thank you, Dot, for your kindness. It means very much to me. This is precisely what I wanted. I was *waiting* for just the right moment for tea and a lemon seed cake."

But she found her throat was thick.

So she took a sip of tea and ate a corner of the lemon seed cake while Dot watched with wide, hopeful eyes.

She might as well chew on her sleeve. Food tasted like nothing.

But Dot lit up and dashed back down the stairs to impart the good news to everyone else.

"ARE YOU CERTAIN you want to do this, sir?"

"When have you known me to do anything rash, Exeter?"

This was, of course, a joke.

And such had been Lucien's sorry state—morose, brooding, stubble-chinned—since he'd removed himself from The Grand Palace on the Thames that Exeter actually offered a small, taut smile.

He'd also brought him a cup of tea.

Lapsang Souchong, of course.

Lucien supposed he'd evicted *himself* from The Grand Palace on the Thames this time, but living in the apartments above Mr. Exeter's offices was like being transferred from Heaven to a cell. Which was an unfair, rather histrionic, comparison—the rooms were comfortable.

He was actually lonely and surprisingly bored, and boredom was a condition he'd always viewed as a luxury. He did not like prolonged periods of leisure for the sake of leisure. He'd grown unaccustomed to that. He liked his minutes filled with things that made him smarter or richer. He'd become quite spoiled by the diversity of company. He liked his room with the blue-and-white counterpane. He liked knowing who was walking down the hall or across the foyer by the sound of their footsteps, and he liked hearing a fat cat galloping up and down the stairs at night, and never knowing whether he would sleep soundly until the morning or whether a coal hod would shatter his dreams with a violent crash. He missed the excellent food and wondering what in God's name Delacorte would say next. He missed, oh God, how he missed, waking to Angelique in his arms, and knowing that she wanted him as much as he wanted her. The taste of her, the feel of her hands on his skin, her soft voice, her laugh. He could not help but imagine these things, but every memory was like a drop of acid trickled onto his poor, raw, ravaged heart.

He had begun to picture a life that felt real and true and completely his—or rather, *theirs*—with Angelique and love at the center of it. Simple and full and happy. But every day that passed felt like he was caught in a riptide, pulling him farther and farther away from her.

It had been a little over a week since he'd seen her or heard her voice. His mind could not conceive of a destiny that didn't include her. It was very like he was in the middle of the sea again, and everything in every direction was one color, and the shore was nowhere in sight.

He went to White's. And to the shock of everyone, he'd apologized, once again, individually and sincerely, to those who had been present for his outburst, explaining that it was no longer reflective of the person he was, but that he had been wounded because the woman in question was dear to him, and would they not do the same for a loved one who had been grievously wronged?

He'd paid for the broken glasses.

He melted hearts all over again. Because Lord Bolt was clearly suffering an age-old problem: heartbreak. And he was doing it with such dignity, with such haunted, shadowed eyes, that even Hallworth consented to shake his hand, and vowed he would not repeat something so scurrilous.

He'd been, after a fashion, forgiven.

After a fashion, he was attempting to fix the unfixable.

But he knew how often a single newspaper was read. How they passed from hand to hand in coffeehouses and pubs and households, wound up tumbling as litter through the city, or wrapped about something breakable to be shipped across continents. The potential for that little snippet of gossip to be read and read again stretched on into perpetuity.

And if he'd shattered Angelique's dream of safety and peace at The Grand Palace on the Thames, he didn't think he could live with himself. If she could not forgive him, if the hurts inflicted by other men had so irrevocably shaped her life as to leave no room for hope or forgiveness for him, he didn't know how to fix that. Perhaps he had experienced their time together one way and she had experienced it another.

In his arrogant, most honest moments he suspected their hearts frankly beat as one and that she could not do without him.

In other moments he acknowledged that even if this were so, it did not mean that she wouldn't. If anyone knew how to endure things, it was Angelique.

And it was this that got him up in the morning, and made him shave his face, and eat food, and otherwise do things humans do. Because any moment of any day he might finally know what to do next.

And then his ship—delayed due to storms and a few bouts of illness on board, staffed by a frazzled crew ecstatic to see land, women, well-cooked food, and money—finally arrived. His cargo of riches, silks, and spice accounted for and undamaged. He'd profusely and personally thanked all of them and ensured their bonuses were doubled, and this was how relationships were cemented. And how the best people wanted to work for and with him. Perhaps people like him and Captain Hardy knew more than any officer behind a desk at the East India Company the dangers, risks, and skills involved in this endeavor.

And as he fingered a bolt of gold silk, so like the one Angelique had worn the day he'd met her, he knew, just like that, what to do next.

It would ensure her future.

And possibly his.

The idea was, perhaps, a little bit mad. Perhaps even a little bit quixotic.

And so he told Exeter what he wanted to do. Exeter was dubious because he was always dubious. Lucien paid the man to be a little dubious.

Hence the dry and anticipated. "Are you certain you want to do this, sir?"

But:

"Oh, yes," he told Exeter. "I'm quite, quite certain."

ANGELIQUE HAD TAKEN a book to the parlor, which was the brightest room at this hour. The Grand Palace on the Thames was still experiencing a rather unnervingly quiet string of days. Nobody new arrived. Everyone inclined to speak in a loud voice or clatter across the marble entry (Delacorte, Cassidy) had gone off to do God only knew what, and everyone inclined to drop things, sing while they work, or bicker in whispers (the maids, and most particularly Dot) was still tiptoeing around her as if she were fragile and would blow over in a bit of a breeze.

It was beginning to work her nerves a little bit, this tender solicitousness. She tried to think of irritation as a sign she might be feeling a little bit more like herself.

She'd gotten hold of a book by a Miss Jane Austen she hadn't yet read and thought she'd see if it was worth reading aloud in the parlor to the guests. She stared at the first page for a good long time. She found her soul was still too wounded and new words and thoughts couldn't seem to enter. And so all she did was sit and stare until something about the quality of the silence in the room seemed to change.

She looked up with a start.

Captain Hardy was standing in the doorway.

"Good day, Captain Hardy."

"Good day, Angelique."

She gave him a little smile. "Ah, is that how it is now? Very well, if we're doing that, I will call you Tristan. Though Captain seems like it ought to have been your Christian name. If anyone ought to have been saluted from the cradle it's you." She laid her book aside.

He smiled at that. "Thank you. I think."

Tristan had found that when brave people, the ones who everyone thinks are strong and un-breakable, were savagely hurt, they had no idea how to accommodate it. So they went about hurting for too long.

As Angelique had pointed out to him once, in some ways the two of them were very alike. He found it profoundly difficult to watch such a proud woman suffer.

That was the day she'd intimated that she knew precisely what he was getting up to with Delilah. And she had warned him, in her inimitable way, what the price would be if he hurt her friend. That was the day he knew that Angelique might glitter like a diamond, but her heart was as soft as her hazel eyes.

And he *had* indeed hurt Delilah, quite inadvertently.

And she had hurt him, too.

Together he and Delilah had made it right.

And he knew he was on the right side of Angelique's goodwill only because he had done right by Delilah.

"Do you mind if I sit down?"

She nodded once, slowly. Eyeing him somewhat cagily. She knew he was not a social animal on most occasions, and he was a man of few words. He was obviously here on a mission.

He sat across from her on a little chair, since she had taken up the middle of the settee.

And to her wide-eyed amazement, he leaned toward her, and took her hands in his.

"Angelique. I am saying this as a man who knows. You have to let him suffer for you."

She inhaled sharply in shock and tried to tug her hands free. "I don't know what you—"

He held on to them, gently. "And if you cannot let him fight all of your battles—and I am not suggesting you should—you have to at least let him be your champion, even if he must apologize later. Because he is in love with you, Angelique. Lucien loves you. And *that* is the kind of love you want. Do you see that? Your pain is his pain. Your heart is his heart. It is all of a piece. Because you're in love with him, too."

He would not let go of her hands. He knew, somehow, she needed that anchor, someone to hold on to her, that she was too proud to ask for.

And before his eyes, slowly, her face crumpled. "Tristan. What have I done?"

The tears started softly, but when they took over, when not even she could stop the sobs from racking her body, he awkwardly took her in his arms and she burrowed in and he patted her back a bit. Hell's teeth.

She needed to be crying, but he was no good at this.

Delilah tiptoed past and peered into the room.

Only to freeze, wide-eyed, at the sight of Angelique sobbing in her husband's arms.

He gestured her into the room with a nudge of his chin.

She crept in quietly and gently, very gingerly, sat down on the settee next to Angelique.

Tristan gently transferred her into Delilah's arms.

Delilah folded her into her body and the weeping continued.

Tristan closed the door behind him when he softly walked out.

"Have I made a terrible hash of everything, Delilah?" Angelique sniffled into her shoulder.

"Maybe."

Angelique laughed and then coughed. "Comforting."

She sat up, and rubbed her palms against her face, knocking at her tears.

"Hashes can be made right, Angelique. And if you know his heart, I expect you know just how to make it right."

Angelique sighed.

She did know his heart. He was brave and bold and maddening, a man unafraid to face his truth, a man unafraid to shoulder her truth for her.

And suddenly she understood that what she'd always considered her greatest weakness was, in fact, a gift, and she knew precisely how to use it to show Lucien how she felt.

LUCIEN WAS RIGHT, Angelique found. Mr. Exeter was an efficient, startlingly useful man.

He also charged dearly for his services, but a person had to make a living somehow.

Angelique understood this all too well, and didn't begrudge him the unique niche he'd carved, given that her own niche could not be more unique.

"She can be found perambulating in the gardens outside of St. Gideon's church, where she goes to perform . . ." and here Mr. Exeter coughed ". . . services for charity."

They exchanged a wry, speaking look.

Angelique poured the tea for him.

(Exeter, of course, hadn't told Angelique that Lucien was living above his offices. He was the soul of discretion for anyone who needed to hire him.)

"She is usually alone for no longer than ten minutes during this time. Her driver awaits her at the church steps and is alert to her presence, but her driver and footmen can in all likelihood be distracted with a bottle of something for the duration."

"I imagine a bottle of something *is* necessary in order to endure her," Angelique mused.

So on a morning when the first daffodils were beginning to open among the graves, Angelique sat on a little bench of St. Gideon's churchyard and waited for the Duchess of Brexford to amble past. She wore a stunning burgundy wool dress and a pelisse lined in fur, and her face above it was stark white. Her hair was sleek and dark, done up simply, and her complexion was ivory fair and blotched in pink. She was handsome, the kind of handsome that commanded attention rather than inspired impassioned poetry.

Angelique rose from the bench and curtsied, long and low in front of her.

"Good morning, Your Grace."

The Duchess stopped short. Her eyes darted about, reflexively seeking the usual servant who protected her from the need to speak to plebeians. When she recalled there were none, she dispassionately raked Angelique head to toe with a glance that made it clear she was as worthy of notice as the trees, the flowers, the ground, the headstones.

She said nothing.

She attempted to circle around Angelique.

And very gracefully Angelique swept into her path and blocked her.

The Duchess of Brexford was nervous now. Even beautiful, well-dressed women could produce a knife or a pistol. "Do I know you, madam? I think not."

"Well, we haven't been formally introduced, but you did try to steal my cook. Fortunately she preferred to be happy, and she is. I do not bring her regards, by the way. She shudders colorfully when she hears your name and we all have a wonderful laugh."

The duchess went rigid with shock. And then her eyes narrowed in fury. "What on . . . what the . . . You've some *extraordinary* nerve. Step aside. Who the devil do you think you are?" Her voice was ice and daggers. Very impressive if she was a duchess of yore, the sort who shouted "off with her head" and that sort of thing.

Angelique feigned a yawn. "For heaven's sake. I don't have to step aside. You're not the *queen*. You're merely a frightened woman of middle years who committed a crime for which you have heretofore not paid, and I am here to see that you do."

The duchess was motionless. And she was impressively impassive, but a fleeting rank fear skittered across her features.

"You are a babbling lunatic," she said tautly.

"My name is Angelique Breedlove. Perhaps you've heard of me? I've lately taken a turn in the broadsheets. I'm also a very dear friend of Lucien Durand, Viscount Bolt, who has also, as you know, spent some time in them."

The duchess's features spasmed before she was able to hold them taut.

She fixed dark unblinking eyes on Angelique. "Ah, yes. Derring's whore." She ignored the mention of Lucien entirely.

"Ohhh, *charming*. And I thought duchesses were supposed to have fine manners. Here's something we have in common, your grace: *you* are about to spend some time in the newspaper, too, if you don't listen to me," Angelique said gaily.

"CLABBARD!" the duchess screeched.

Her voice merely echoed in the churchyard. Clabbard, her driver, and the footman who traveled with them, were passing around a bottle of good whiskey on the opposite side of the church gates.

"I would like to make something clear. I think you're a thoroughly awful person, Your Grace. People are sometimes awful because they're frightened, which is, of course, the same reason adders bite. One can understand the nature of the adder whilst knowing they're dangerous to disrupt."

The duchess's jaw dropped. "What rot you—"

"Ah, ah, ah." Angelique waved a finger. "I'm here today because I've decided to write my memoirs!" Angelique said brightly. "I was a governess,

Lady Brexford. I write *beautifully*. And the first thing I intend to write about—a little item I intend to share with the broadsheets straightaway, in fact, to give them a taste of what's to come—is that you paid a man to lead Lucien Durand into a trap in order to drown him. Thereby ensuring evidence of your husband's, shall we say, affection for another woman would be effectively erased."

She allowed her words to ring in silence. The duchess's breathing was shallow now.

Two angry red blotches rode high on her cheeks.

"He was a drunken wastrel and fell into the water. *No* one will believe otherwise."

"He was a young man, abandoned by his father. He is an extraordinary adult now. I suspect people will want to believe that you ordered it, simply because it's amusing to believe things about duchesses, especially because you're so awful. But there's more. My memoirs will feature the time I saw your husband at the Earl of Derring's little parties, during which mistresses climbed into the laps of titled men the way kittens do. And so. *Much*. More. I expect they'll make me a wealthy woman and you a laughing-stock."

The Duchess of Brexford's nostril flared and closed again, like an angry bull. Her dark eyes were pinpoints of terror. And her complexion was now all over blotches of red.

And then, to Angelique's astonishment, she

covered her face with her hands in despair. For a long, silent moment Angelique watched her.

Finally the Duchess sighed and brought her hands down.

"Mrs. Breedlove . . . have you ever had a child?" Her voice was frayed now.

"I haven't, yet. No."

"When and if you do . . . you may find that you'll do anything you can to protect that child, and that child's future from someone who would besmirch the family name."

"That may very well be," Angelique said gently. "Excluding murdering another woman's child, of course."

The Duchess's eyes flared.

And then she slowly closed them. And heaved a sigh. "She was so beautiful." Her voice was strained. "Just a peasant, really, but I saw her once from a distance, and I've my fine qualities but I could hardly compare. And Lucien's hotheaded recklessness . . . never a moment's peace from the gossips . . . What sort of life would that be for me, for Robert, my son? It was *hell*. I never meant for Lucien to be killed, you must understand. I only wished for him to be *frightened*."

Angelique remained stonily silent. They both knew the odds of perishing in the Thames in the dead of night whilst drunk were quite high.

A bird trilled something heartbreakingly lovely into the silence.

"I love him, you know. The duke. Fat lot of good

that does me. And perhaps you know, but love can be pain." She looked up fiercely at Angelique for some sort of approbation.

Angelique knew that much too well, but her compassion could not extend to a woman who had tried to do away with the man she loved.

But she was not made of stone.

"Would you like to sit down? You don't look as though you're feeling in the pink of health."

The duchess sat heavily on a stone bench.

Angelique remained standing.

For a moment they studied each other in silence.

"You don't know who you're dealing with," the duchess tried. It lacked conviction. She looked weary.

"Oh, but I do. And you won't be able to dump *me* into the Thames. I seldom take walks by the river. And I never frequent gaming hells. And you should *see* the men who live in The Grand Palace on the Thames. I'd wager all of us against you, any day. And even if something were to become of me . . . the damage done to your reputation will ripple on for ages. The whole of London will be enthralled. And your son's future would be quite tainted."

Angelique said all of these appalling things in an entirely reasonable tone.

The duchess's bodice rose and fell, rose and fell with her breathing.

"Or . . . I suppose there's another way we can address this . . ." Angelique tipped her head, as though she'd had a sudden inspiration.

The duchess's head shot up. No fool and no stranger to negotiation, she was ready to bargain.

"What the devil do you want?" she said resignedly.

"I'm *so* glad you asked."

And she told her.

A few days later ...

LUCIEN HAD ENSCONCED himself at a desk in Exeter's office to review a satisfying stack of bills of lading—wealth was a lovely thing—when Exeter's voice interrupted.

"A package has arrived for you, sir."

Lucien didn't look up. "What is it?"

"The nature of packages is that they are often inscrutable, sir."

"Ha, Exeter. You ought to go on stage. You entertain me endlessly." He did look up, then.

"It is wrapped in brown paper and tied in string. And it is addressed to you, but the sender is not noted anywhere on the package."

He slid it over to Lucien, who produced a knife and cut the string, which he handed over to Exeter, because Exeter never wasted a damn thing.

He made short work of the paper, tearing it and tossing it aside.

Exeter scooped it up.

Inside he found a little wooden crate, not much

bigger than a loaf of bread. Exeter handed him a hammer and Lucien, with a grunt, prised up the lid and found a great quantity of straw, and quite ironically, an equally great quantity of wadded scraps of old broadsheets.

He dug through all of that, feeling a bit like Beacham's spaniel, and finally was able to peer at what was inside. He went still. It couldn't be.

His heart pounding, he reached in.

And lifted out his mother's ormolu music box.

He stared at it.

His father didn't know a thing about Exeter. He couldn't have possibly known where Lucien was staying.

That left only one possibility.

He ran gentle hands over the surface of it, the amber and the carnelians that had fascinated him as a boy, that had made both him and his mother feel rich indeed, and found the hidden indentation. He pressed and tugged, and the false bottom, a little tray, slid free.

Inside, alongside his own curl of hair, and the curly dark one from his mother . . .

. . . was a lock of shining hair, the color of a doubloon.

It trembled in his fingers when he lifted it.

He closed his eyes, and held it beneath his nose, and breathed it in.

And *that* was the moment Lucien Durand, Lord Bolt, was truly resurrected.

He opened his eyes. And beneath the locks of

hair was a little scrap of foolscap. In a beautifully precise script, it said:

> *Lucien,*
>   *I wanted to show you that I will do anything for you, too.*
>   *I need you, now and always.*
>   *Please come home.*
>   *Angelique*

He could *hear* her voice. The dry wit. The soft yearning. The forgiveness.

The love.

Home.

"Are you going to cry, sir?"

Lucien had completely forgotten that he wasn't alone.

"Don't be ridiculous, Exeter." His voice was hoarse.

"I charge more for watching you cry."

"Did you just make another joke, Exeter? Do you charge more for jokes?"

"Of course, sir. I charge for everything."

Funnily enough, Exeter sounded hoarse, too.

And a few days after that . . .

IN THE DAYS after she met with the duchess in the churchyard, the very world seemed to hold its breath.

The duchess had sent a one-word message—
"Done"—to Angelique, indicating she'd made
good on her promise, one day after they'd met.
And Angelique had gently and carefully packed
the music box and written a note on a scrap of
foolscap (she had that in common with Exeter—
they never wasted a thing) and sent it to Lucien,
care of Exeter's office address.

But she still hadn't heard from Lucien.

The tension of anticipation in The Grand Palace
on the Thames was such that a dome of crystal
seemed to enclose it. Angelique would not be surprised if she could reach up and tap a *ping* out of
the very air.

Hope seesawed with despair.

Finally she could bear it no longer. She knew
of only one thing to do while she waited. It was
the one thing that might offer her a clue of what
Lucien was thinking.

"Delilah, will you take a walk with me?"

Delilah knew precisely where Angelique
wanted to go.

But when they went to fetch the key the estate agent gave them the bad news: "I'm afraid
it's been sold, ladies. The transaction was final
today."

In the following three seconds Angelique's and
Delilah's emotions were a bit like a weathervane
in a windstorm. They of course presented pleasantly inscrutable expressions to the agent.

"Well, *that* is disappointing," Delilah said, because she was the one who could actually speak. Angelique's heart was hammering too distractingly. "Would it be possible for you to share with us the name of the purchaser?"

"I'm strictly not at liberty to say, I'm afraid. And besides, I believe the purchaser intends to transfer the property into another's hands straightaway, anyway."

Angelique and Delilah exchanged a speaking glance.

And Angelique's heart kicked off one of its shackles.

Angelique cleared her throat. Still, her voice emerged on something like a whisper.

"Did the new owner say anything about . . . about opening a gaming hell?"

He snorted. "Ah, if only. He said rather the opposite. He said he expected it would be heavenly."

And hope, that fickle flower, bloomed brilliantly. It was precisely what she'd said to him that day when he'd found her staring at a bare tree stuck out of the ground.

Neither Delilah nor Angelique could speak for smiling. Delilah reached for Angelique's hand and gave it a squeeze.

The estate agent narrowed his eyes at Angelique.

"Pah! Look at you now, madam. Sure, and *I* am the one who ought to be weeping. The docks are going to be right dull, at this rate, thanks to you lot."

That night . . .

A LIGHT RAIN ticked against the windows and made the crackling fire in the parlor spit and dance a bit, so Captain Hardy got up to give it a good poking. Despite his efforts, the flames sullenly resisted roaring. But all the guests of The Grand Palace on the Thames were well-fed and in for the evening, and the room was warmer for it. Coverlets and scarves unfurled from knitting needles. Mrs. Pariseau was at the chessboard, learning how to play from an exquisitely patient Mr. Delacorte. Mr. Cassidy was reading aloud from *Rob Roy*, and a fine voice he had, a baritone that caressed the ear, everyone agreed, though he needed a little work on the female voices. Dot was listening to the story so raptly—and admiring Mr. Cassidy's cheekbones—she had inadvertently embroidered the "B" from "Bless" right directly onto her lap. Mrs. Locksley was surreptitiously drawing Mr. Delacorte. So far he looked like the letter "D" on two stocky legs.

And then came the knock on the door.

Delilah and Angelique exchanged swift glances. It had been nearly two weeks since anyone sought lodging at The Grand Palace on the Thames. One person had arrived in the dead of night searching for The Vicar's Hobby, and they were gently told that this was no longer a palace for rogues, thank you very much and shame on them. They had no way of knowing whether the broadsheets had influenced this little drought in visitors. Perhaps in another week they could draw conclusions.

"Would you answer the door please, Dot?" Mrs. Hardy said calmly.

Dot leaped up.

They listened to her feet click across the foyer.

Then the click of the latches seemed to echo as she unlocked the door.

There was a silence.

Followed by what sounded like a stifled "Oh!" of pure delight.

Angelique froze.

She somehow knew. She knew.

She closed her eyes and leaped like a falcon sent skyward.

She knew.

Even before she heard his footsteps, measured, slow, across the marble foyer.

And so when Lucien Durand, Lord Bolt, appeared in the room, she was already trembling.

Later everyone present claimed they knew the moment his gaze collided with Angelique's. Because the dying fire ignited with a whoosh and blazed to light the room like the sun.

The only thing brighter in the room was Lucien's and Angelique's dazzling faces.

And just like the very first time Lord Bolt entered the room (or entered most rooms, really), everyone was frozen in place like so many statues littered about, staring.

A collective gasp when he suddenly dropped to one knee before Angelique.

"Lucien," she said hoarsely. Her hand flew to her heart.

"Angelique . . ." His voice was low, soft, soft as the voice from the next pillow. "You once told me you would never hold me to promises I can't keep, and I took you at your word. But it is so easy to make these promises to you: I will keep you safe. I will make you laugh. I will make you beg for more."

"Oh, my," Mrs. Pariseau murmured, and fanned herself.

"I will make you certain that you know that you are loved every day of your life. I will teach our children to fight, to love, and to be kind, and to forgive. And if I should ever again hurt you, I will do anything, *anything* to make it right. Because only two imperfect people could create such a perfect love. I am yours and you are mine."

He reached for her trembling hands and brought them to his lips. And his voice cracked on a sort of awestruck amusement, an acknowledgment of pure surrender. "I would have come at once, but I wanted to have something to offer you. The building is yours. Angelique . . . I love you so."

The words were scarcely more than a whisper.

"I love you, too." She whispered it, too, inches away from his beloved face. As if this was a miraculous secret that only the two of them could share or understand. This love of theirs.

Her tears glittered like little diamonds on her eyelashes.

And then his beautiful voice rose, just a little, but it was for everyone to hear.

"Angelique Breedlove. It would be the honor of my life if you should entrust me your heart. And if you would consent to be my wife, I shall endeavor all my years to deserve you. Will you be my wife?"

She allowed those words to echo, to reverberate through her.

"Oh, yes," she said, her voice cracked and joyous. "Please, thank you, yes."

A great cheer went up and everyone rose to their feet and fell upon each other in happy congratulatory embraces as Lucien drew Angelique up to her feet and kissed her so thoroughly yet reverently it brought tears to everyone's eyes.

"AND THAT'S WHY," Dot told all the maids later, "living here is much more entertaining than the broadsheets, and I don't even bother reading them anymore."

Epilogue

❦

Some months later ...

Dᴏᴛ ᴅɪsᴄᴏᴠᴇʀᴇᴅ to her delight that the news part of the newspaper could be just as interesting as gossip, when heretofore she'd thought of it as the cod-liver oil to gossip's blancmange.

For instance, in an article about a surge in aristocrats supporting charitable causes and donating to charities, not typically the liveliest of topics, she found this to read aloud to the maids in the kitchen:

> *The recent surge of charitable giving can be attributed in part to the ton's general awe of the piety and humble generosity of Lord Geoffrey Cuttweiler, who took it upon himself to join a five-year missionary excursion to the South Seas and donated half of his fortune to various causes supporting orphans and the poor in London ahead of his departure.*

As it turned out, Lucien's own sense of charity could not quite extend to the need to be civil to Cutty every time he visited White's, or anywhere else, really. It seemed he could, after a fashion, forgive, but forgetting was quite another thing altogether. The solution he'd arrived at accomplished the twin objectives of amusing him and horrifying Cutty, but he'd presented it as nonnegotiable, so off Cutty went. Lucien's own character had been built across the world; with luck, Cutty would return with some character of his own, if he was not eaten by cannibals.

"Ain't he kind to do that, then?" the new maid, Rose, who'd been hired on to help with the duties at the Annex, said dreamily. "Lord Cuttweiler. Are all lords kind?"

"'Aren't,'" Dot corrected gently, but a little grandly, after the fashion of Lady Bolt, Angelique Breedlove Durand, whom she admired fiercely. "And good heavens, no. They most certainly are not all kind."

"Aren't," Rose repeated dutifully, because she was a little in awe of Dot, who was clearly so important to the running of The Grand Palace on the Thames and so close to the kind proprietresses with their very tall, grand husbands.

She raised her head to see if Mrs. Breedlove or Mrs. Hardy were coming. They were safe for now, so she read on.

And in an article about new travel destinations, Dot found this fascinating sentence:

Whereas her contemporaries favor trips to sunny Italy, the Duchess of Brexford claims

*Russia is her favorite travel destination and
will undertake her journey at the start of June
and is uncertain as to when she will return.*

"Thank goodness. Russia is so *very* far away,"
Helga said, indulging in a bit of martyred self-
satisfaction. One of the burdens of being a culi-
nary artist was the fact that she had been lured
to work for a *duchess*, of all people. She was a hid-
eously difficult woman.

Since Angelique longed to one day visit Spain
and she was fond of Italians, she disliked the
notion of inflicting the duchess upon them. She
suggested—she did not insist—that Russia might
be a fine place for her to retreat to for the time being. How gratifying that the duchess had taken
up her suggestion, Angelique thought dryly.

Gossip at White's—Lucien returned with it and
shared it with her—had it that the baffled Duke of
Brexford wanted none of his wife's Russia madness. He liked things to go on as they were. No
country could possibly be more interesting than
England, and given that he had a grand bloody
house in London and houses scattered all over
the country, what *more* could a woman possibly
want? He would be staying; he would allow his
wife to go, because she would not be quiet about
it. His son, the marquess, could write letters to
his mother in Russia. He was nearly fifteen years
old and at Eton; surely a boy didn't yearn for his
mother anymore at that age?

Angelique had known how that had sounded to Lucien. And while he agreed that the duchess did indeed have to go, he spared a thought for his half brother.

"Shouldn't you ladies be dusting?"

Angelique had a wraithlike ability to sneak up on the slothful.

The maids leaped and squeaked and scattered like mice confronted with Gordon the cat. Nothing was allowed to settle for long at The Grand Palace on the Thames, and that included dust, maids, and dirty dishes, but excluded the guests and said cat, who worked all night and could therefore be allowed to sleep all day if he chose.

"Sorry, Mrs. Bree—Mrs. Durand," Dot said sincerely.

Angelique had decided she quite liked the sound of Mrs. Durand rather than Lady Bolt in her role as proprietress of The Grand Palace on the Thames, which suited Lucien. It was his mother's name, and his own. He was proud of it and of her, and he was honored she wanted to use it.

There were so many new things to remember, Dot reflected. Names becoming other names, like when Lady Derring became Mrs. Hardy and now Mrs. Breedlove, new servants hired—Rose was just one of *three* new maids taken on to help with the anticipated business of The Grand Palace Annex—and soon there would be footmen, two of them, the prospect of which was nearly unbearably thrilling, because she would be allowed to be present for the interviews.

"Anything interesting in the newspaper today, Dot?" Angelique peered over her shoulder.

Newspapers weren't cheap. This one would be read a full dozen times by anyone who could read. They liked to keep them available for guests, and when it had been spilled upon, torn, or smeared beyond recognition, they were employed in other ways.

"So *many* things," Dot said delightedly. "And the more words I know, the more interesting things get."

Angelique smiled. "Words to live by, truly, Dot."

She slipped the newspaper out of Dot's hand, Dot's cue to scramble back to work.

She knew what it said, and she was going to save it for her husband. Perhaps even have it framed. Or maybe it was best to use it for kindling, allow the ashes of that part of his life to rise from the chimney as smoke, to mingle with the smut of London, and perhaps blow off to sea.

"THERE SHE IS, lads." Captain Hardy's voice was only a hair or two less warm than the one he used to say the word "Delilah."

Lucien, Captain Hardy, and Mr. Delacorte stood on the dock and looked up with great satisfaction at the *Zephyr*, that beautiful vessel of commerce.

Her sails were furled for now. She looked restive, as though she yearned to be cresting waves on the way to India.

After many conversations over brandy, some of them arguments that ultimately entertained them more than resulted in any sort of lasting rancor, Captain Hardy and Lucien had decided to combine efforts under the Triton rubric, and Mr. Delacorte had been invited to be a partner as well. With his unique knowledge of merchants up and down England, his niche for cures and potions and so forth, and a portion of his tidy little savings, he'd been a surprisingly astute addition to the group.

The dock was its usual swarm of workers, sailors, merchants, prostitutes, pickpockets—a mass of humanity.

Delacorte suddenly peered at the end of the dock. "Who's the lad in the fancy coat dressed like a little lord? Good God, he'll be eaten alive out here. They'll strip him like locusts for his boots and buttons. HO, LAD! LOSE YOUR MUM?" Delacorte, being Delacorte, managed to be genuinely concerned and offensive all at once.

"Whoa," he said at once. Taking a step back. "That lad about singed me eyebrows off with a look, even from this distance. Reminds me a bit of the way you look sometimes, Bolt," he said cheerfully.

Lucien went still.

He pivoted abruptly. And shaded his eyes and peered out at the tall, colty young man standing at the end of the dock, radiating indecision and diffidence and staring unabashedly at them.

He exhaled at length.

"That's my brother."

Seldom had a word been so complexly inflected with so many different emotions. Exasperation, resignation. Wariness.

And yet he was surprised by how much he enjoyed saying them.

"Half brother," he corrected, absently.

Tristan and Delacorte remained absolutely silent.

While a pair of gulls squawked and squabbled over a bit of bun left on the ground next to him, the future Duke of Brexford lifted a hand and tentatively waved it at Lucien.

Lucien sighed.

"Gentlemen, if you'll excuse me for a moment?"

Lucien strode down the dock so rapidly Robert blinked.

"Er, h-hullo, Lucien."

"Good morning, Robert."

There was a little silence.

"I went to The Grand Palace on the Thames first," Robert said cheerfully. "The maid who answered the door—she has big round eyes, a bit like a child draws—said you were here."

It was a fantastic description of Dot.

"Robert, you ought not to be here at all. First of all, how on earth did you get here?"

"I took a hack," he said proudly. "Father would have had apoplexy if I took a carriage out."

"I'm not certain a hack to the docks is a good use of your allowance. And I'm certain you get an allowance. Does your father know?"

"Of course not."

"Robert, I say this sincerely. This is not a safe area for the likes of you, no matter how skilled your fencing master is. You'll be stripped of your boots and buttons in no time."

Robert was just a little irritated. "I know. Or rather, I gathered it's not entirely safe. I'm not utterly stupid, Lucien."

"But," Lucien added, "it was brave."

Because damned if it wasn't a little.

Robert beamed at him. He clasped his hands behind his back and dragged the toe of his boot to and fro. "Lucien, I heard that you were married. My friend Alfie—his father is Lord Beacham—he heard his mother and father talking."

"I am married now, yes." Married. The word still held a delicious magic for him. It shimmered and he paused to indulge in a reverie nearly every time he said it.

"I w-would like to offer my felicitations," Robert said gravely.

"Thank you," Lucien said, just as gravely.

There was a little silence.

"Is she pretty?" Robert asked hopefully.

"More beautiful than the brightest star in the sky."

Robert grinned slowly at that. It lit his entire face. And Lucien could almost see this young man's future unfurling, all the women who would hurl themselves at his feet. The sound of hearts breaking when he strolled by.

"Her name is Angelique," Lucien added. He wanted to say her name, like a talisman. In moments like this he still could not believe she was his. He had surely done nothing to deserve such good fortune, rather than survive fortune's slings and arrows. "She is clever, and very witty and kind, and I am very grateful for her. A man is fortunate indeed if such a thing happens in his lifetime. It is rare."

Robert listened to this raptly.

No matter what, Lucien wanted him to hear that men ought to be grateful for the loves in their lives. For the women who add grace, beauty, softness, and kindness to it. He wanted him to understand that women were not commodities; they were to be cherished. He would certainly never learn it from his father. He doubted his parents were shining examples of marital bliss.

"You look very happy," Robert said astutely and cheerfully.

"I am." Lucien smiled; it could not be helped.

Another little silence and then Robert thrust his hand into his coat pocket.

"Alfie told me her name. I heard. I . . . I brought you a present."

It was the very last thing in the world he expected his brother to say. He was motionless for a moment, assailed, only briefly, by darker more unworthy from *this boy got his money from our father.*

"Robert . . ."

"You d-don't have to take it. I shall not be offended. But I saw this in the window in a shop at the Gallerie and I thought maybe you could give it to her because she's after a fashion my sister now, too."

He withdrew something from his pocket and pressed it into his hand. Lucien looked down.

It was a tiny crystal angel. Delicate wings unfurled like the sails on a ship, her robes flowed in pleats to tiny bare feet, her hair poured down her back. Not more than four inches high.

It was a long moment before Lucien could look up.

And he thought, *I only bought her a building, but this angel will likely break her heart in the sweetest way, like he's breaking mine right now.*

Finally he raised his head to Robert's anxious face.

"It's beautiful and she will love it, Robert, and I will tell her it is a gift from you. It was a very kind and gracious gesture. Thank you."

Robert was rosy with pleasure. He fidgeted a little, his hands fiddling with the fine buttons on his fine coat.

"If I'm not mistaken, Father will want an accounting of your expenditures and you'll be hard pressed to explain this one."

"I earned a little more money by helping with schoolwork and . . . well, we played Faro, and . . ."

Lucien laughed and then thought maybe he shouldn't have. "Resourceful."

Robert beamed.

"But you ought not gamble." He said this strictly as a Quaker.

Robert looked uncertainly up at him. "But . . . but you . . ."

"I can speak from experience that gambling is an unpleasant road, indeed."

"Oh. I see. All right."

There was another little silence.

"Lucien . . ." He cleared his throat. He turned away a little, and blushed. "I wondered if I could write to you, like? From school? Or maybe I could come to visit you . . . and have a look at your ship?"

He gazed yearningly up at the *Zephyr*.

Hell's teeth.

Lucien stifled a sigh. What did *he* want?

He was stunned to realize that he wanted what Robert wanted: family. The surge of hope and joy he felt when he pictured his own sons and daughters with Angelique.

"I am afraid our father would never allow it. He would discover it and you would be punished. And he would be angry with me, indeed, with just cause, I might add, if he thought I encouraged you to disobey him. It's complicated, but our father and I do not . . ." what was the kindest way to say it to this child? ". . . rub along."

"But when you were younger, you broke *every* rule!" Robert enthused. "The races, the wagers, the—"

"Robert." He said this so sternly, the boy gave a start.

"I will tell you something that may be difficult to understand from where you are. Not because you aren't obviously clever, but because it's . . . like a language you haven't yet learned. Think of life as a school. These lessons will come. So you must trust me when I say that reckless people are seldom happy people. You will find there are other ways to rebel. You may have to negotiate. Strategize. Do I look prosperous and successful to you? Do you suppose I have learned a useful thing or two?"

Robert nodded, subdued. He would make his own decisions and draw his own conclusion, Lucien was certain. But he could not resist giving him a steer.

Robert turned away briefly, twisting the hem of his coat in his hands.

"Couldn't you talk to him again?" he asked desperately. "Our father."

"I'm afraid not."

Robert swallowed.

"My mother has gone to Russia. And my aunt

has come to stay, you know, and she's not bad. But the house is so big when I come home and it echoes and it's like a mausoleum, don't you think? Far too shiny. Right dull it is."

Oh God. He thought of Robert rattling around in there, lonely and bored, and what a lonely and bored and clever child could get up to.

And then all at once Lucien knew he could handle anything the duke would say or do even if he did disapprove of Robert speaking to Lucien. And perhaps—just perhaps—he could speak to the duke again, now that he'd come to terms with the fact that the duke was not and never would be the sort of man Lucien wished he could be. He would speak to him as one man to another. Perhaps. It would bear more thinking.

Life was a series of adjustments and negotiations. It was a balance sheet that, in the end, ought to be reconciled to one thing: love. If at all possible.

He thought of Angelique, and what she would want him to do.

And it was precisely what he wanted to.

And then he looked back at Captain Hardy and Delacorte. Strength and wisdom and discipline. Kindness and openness and joie de vivre. He could think of no two more diverse, or better, examples of the various shades of a good man. God only knew one could learn patience and tolerance from simply being near Delacorte.

He sighed. "Would you like to see the ship?"

Robert's jaw dropped. He was speechless with joy for a full two seconds, his eyes like lamps. It was impossible not to smile at that.

"Cor! *Would* I!"

Lucien sighed heavily and gestured with his chin for his brother to follow him to where Captain Hardy and Delacorte waited.

WHILE LUCIEN AND Captain Hardy and Mr. Delacorte—perhaps the most unlikely trio ever to combine forces—went down to the docks, Angelique went back up to the sitting room with Delilah to take up some of the never-ending mending which was, actually, one of her favorite things to do. So satisfying to transform something torn into something whole, just like that.

The past few months had been the most joyous and chaotic and full of Angelique's life.

While Captain Hardy had moved with alacrity into Delilah's little room at the top of the stairs—he was accustomed to small, cramped quarters and was frankly happy to sleep anywhere, as long as Delilah was in the room with him—Lucien was less certain he wanted to live in a room half the size of the one he'd paid three guineas for and reserved with half a token. He wanted lovemaking to be noisy and abandoned, but not necessarily overheard. But they soon discovered that lovemaking needn't be confined to only one bedroom, or even to a bed. They were resourceful and discreetly tested the acoustics

of every room in the Annex as it underwent its
transformation.

They would stay in the room at the top of the
stairs for now, where Angelique had slept from
the moment she'd arrived at The Grand Palace
on the Thames. They seldom used it for anything
apart from sleeping, anyway. They were both so
delightfully busy.

And besides, there were larger rooms at the
top of the stairs in the Annex; perhaps one day
they would move into one, when the buildings
were cleverly connected with an enclosed walkway enabling servants and guests to move to
and fro freely, no matter the weather. For they
still wanted everyone to eat together, when at all
possible. They still wanted everyone to gather in
the drawing room. She and Delilah had earnestly
discussed the rules, and decided that all of them
would stand. Including the jar.

And while an unnerving lull in guests did
indeed follow in the wake of the item about Angelique and Lucien in the broadsheets, it was difficult to know whether it could be attributed to
that item or was just part of the general ebb and
flow of life.

"If anyone who looks a bit shifty eyed comes to
the door—"

"Shifty eyed?" queried Dot.

"Shifty eyed," Angelique reiterated, demon-
strating by shifting her eyes, "should come to
the door, they are likely from the newspaper and

looking for more gossip, hence the shifty eyes. And if they ask for Mrs. Angelique Breedlove, you may tell them that no one by that name lives here or has ever lived here."

It was an ingenious solution, because this wasn't entirely untrue. She had never been a Mrs.; her real name was Anne; she was now Mrs. Durand, Lord Bolt.

And someone had indeed come looking for Mrs. Angelique Breedlove. Dot dispensed with them with alacrity with the instructions she'd been given—"Nobody by that name lives here, and good day to you, sir." Her native resting expression—confused, a little dreamy—helped make this assertion very convincing. The hopeful gossip writer went away and did not return. It seemed an unlikely place for a doxie to live, anyway, this shining white building by the docks. Obviously a respectable place, even if it was adjacent to a pub called The Wolf And, with some vestiges of a word that looked like "Rogue" visible beneath the painted sign swinging on chains above the building.

But that afternoon, shortly after Angelique had scattered the maids and she and Delilah had repaired to the sitting room at the top of the stairs, Dot appeared.

"Mrs. Hardy. Mrs. Durand." Dot was whispering.

"What is it, Dot?" Angelique whispered, reflexively, and felt a right fool.

"There is a woman downstairs who is asking for Miss Annie Breedlove. Not Mrs. Angelique Breedlove."

Angelique went still. She exchanged glances with Delilah.

Very few people knew her real name was Anne. She'd called herself Angelique some years ago; it seemed to fit. She would not abandon it for the world, especially given how Lucien could turn every syllable of it into sensual music when he whispered it into her ear, in longing, in pure awe.

"What does she look like, Dot?"

Dot cleared her throat. "She looks very much like you, Mrs. Durand, but there is a good deal more of her, if you take my meaning. She has blond hair but some of it is gray and her eyes are blue with gold in them. She has a kind face and there is a small bird on her bonnet. And she looks worried."

Angelique went still.

"Delilah . . . oh, my . . . I think I know who that is." Angelique's heart lurched. But it was hope, a painful hope she hadn't even known she truly harbored. Nervously. Her palms were damp.

"Shall we go down and see together?" Delilah suggested gently.

"She's in the reception room," Dot said brightly, in a normal voice. "I'll bring in tea."

Angelique paused on the threshold of the drawing room.

The woman was turning this way and that,

admiring the reception room, a little wondering, bemused smile on her face, the way most people looked about the reception room of The Grand Palace on the Thames. She was indeed wearing a bonnet decorated with felt cherries and a small bird.

"Annie?"

"Aunt Lizzie?" Angelique's voice was a thread.

"Oh, my little Annie. It *is* you!" Her aunt's face suffused with a wondering light. She pressed her palm against her mouth and tears filled her eyes. "Oh, my goodness. You are so lovely. Your mother would have been so very proud. How I miss her! And you!"

Angelique yearned to move closer, and closer, and then to launch herself into the arms of her mother's sister. She'd once been like a second mother to her. But she'd been hurt so gravely when everyone had turned her away when she'd needed them most.

She could not, she could not bear another heartbreak. She could not bear to reach out if she was pushed away yet again.

Aunt Lizzie understood. "Anne, my dear, my husband, that supercilious, hypocritical old toad, forbade me to write to you or to take you in. How I wish I'd the courage to stand up to him or for you, but I'd children to raise and I depended on him. And then I did not know where you had gone, and I was so very worried. He died last year, rot his soul."

She said this with surprising equanimity. Not one woman in the room blinked. Both Delilah and Angelique had learned the kind of liberation that could be had when a such a man dies.

"Your charming husband wrote to me and I came straightaway, without even a reply. I had to see you. I hope . . ." she paused to whisk out a handkerchief and aggressively dab at her eyes, which sent the felt bird on her bonnet bobbing merrily ". . . oh, my dear, you can find it in your heart to forgive me."

Angelique swiped at her eyes with the back of her hand, while behind her Delilah and Dot did the same thing. "Auntie Lizzie. Of course. Of course I forgive you."

She did not step forward. Not just yet.

"My dear, I understand full well the kinds of decisions women are compelled to make. There is a good deal of our family history I daresay you know nothing about. I have always loved you and wanted the best for you. I can see from your very radiance that you have that. And I am so glad."

Angelique glowed clear through to her soul, and some lingering weight she hadn't known she was carrying detached like a fall leaf and sailed away.

Was it possible to love her husband even more than she did? She imagined there were no boundaries to it. It was like the very air she breathed, this love for Lucien.

"I am indeed happier than I have ever been."

Her voice trembled. "But you have made my happiness even more complete, Aunt Lizzie. Thank you for coming."

And then she did step toward her aunt, who was moving forward, and they fell into each other's arms and hugged and wept a little.

Angelique, however, was never going to love histrionic displays. She stepped back and cleared her throat.

"Allow me to introduce you to my dear friend and partner, Mrs. Delilah Hardy. And this is our maid Dot, who is very important to The Grand Palace on the Thames, and who almost never forgets to bring in tea."

Dot gave a squeak and scampered off, sniffling and beaming. She did love a happy ending.

ANGELIQUE PROUDLY TOOK Aunt Lizzie for a tour of The Grand Palace Annex, as they'd decided to officially call it. Lucien had had no objection to her straightaway putting the building in both her name and Delilah's. It only seemed fit, since Delilah had done the same with The Grand Palace on the Thames when it was virtually the sole possession either of them had. She had given Angelique hope and a future.

They hadn't a vast store of savings, so they'd used the same ingenuity—begging, bartering, sewing, repairing—to hire a crew to do the most difficult parts of the cleaning, the vanquishing of spiders and the like, and to replace rotting boards in the floors, and to scrub, polish, and oil them once they were whole again, to peel old paper from walls and paint and put up new paper, to hang curtains and repair sconces and hinges and doorknobs, to polish the ballroom until it glowed like a golden sea. But all of the men in their lives had thrown themselves handily into the process, too, seeing an opportunity to get dirty, make noise, and hit things with hammers. Mr. Cassidy was particularly helpful in that regard; he'd helped build his family home from timbers, he said, beginning with when those timbers had been trees. He knew a fine building when he saw one.

Delilah and Angelique made decision after decision, swiftly, deftly, and secondhand rugs and settees and chairs and the like were acquired and given new life and proud place in the large suites and the little sitting rooms. All the suites were clean, but only one was officially ready for tenants, complete with comfortable beds, fluffy pillows, counterpanes as welcoming as hugs, little writing desks, and a rather compact sitting room, with chairs and a settee, that a family could loll about in when they weren't joining the rest of the guests of The Grand Palace on the Thames.

Some construction was still underway in the bottom corner near the little kitchen, next to the scullery, and it was roped off with tarps and the like so one couldn't trip on a loose board or get pierced by a nail, so Angelique steered her aunt away from it. Angelique and Delilah had discussed the notion of one day, possibly, needing an additional cook. It wasn't a topic they looked forward to broaching with Helga.

Aunt Lizzie was delightedly breathless by everything she saw. "You always were the most efficient girl, Angelique. So very clever and good. I am not surprised at all you live in a grand palace and have a viscount for a husband."

Angelique laughed.

But even as they strolled through she was aware they still had a good deal more work to do; they couldn't expect servants, especially the young maids, to run to and from buildings in inclement weather; they would need footmen to do some of the heavier work, though Dot had been assured that she was the Head of Answering the Door. She anticipated that interviewing them would be entertaining, indeed. Well. Operatic, she'd called their life here. What need had they for musicales, when life was so varied and splendorous from moment to moment?

But they would need tenants soon. Annexes did not pay for themselves.

She heard Dot coming at a run. "Mrs. Bree— Durand. Mrs. Hardy sent me. There's a family you see . . ."

Dot paused to suck in a few breaths.

"A family?"

"A family that wants to stay!" Dot was beside herself with glee.

"Oooh, a family! How exciting, dear!" Aunt Lizzie said.

"We expect the word has gotten out about our exceptional service," Angelique said regally. But frankly she was excited, too.

"THERE WAS A snake, you see—" Lord Vaughn's hair seemed to have been combed with a rake, and his eyes were still a bit wild.

"And Papa thought he might try to shoot it." This came from a young woman of about seventeen or eighteen years old. She had clear gray eyes and red-gold hair bound up in plaits. "I'm Claire. He shot a hole through the wall, and through the ceiling."

"And lest you think I'm one of your eccentrics, well, I'm not in my dotage yet and this was not one of our little English adders, oh, no. It was a dangerous sort of snake, brought here alive from the jungles, I believe, by a naturalist bloke, and St. John won it in some kind of wager and brought the poor creature home, whereupon it escaped. St. John is a blight upon us all."

He said this with an interesting blend of long-suffering bitterness and affection and fixed a baleful gaze.

"St. John is bored," said St. John, who, far from being a blight, had the sort of good looks that could cause whiplash, a wicked gleam in his eyes, and a way with an indolent slouch. "And I've scarcely slept for days. I didn't mean for the

poor creature to get *out*. I would have brought it
back to where I got it. Only meant to put the fright
on Claire and Lillias. And it worked, too. I wondered when we might be shown to our rooms?"
He turned to Delilah and Angelique.

They politely ignored him for now. They knew
St. John's type.

"That poor creature won't last a day in our
English weather," his father said. "Unnatural."

"Ha! I'd like to see that snake survive here at the
docks," said Claire, with a certain amount of relish. "It's tremendously thrilling. Did you see the
man who was relieving himself against the—"

"That's quite enough," said Lady Vaughn. Her
voice was quiet, stern, loving, and she managed
to put a stop to the chatter just like that. She was
hollow-eyed from lack of sleep and one got the
sense that her coiffure was usually flawless, but
right now it was a bit fuzzy. She was clearly the
source of her daughter's coloring.

One also got the sense that one did not argue
with Lady Vaughn.

"So it will be us," she told Delilah and Angelique, once she'd created a little quiet. "Our
family. My husband and I, our son, our daughters Claire and Lillias, and we hoped you'd have
room to house us all whilst repairs are underway.
And our lady's maids and . . . Where the devil is
Lillias?"

She looked at her husband.

Whose gaze ricocheted about the room.

"I hope Lillias isn't another snake?" Angelique said gently.

"Same difference," St. John said, with a yawn.

"Our oldest daughter," Lord Vaughn corrected, scowling at his son.

"We've some rules we expect our guests to follow, but they're meant to foster camaraderie, rather than make a guest feel restricted, and we find all our guests typically embrace them."

"We agree to them," Lady Vaughn said at once. "All of them."

St. John had gotten hold of the little card printed with rules, and he looked alarmed. "Now hold on one moment. There's a *curfew*?"

"Of course," Delilah said pleasantly. "We want all of our guests to feel safe and snug, especially those with young daughters."

"Sound practice," Lord Vaughn said.

"We've an epithet jar, and we charge one pence. But we've considered instituting an insolence jar," Angelique said.

St. John frowned a little. Wary now.

"I wish you would," Lady Vaughn said fervently. Irritably.

"I'll leave you with the rules and your tea, and Mrs. Hardy and I shall go and discuss whether we think you'd be happy here as guests of The Grand Palace on the Thames."

Which was of course a diplomatic way of saying they were going to go off and talk about whether they thought they could tolerate the Vaughns for any length of time.

Delilah and Angelique repaired to the drawing room across the foyer to have their usual whispered conversation.

"Somehow we failed to discuss whether we needed to like *all* of them in order to allow a family to stay with us," Delilah said.

Angelique laughed softly. "I'd wager on the mother that she keeps them more or less in line. I can imagine what Lucien and Tristan would do to St. John."

"It might be amusing."

"Or carnage."

"And who is this Lillias?"

"Another daughter, and a mystery as of now."

"I do not think we can turn them away, Angelique."

"Not the least because we'll be charging them dearly."

"Shall we vote quickly on a new rule? Families deemed too insufferable will be evicted without notice. All in favor . . ."

"Aye." Angelique raised her hand.

"Aye." Delilah raised her hand. "But won't it be a bit awkward until we've hired on the footmen, to ferry things from building to building? And to manage dinners and the like?"

"Life is always a bit awkward. We will triumph, Delilah. Don't we always?"

HUGH CASSIDY GAZED wistfully out the window of his comfortable room at The Grand Palace on the Thames. Bolt and Hardy and Delacorte had tried to persuade him to come along to the ship with them today, and he'd frankly wanted nothing more. But he had the sort of business to attend to that couldn't wait, and Hugh could give Captain Tristan Hardy a run for his money when it came to a sense of duty.

Hugh was not yet thirty. Those three men were older and more established. But witnessing them moving forward with their endeavors, building a business and a legacy, not to mention wealth, made him restless. He felt the tidal pull of their ambition; it echoed to his own. In other circumstances he would have leaped at the opportunity, because he knew at least two of those men were formidable and would triumph over any obstacles. The other was purely a good man, and those were rare enough in the world. But his own future was in America.

So odd that the two countries so recently ruled by one crown could be so very distinct in identity. He yearned for his New York home, for the woods and rugged coasts and people who were more direct, where a man who had no social status or fortune could build an empire from his wits, charm, and will. And whose will was stronger than his?

War tended to knock frivolous impulses from a person and quickly distill the things that mattered. He knew how to hunt, build, farm, seduce, and fight to win. He'd also learned that, no matter how battle hardened the man, a woman could still run his heart through a meat grinder.

Which brought him to today's business.

> *Dear Mr. Woodley,*
>   *I've made a dozen or so discreet inquiries throughout London, and they've been fruitful. I've heard a credible account that Amelia might have gone to Dover, though I do not know why. I am in London now. I will investigate and write the moment I have news. I will bring her home.*
>   *Yrs,*
>   *H. Cassidy*

Woodley was wealthy and had good cause to believe in Mr. Cassidy's tenacity, because he'd witnessed it firsthand. "Like a damned bull," his brother had half groused, half enthused, about Hugh, once upon a time.

His brother was dead, killed in the war. Hugh had shouldered his responsibilities back home. Woodley's reward money would be the beginning of . . . everything. Perhaps in more ways than one.

He would post the letter to Mr. Woodley this afternoon. And then he was off to Dover. Walking away from Helga's cooking for even a day seemed a veritable cruelty. And while Hugh's common sense and sense of honor kept him from dalliances in a place he didn't intend to put down roots, Mrs. Locksley's limpid blue eyes were undeniably more pleasant to look into than Delacorte's.

He sighed, sprinkled sand, and sealed his letter.

And then he bolted down the stairs, savoring the feel of that wood banister sliding beneath his palm. He stopped short in the foyer beneath the huge chandelier. In the reception room Mrs. Hardy and Mrs. Durand were speaking with what appeared to be a veritable crowd of people.

He brightened. Things were *never* dull around here.

"Dot," he whispered, as she came up the kitchen stairs with the tea. "Who are the new guests?"

"They're for the Annex!" Dot bit her lip with excitement. "It's Lord Vaughn and his family."

"*Ohhh*, another lord. This should be good."

He and Dot exchanged grins and he went out the front door.

But the mention of the Annex made him stop.

He veered, on impulse, toward it.

Delacorte had shown him and Bolt the tunnel entrance that connected The Grand Palace on the Thames to the livery stables. Hugh was positive—though it wasn't much more than a hunch, just something about the feel of the place—that some sort of tunnel connected the Annex to The Grand

Palace on the Thames. Given its history, and all. He thought he'd have another look before he posted his letter, and circled around back to where the scullery had been laid open and the walls were being repaired.

He went still when he smelled smoke.

Cheroot smoke. And not the sort of usual foul nonsense the average fellow would roll up and light. *Good* tobacco.

There ought not be anyone in there at this time of day.

Wary now, he crossed the new boards toward the scullery, and slipped around the tarp hung there.

And in the dusty half-light, leaning against the half-repaired wall, was the most beautiful girl he'd ever seen.

Her hair was a shining mahogany; it was heaped up onto her head in some sort of artful pile that probably only a fine lady's maid could achieve. Little spirals of it traced her straight jaw, turned three quarters away from him. A long, pale throat rose from a silk dress the shade of old roses.

She was smoking a cheroot.

She noticed him.

If she gave a start, she disguised it well.

She turned her head in a leisurely fashion and fixed him with bright eyes, silvery, almost like Captain Hardy's. She'd a nose straight as a blade and a mouth wide and soft like a pillow, the precise color of cherry blossoms.

Her gaze traveled over him. Taking in his clothes, his build, his face. Drawing the kind of conclusion people the world over did about class and money and so forth.

Her expression settled into faintly amused, perhaps even a little contemptuous, lines. But he'd seen her pupils flare. He was very aware of that fixed regard. It was the sort of thing that could not be helped. Hugh Cassidy might be from one of the poorer families in New York, but he knew very well his own appeal. He'd been making female pupils flare since he was a teen.

"You might as well stare. They all do." Her voice was low, a surprising husky velvet. Cynical.

He somehow couldn't quite speak yet.

"I'm Lady Lillias Vaughn," she added. She said it as though he ought to know what that meant.

"My father is an earl," she prompted as though he were slow.

"Ah. I see. I'm Mr. Hugh Cassidy."

There was a little silence.

"Aren't you going to bow to the daughter of an earl, Mr. Cassidy?" It seemed to amuse her more than anything.

She thought he could be played with.

"Why waste a second doing that, when I can remain upright admiring you?"

Her expression flickered. Eyes widened as she reestimated him.

She studied him in silence. Her mouth curved slightly. "American, Mr. Cassidy?"

"Why, yes. I've noticed the English do like to announce whether they think someone is American or not. A bit like a child pointing out shapes and colors."

Lillias Vaughn blinked then.

Hugh indulged himself then in a swift head-to-toe inspection of her, swifter and more expert than hers, and the bands of muscle tightened across his stomach ever so slightly. The lines of her body seemed expressly designed to shorten a man's breath.

She noticed.

And now there was something breathlessly anticipatory about her.

He approached her slowly, slowly. As though she might spook and flee like a doe.

She didn't move at all. Her chin did go up just a very little.

Finally he was close enough to smell the soap scent that rose from her body, something floral and French and fine. To see her pupils flare, and how breath, swifter now, flutter the little curls at her temples. If he wanted to, he could close those few inches between them and lay his lips against hers.

He reached and plucked the cheroot from her fingers, dropped it to the floor, and crushed it beneath his boot heel.

"Go inside, little girl," he said softly. "I'm off

to tell your father you were smoking a cheroot. It isn't anywhere near as daring as you think it is. You wouldn't know 'daring' if it bit you."

And he left her the way he came.

AUNT LIZZIE WAS comfortably installed in a room in The Grand Palace on the Thames. The oldest Vaughn daughter had been located, thoroughly scolded—a cheroot! Angelique rolled her eyes. Mr. Cassidy had pulled her father aside and told him this regretfully, man to man, and she'd been fetched in and thoroughly castigated.

The entire exhausted family had been settled into the suite, fed, tea'd, warmed by fires, and every last one of them was wearing a dreamy little smile, even the clearly-going-to-be-trouble Lillias, when she and Delilah stopped by to see how they were. Every now and then all anyone needed was someone to lift their burden, if only for an hour or two.

What an exhausting, thoroughly rewarding day.

Angelique walked out to admire, yet again, the place where that dead, bare tree had poked up from a patch of dirt between The Grand Palace on the Thames and the Annex. It had been replaced by a patch of riotous greenery, lovingly, laboriously planted and chosen for its beauty and projected survival skills, and surrounded by a wrought iron fence in the fierce hope the winds off the ocean wouldn't uproot them and blow them all away. The one impractical choice was the little apple tree planted in honor of Lucien's mother; it was hardly the best spot for it to thrive. Inside the wrought iron fence was a little flagstone path. It led to a surprise she had for Lucien, which had also arrived today.

And so she waited, the wind lashing at her, pelisse whipping about her ankles, for her love to come home.

The sun was gilding the gargoyles presiding over The Grand Palace on the Thames when three men came into view, two very tall, one short.

It was all she could do not to hike her skirts in her hands and run to Lucien like a girl.

When he was ten feet away and she could see his smile, she realized she could feel anything she wanted to feel now and show it, and off she ran.

He scooped her up easily in his arms.

Delacorte and Captain Hardy grinned at them and left them to it, pushing open the door of The Grand Palace on the Thames and vanishing into its cozy warmth.

Lucien put her back down on the ground and kissed her as though he'd just returned from the war, and who could possibly feel the chill off the ocean when she was kissed like that?

"I want to show you something," she whispered. She took him by the hand, and led him to their little green area, and turned the key in the wrought iron gate.

There on a modest bench she'd gotten for a bargain was a little plaque that read:

HELENE DURAND PARK

He gave a short, stunned laugh and sat down hard on the bench.

Never mind that their park was about the size of four picnic blankets sewn together. It was a miracle it was growing at all. It was a miracle they owned two buildings. It was a miracle she was in the arms of a man the *ton* once claimed had devil's blood.

"Oh, my love," he finally said.

He pulled her into his lap, and buried his face against her hair, and they held each other. She loved that she had the power to move him. They luxuriated in closeness a minute.

"Aunt Lizzie arrived today."

There was a little silence.

"Ah. Did she? A woman of alacrity. I like alacrity in a woman." He added hurriedly, "You do not mind that I wrote to her?"

She laughed. She was not going to weep again. "She is wonderful and she loves it here and I imagine she'll love you, too, when you meet."

"Women invariably do, given enough time."

She nudged him. Then sighed contentedly. "I don't know how to thank you, Lucien."

"There is no need. If only you knew what a gift it is to me to be able to make you happy, Angelique."

She could not *believe* she'd actually had the

great good fortune to marry a man who went about saying things like that.

"If you like, we can visit Devonshire to see the rest of your family. I've a house there. Perhaps, if it isn't yet falling down, it would make a good country inn."

"Perhaps one day," she murmured contentedly.

"I've something for you, too."

He pulled the angel from his pocket, where he'd wrapped it, very carefully, in scraps of newspaper and his handkerchiefs.

"It's a gift to you from my brother. He brought it by the ship this morning."

She gave a soft laugh. "Lucien . . . I . . ." She couldn't speak.

She touched the angel's little face, its delicate wings. She thought about Robert searching for family and his tender heart that hadn't yet been crushed, or turned to stone by his father and mother. Tears stung her eyes again. And if she felt this way, she knew how Lucien must have felt.

Things were complicated.

No matter what, they'd see it through.

She looked up into his face. Shadowier now that the sun had nearly set all the way.

"So you had an interesting day, too," she said dryly.

He gave a short laugh, then sighed, but it was the sigh of a man who was more or less replete. "I will tell you about it inside."

She tipped her head back.

"Oh . . ." she breathed. "Lucien! Look!"

Visible now in the near dark, the apple tree they'd planted in honor of Lucien's mother was proudly sporting a single white bloom.

"A little like you. A beautiful thing improbably blooming here by the docks," he said.

She shook her head and smiled.

"It's like the first star you see at night," she said softly. "Perhaps we ought to wish on it."

He touched the blossom gently. "I wouldn't know what to wish for." He laughed ruefully. "I have everything I want."

"Perhaps you ought to wish your wife would kiss you in the dark beneath an apple blossom before we go in for the evening."

And because it was clearly a magical tree, that wish was instantly granted.

*And don't miss the first
book in Julie Anne Long's
Palace of Rogues series,*

LADY DERRING TAKES A LOVER

*D*elilah Swanpoole, Countess of Derring, learns the hard way that her husband, "Dear Dull Derring," is a lot more interesting—and perfidious—dead than alive. It's a devil of an inheritance, but in the grand ruins of the one building Derring left her, are the seeds of her liberation. And she vows never again to place herself at the mercy of a man.

But battle-hardened Captain Tristan Hardy is nothing if not merciless. When the charismatic naval hero tracks a notorious smuggler to a London boarding house known as The Rogue's Palace, seducing the beautiful, blue-blooded proprietress to get his man seems like a small sacrifice.

They both believe love is a myth. But a desire beyond reason threatens to destroy the armor around their hearts. Now a shattering decision looms: Will Tristan betray his own code of honor . . . or choose a love that might be the truest thing he's ever known?

LYNSAY SANDS

The Highlander Takes a Bride

978-0-06-227359-8

Raised among seven boisterous brothers, comely Saidh
Buchanan has a warrior's temper and little interest in
saddling herself with a husband . . . until she glimpses
the new Laird MacDonnell bathing naked in the loch.
Though she's far from a proper lady, the brawny
Highlander makes Saidh feel every inch a woman.

Always

978-0-06-201956-1

Bastard daughter to the king, Rosamunde was raised
in a convent and wholly prepared to take the veil . . .
until King Henry declared she would wed Aric, one of
his most valiant knights. While Rosamunde's spirited
nature often put her at odds with her new husband,
his mastery in seduction was quickly melting her
resolve—and capturing her heart.

Lady Pirate

978-0-06-201973-8

Valoree has been named heir to Ainsley Castle. But
no executor would ever hand over the estate to an
unmarried pirate wench and her infamous crew.
Upon learning that the will states that in order to
inherit, Valoree must be married to a nobleman—and
pregnant—she's ready to return to the seas. But
her crew has other ideas . . .

LYS8 1016

*At Avon Books, we know your passion
for romance—once you finish one of our
novels, you find yourself wanting more.*

May we tempt you with . . .

- **Excerpts** from our upcoming releases.
- **Entertaining extras**, including authors' personal photo albums and book lists.
- Behind-the-scenes **scoop** on your favorite characters and series.
- **Sweepstakes** for the chance to win free books, romantic getaways, and other fun prizes.
- Writing **tips** from our authors and editors.
- **Blog** with our authors and find out why they love to write romance.
- **Exclusive content** that's not contained within the pages of our novels.

Join us at
www.avonbooks.com

AVON

An Imprint of HarperCollins*Publishers*
www.avonromance.com